THE EINSTEIN OBJECT

BOOK ONE OF THE SPYNNCASTER SEQUENCE

KEVIN HINCKER

FOREWORD

Writing good software and writing good novels are similar jobs, I have found. The first step, and the ongoing struggle in both cases, is organizing all the information. While I have always written novels (not when I was a baby, but after that) I have also occasionally founded software companies, and I've written a LOT of code.

The mobile game in this book is something I built and played with my own son, years ago when he was 12, just as Oliver is in this book. My plan is to release the game when I publish Book Two in the Spynncaster Sequence. If you'd like an advance look at the navigation, game play, art, consider joining the mailing list at kevinhincker.com and checking the box for Einstein Extras. Happy reading!

CHAPTER
ONE

Today was Preston Oliver Nowak's 12th birthday. Two days earlier he had seen a fruit branded shopping bag in the trash, so he knew that the small, rectangular present hidden in the broom closet was a cell phone. And Preston was certain that the moment he took personal possession of his cell phone, his life would be complete. He was sure that the nagging, poorly-defined *something* he felt, setting him apart from other people in the world, would vanish, and that he would at last fit in. Though unfortunately for Preston, none of those things were going to happen.

But he was getting a phone at last, he knew that much. So now he had a new problem — and there's almost always a new problem, often created by the solution to your old problem, a truth Preston was only now starting to understand. The new problem concerned a Nowak birthday tradition: presents were always opened *after* all party guests had gone home. But what was the point of becoming a person with a cell phone if it happened too late to meet your guests at the door, casually voting down a meme, or linking to a hilarious video? There was no point. With birthday presents, timing is everything.

"Mom—" Preston was in the kitchen saying to his mother, while she mixed batter with focused enthusiasm.

"Preston, honey," she interrupted, "we open presents at the end of the day. After the cookies and the party. That's the schedule. It's family tradition."

"I know the family traditions, for sure," he nodded. "But I think this one's from the old days—like a bygone tradition I think?—plus even if it's not bygone you know what everyone says about traditions."

His mother tilted her head as she mixed. "No. What do they say?"

"Traditions are made to be broken."

"Oh, I see no, you're thinking of *rules*. They do say that about rules. Criminals, in any case." She pointed. "Will you get the cookie sheet?"

He held the sheet out without putting it on the counter so she had to turn and face him. "I'm changing. I'm twelve now," he told her.

"Yes you are."

"I'm maturing and changing and I think I should take more responsibility. I should pull weeds without being asked."

"That sounds wonderful."

"I should learn how to do the dishwasher to save you and dad your arthritis."

"Neither of us have arthritis dear, but that's a marvelous plan."

"Right, that's the thing about all changes, they're *marvelous*, so I think we should change our tradition, since everything changes, so why not traditions... " and here Preston felt his mouth take on something of a life of its own, and wondered, for the first time in his life, if he wasn't rambling, which is the sort of questioning that begins around your twelfth birthday, in high stakes confrontations with forces beyond your control, " ... because I'm getting *older* is the main thing changing now, even *you* say changes are happening to me so fast, right before your very eyes, I'm not a kid, pretty soon I'm going to leave home, no stop wait mom, I'll probably go to college or join

2

the foreign service or something and then I'll come home and take over Nowak Family Shoes from dad and then get old and die, and all the changes and responsibility I have from getting older means *I totally need a cell phone as soon as possible...* I'm... "

His mother was smiling but frowning and shaking her head. She was blinking like she might cry, which was absolutely the opposite of what he wanted. Then she hugged him.

"Stop reminding me how much *older* you are," she sighed. "And listen to me, I know what this is, all your friends have phones and you want to fit in, but you do not need a phone, or anything other than your wonderful personality, for people to like you."

"Oh I totally know that," he agreed.

"They'll like you because you're *you*."

He nodded vigorously, though what she was saying was ridiculous and absolutely not true. He nodded because he felt a change coming. His mother sighed again and hope rose in his chest. When it did he grimaced, which is also something that begins at about twelve. All through your life hope will have risen in your chest this way, but around twelve you find that process start to become painful.

"OK, you win," his mom said. "Let's go find your father and tell *him* about all your upcoming responsibilities."

What followed were a string of very amazing moments. Peak moments, these are called. It all seemed like a wonderful dream to Preston, though of course it was not a dream, and if he had known what lay in store for him he would not have called any of it wonderful. But since Preston did not live in a magical world where people told you the future, or voices issued timely warnings out of thin air — or at least he didn't live there *yet* — he still had no idea of the pain, the terrible choices, and the upcoming coma which this phone would force on him. All he knew was that he'd wanted a phone forever and at long last was getting one.

He and his mother went to the living room where his father sat reading *Architectural Digest*. People in the neighborhood might have been surprised to learn of his father's fascination with architecture, considering the condition of the roof and the infrequent home repair at 4332 Fair Oaks Ave. His father claimed their house, which had been owned by his own father, possessed what professional designers called *authentic small town charm* and that the neighbors might one day thank him for pushing their home prices higher with authenticity.

He looked up when Preston came in.

"Hey, birthday boy!" Then he looked closer and put down his magazine. "What's up?"

As the new order to the universe was explained to him, Preston Sr. appeared disappointed. But once the proposal had been fully outlined, he shrugged.

"Well why not?" he said. "Traditions are made to be broken, after all."

The back of the highest shelf in the broom closet was the hiding place for all presents, all Valentine cards, all surprise plane tickets and, once, an unlucky Easter gerbil. From that shelf his mother pulled the small box, carefully wrapped. She handed it to Preston. He did not remember unwrapping, or breaking the packaging open, or lifting the phone into the air. All he remembered later was gazing in astonishment, holding the phone in both his hands because phones are slippery and if you drop yours, you're unlikely to get another until you're sixteen.

"You look like a regular grownup," beamed his father.

"He looks twelve years old," his mother said, "why is everyone... he's not... he's a baby... " Then she turned and went back to the kitchen to remix the birthday cookies.

Preston flipped the phone on. The chime gave him a thrill. Under his father's watchful eye and moving as quickly as he could, filtering out his father's stream of hints and mistaken suggestions, Preston began to set up the device. His dad peered through glasses at the instruction booklet, trying to show the illustrations to Preston. But

Preston had read those instructions long before. He'd searched them out on a forum in preparation.

"We added you to the family account," his dad said, "so let's see... enter this code — "

"I know."

"Ok now tap the — "

"I know, Dad."

"The red exclamation mark gets you to the next — "

"No it doesn't — Dad! This might go faster if I did it myself. You can watch. Do you want to watch?"

His father raised his eyebrows like curious dolphins arching above his glasses. His son knew that Preston Sr. was digitally handicapped, and nothing could ever change that fact. Preston Sr. had no idea how electronics worked and the family just worked around it. But now the birthday party was almost here, and many settings still had to be toggled, passcodes created, and avatars and ringtones selected. A lot of pressure. Preston didn't have time to help his father help him with technology.

"I'll just leave you to it, and I'll go have a birthday cookie," his father said with a smile, expecting to be called back to help soon enough. He imagined it was technology that was the problem, and not him.

As he left the room his father said, "Let me know if you get to the part where they assign you a phone number. I want to be the first to call you."

Once the field was clear of adult assistance Preston's progress was headlong, which is often the case with twelve year olds, with phones and many other things. He confirmed that he'd been added to the family account. Yes, Preston Oliver Nowak. The same name as his grandfather, a man Preston had never met, who'd died years ago and burdened Preston with a name.

He flew through the setup process until, finally, he came to the screen with the phone numbers. He expected to choose from a list, but the progress icon stalled for what felt like hours, and he did not get a list. He was given one, single choice: 323-213-7079.

Activate, he tapped.

Your new number is being processed and should be active within 30 minutes, he read on the screen.

～

THE PARTY STARTED PROMISINGLY. He greeted his guests as each arrived, opening the door while looking down at his phone as if reviewing an important communication, before noticing his visitor. The guests all leaned close to see what he had, what his background image was, what games were installed. He wanted to pass out his new number, but his activity meter was still whirling.

"The number's processing," he told each guest, hiding his disappointment, "it'll activate any second."

But seconds passed and passed and no activation happened. Pizza came and went with soda and cake and he knew that he was being what his mom would call a *bad host* though no one seemed to notice or care other than his mom. All he wanted was for the spinning to stop and his life to begin. His guests were having a fantastic time without him, which somehow made everything worse.

Then the group began a multi-console game free for all. This had never happened at Preston's house before. And for a moment he had a purpose, since he was needed to find the remote controls, and as host was empowered to pick the games. He almost managed to forget to wait for the most important chime of his life as they launched into rounds of Final Fantasy, Zelda, Call of Duty, some new Battle Royale. At one point playing Gran Turismo he really did forget what he was waiting for, because for one shinning moment it seemed as if he was going to beat Andy Margolis on the Grand Valley Speedway.

It was basically impossible to beat Andy Margolis playing Gran Turismo. All Andy ever did was play GT, every chance he got. He obviously played it instead of doing homework, and it was his only real skill as far as Preston knew, except judo kicks and spitting in school drinking fountains. Andy formed a kind of psychic connection with the controller in Gran Turismo. If you managed to finish a race within ten seconds of his car, it was a good day.

There were six others kids at the party and one after another Andy dispatched them, while Preston held back to postpone the beatdown. But finally he put his phone on the coffee table — to keep an eye on the screen — and picked up a controller. Andy grinned. He took special pleasure in beating Preston, for no reason Preston understood.

The race started. The one good thing about racing Andy was that if you stuck behind his car you almost always ended up coming in second. Even the AI drivers couldn't keep up with him. Andy steered the shortest lines through every corner, braked and shifted, throttling up and down like a machine. But this afternoon Preston found himself sticking behind Andy like glue.

The Grand Valley Speedway has 3 sections. Through Section 1 Preston was right on Andy's tail and he could tell Andy noticed. Usually by the beginning of Section 2 Andy would be a minimum of 2 seconds ahead of anyone he was racing, but today Preston was right on his bumper. Andy slotted Turn 7 and nailed the gas and spun an unconventional path through the corner high and right, to leave Preston trapped by an AI Lotus, but somehow Preston managed to pass the lotus on the *left*, dropping back, right on Andy's rear.

The room started to buzz. The guests gathered. Was this luck? Had the game been updated somehow, and they hadn't heard? How was this happening? They began urging Preston on because everyone wondered, what would happen if Andy, prone to demonstrations of martial art, lost at GT to *Preston*? Andy's face darkened. Suddenly it was war.

Andy began destroying the track, throwing his car into every turn, leaving computer drivers far, far behind. He found impossible openings, geared up and down so fast into hairpins it seemed the plastic on his controller might melt from friction, and every step of the way Preston matched him. He couldn't pass Andy. But Andy couldn't lose him.

The racers leaned forward on the couch, poised and tense. The looks on the spectators' faces said everything. It was historic.

Then Andy made a mistake.

Flying into Turn 15 with Preston in his wash, Andy needed a late brake, and a hard spin right to set up the next turn, and Preston was following, waiting for Andy to slow, nano seconds flashing and track blurring, until finally Preston couldn't wait another yard and slammed his own brakes, sliced a path, and exited the curve.

And realized that Andy was *behind* him; Andy had waited too long and lost a whole second on the turn. Preston was ahead. Ahead!

It was the final leg. Only three more turns. Andy followed Preston now, thrashing his car, desperate for speed. Preston swayed, squared through another turn — still ahead. One turn and the race was over.

Time slowed. From the corner of his eye he saw guests open mouthed, riveted. Then from the table in front of him came a chime. His phone. A text notification. Did that mean...

And in that high-speed, slow-motion second, he lost focus and tagged the rail into the final straightaway and his car, going 220 miles per hour, pitched sideways. Somehow, through some magical flow state combination of braking and over steering and drifting, Preston kept his machine from spinning into the other wall and exploding into a million pieces. But Andy flashed by him. No way to catch him. And Preston lost by 20 seconds.

"No texting while driving!" his guests shouted, laughing so hard they collapsed. Defeat torn from the jaws of victory was how it would be described in a racing journal. A career shattering failure. Andy was victorious and exultant, then started playing the whole thing off like he'd never felt threatened.

And all Preston could think was, a *text*. A text! That meant his number was active! He grabbed the phone and thumbed up the message app.

It was spam from an 800 number: *Learn Computer Programing, TAP HERE!* the message read. He felt a new kind of wild joy. When you get your first piece of cellular spam it can be very exciting, though as with many of the privileges of growing older, the novelty wears off fast.

"Guys," he called over their laughter. "Hey GUYS! My number's live. Text me!"

They all went for their devices, firing texts at Preston in a contest to be the first to reach him, because making everything a contest is a cruel team building exercise certain people learn when they are twelve. In this case, Preston was happy to be the prize the competitors fought over.

But one after another, they all shook their heads.

"The number can't be reached it says," was the general report.

It made no sense. Preston knew how phones worked. His wasn't on the wifi network. The text had come over the cell network addressed to his phone number. But none of the other kids could reach him. It took no time at all for the guests to forget to compete for him, a contest they hadn't particularly cared about winning in the first place. Preston sat on the couch, carefully relaunching the mobile provider app, where his number continued to be *Processing*.

A haze settled over the proceedings then, and it lasted for the rest of the afternoon. And Preston was left, after his last guest went home, with a certain *something* still setting him apart from the world, apart from what people called *regular life*. Though, as Preston was soon to discover, people really have no idea what they are talking about, when it comes to *regular life*.

TWO

After everyone was gone, and Preston had tried everything else he could possibly think of, including reading the manual again even though he basically had it memorized, he had been left with no choice but to let his father explore the phone problem, which made his father feel slightly smug. Preston's stomach dropped as he watched his father gesture with the phone, flinging his hand about and expounding about *persistence* and a *methodical approach* being the secrets to solving every problem. But these secrets did not apply to cell phones, as it turned out. Within a few minutes Preston Sr. had been reduced to saying, *huh,* and squinting into the past where he had done something with his own phone, once, if he could only remember...

"Dad," Preston suggested, handing his father's own phone to him with as much patience as he still possessed, "you could call the cell company on *your* phone."

"Oh. Sure. Let's see, they're going to ask for your number, ah... " He poked uncertainly at the screen in his hand until Preston stepped up and opened the settings app. His father looked over his glasses, surprised and impressed, then got a pencil to write down Preston's information.

He stared when he was finished writing.

"Huh," he said. "Now why does that number look familiar? 323-213-7079. I should call it." He began looking for his phone, which he had set on the side table. Preston handed it to him again.

"It won't work. I think you should call the company," he said.

"It's funny," Preston Sr. stared at Preston's phone. "I feel like I should remember that number. Hmm... " He even shook the phone a few times, and though Preston didn't roll his eyes at this, he did momentarily cover his face with one hand.

"That's not going to help," Preston said. "They don't do anything if you shake them."

"I know, Pres. Wow, it's really going to bug me. I should remember the number. I never forget a number you know."

Then he gave up his lost memory and Preston listened as his father cycled through the cell phone customer service system, confusing everyone he talked to. He gave Preston several reassuring thumbs-up, listened intently to people telling him things he did not understand, and at last smiled and said, "Oh ok. Perfect. Thank you!" He hung up and turned to Preston.

"It's processing," he explained.

"Dad, we know that. It's been processing since breakfast. We needed to know why."

"They say the number doesn't become active until it finishes processing."

"But Dad I got a text on my number, how could the number be processing if I got a text? How come nobody *else* can text me?"

Preston's dad looked at him. His mouth moved a little bit, the way an aquarium fish moves its mouth while waiting for the helpful bipeds to approach and dazzle it with food. Then he looked up at the ceiling. There did not seem to be any additional mobile phone information up there. After a moment he looked back down, nodded knowingly, handed Preston his phone, and patted him softly on the shoulder. Then he said, "Let's just wait. Should we go see if Mom has dinner ready?"

~

THE GREAT SCIENCE fiction writer Isaac Asimov died long before Preston was born—although they still make his books into movies today, which is how you know he was a great writer. Issac Asimov liked writing down rules. He wrote some rules about robots, which many people who are afraid of robots know. And he wrote an important rule about magic. And if Preston had ever read any Isaac Asimov books he would have known this rule, and maybe saved himself a lot of trouble, but unfortunately Preston didn't read science fiction books. Asimov's rule about magic went like this: "Any sufficiently advanced technology will seem like magic."

This is pretty obvious once it gets pointed out to you. A teleportation machine might seem like magic to Preston. And if you went back to ancient Egypt and showed your mobile phone to King Tut, he might have called you a magician. *How is this possible?* King Tut might have wondered, taking a selfie or reading a text? *What kind of spell is this?* To him the obvious — the *only* — explanation would have been *magic.*

There's also the rule Asimov *didn't* write. Preston didn't know this rule either, which just goes to show you that learning a few rules can be a good idea. Knowing this one might have saved Preston from all the school he was about to miss and all the leg cramps you can get being unconscious in a coma. Because Isaac Asimov's unwritten rule says: "Any real magic, any real magic *EVER AT ALL*, will seem like the most unbelievably advanced technology to a person living in a house in Pasadena today."

Anyone in Pasadena who is confronted with magical events will explain them with the most obvious theory, just as King Tut did, and for modern people the explanation would be technology. In Pasadena, in the time of Preston Oliver Nowak, scientists and engineers had brought to life wonders unimaginable. You could not predict what they would make next with nothing more than microchips and glass. You grew to expect the unexpected, and to shrug and call the amazing, magical things "technology."

But those were all rules that Preston had, and had never thought about what magic might look like if he stumbled across it, so he had no chance at all to stop or change any of the things that were about to happen to him, sitting on his bed after a very disappointing birthday dinner, alone and in his pajamas.

His lights were supposed to be out since tomorrow was a school day, but he had a small reading lamp turned on. His phone lay on the covers beside him. It was still *processing*, although it could connect to the house's Wi-Fi network and he could go online. But to him, it was dead. He did not have what he wanted, which was a phone number where he could be contacted, and cellular data he could use anywhere in the world.

He wondered for a moment if he was cursed, and picked his phone up and almost shook it the way his father had. It just didn't make sense! Nine hours of processing. And what about that text that had come through and ruined his chance to beat Andy Margolis at Gran Turismo? How could that come to his phone number when his phone number wasn't even active?

In irritation he flicked open the messages app and read the text again:

Learn Computer Programing, TAP HERE! Following that was a link.

"How did u get this number?" he keyed.

An answer came back instantly. The exact same words. *Learn Computer Programming, TAP HERE!*

Tell me how you are messaging me, he wrote, his aggravation rising. *This number is not active!*

Learn Computer Programming, TAP HERE! the response came again.

It was just a bot, he thought. He tapped the link in the message. His messages app slipped away and a browser window loaded.

At the top of the page, in deep blue capital letters, was a word: *SPYNNLANG*. And beneath this were bullet points noting the benefits of the offered course in computer programming. Classic spam, he thought, until he began to read over the list.

Surprisingly, the reasons a person might want to become a computer programmer included things like *Live Forever* and *Enjoy Fabulous Riches* and *Destroy Your Enemies*. He scrolled through, all the way to the end, trying to understand what was actually being proposed, and how *Command Vast Armies* and *Sire Formidable Heirs* could be selling points for a programming course. It seemed more like a course in taking over the world.

When he had scrolled all the way down he came to the footer text:

Computer Programming is your path to boundless power and life-long happiness. Walk that path and live the life you always wanted — TAP HERE TO START.

No email address. Maybe on the next page? He tapped the link.

A popup appeared.

You seem to be on a mobile device. This coursework is more effective on a desktop screen. This coursework will now be transferred to your computer. And below that, a button that read *OK*.

Preston looked across the room at his old iMac. He did not use it much. The keyboard had a few keys chipping, though it was useful for playing Steam games and watching YouTube. Sometimes for writing book reports. He tapped the *OK* button on the phone, expecting to be asked for an email address where the link could be sent, so he could open it on his desktop browser. But that is not what happened.

The second he tapped *OK*, the phone became molten hot in his hands — instantly, fingers on the grill, fry-the-skin-off-your-palms *hot* — and he thought he saw the screen of the iMac flicker on before a powerful white flash from the phone blinded him. He cried out and dropped the phone, shaking his hands wildly to dull the burning. The pain subsided, but afterimages from the flash, brighter than a thousand flashbulbs, coruscated in his eyes like snakes and he spent a moment just trying to clear his vision. When he could see again he turned to his desk and stared at the iMac. It had turned itself on, and it seemed to have loaded a web page.

From the bed Preston could see the large blue Spynnlang logo at the top, though he was one hundred percent certain the computer had been turned off. He looked back down at the phone on his covers. The screen was dark. Very carefully he touched it. It was still hotter than usual, but seemed to be cooling. Then he noticed that the battery was almost dead, though it had been at 98% just seconds before. He took it with him as he slid off the bed and padded toward the desk. As he came closer he could read the greeting at the top of the Spynnlang page.

"Welcome to Lesson One, Preston Oliver Nowak!"

He plugged in his phone and put it in the desk's storage cubby. Lesson One? He pulled out his chair and sat, rubbing his still raw hands and reading the fine print beneath the greeting. *If you are not Preston Oliver Nowak then you are legally obliged to stop breathing and set fire to the device displaying this greeting. Continued breathing constitutes legal agreement to these Terms and Conditions.*

His head was feeling a little light. He had never passed out in his life, as far as he knew, but he suspected you might feel exactly the way he felt right now just seconds before you fell over and hit your head on a desktop. He forced himself to focus on the words on his screen.

You will not be sorry you signed up for this course! Before we begin, a note: do not believe the things other courses tell you about Computer Programming! Computer Programming is very, very hard — unless you are named Preston Oliver Nowak! This is fantastic luck for you. Since this is the first time you will be doing Computer Programming, you are also lucky because you will not have to UNLEARN all the useless "skills" that other courses propagate! You will learn Computer Programming the

RIGHT way, the FIRST time! Start by holding your hands out over the keyboard without touching it!

There was nothing else on the page. Just a bunch of white space below that last sentence. Preston's head was really starting to pulse now, and the burning sensation in his hands, which had seemed to fade after he got off the bed, was returning full force. He held up his hands to see if they were red or swollen or covered with biting ants. As he did that the pain spiked; the fire started sliding down from his fingertips toward his wrists like he was performing a slow-motion dive into a pool of bubbling lava. Despite himself he groaned. He waved his arms and blew on his skin but this only made them burn hotter. What in the world was going on? He thrust both hands out over the keyboard toward the screen as if to say, here, look how much this hurts right now!

And the moment he had his hands suspended over the keys, the pain went away.

Very nice job! The words faded in on the screen. *This is your first Computer Programming lesson! Your hands must always start out in front of you, near enough to the keys so you can touch them! Beginning programmers will often attempt coursework from across the room or while riding a pony or showering! But proximity to the keyboard is essential! Now lower your fingers until they touch the keys!*

Preston waited. His dizziness was not going away, and after a minute or two his arms began to tire, but he was suddenly uncertain about following the onscreen instructions. At the same time, he had no desire to pull his hands away from the keyboard and risk excruciating pain. A small part of him was urging, *YELL! Yell for mom and dad!* But another part of him wondered what he would say to them — please help me move my hands away from the computer without setting them on fire?

One of the many interesting lessons you learn as you get older is that the more reasons your brain manufactures for you not to call for help in a given situation, the greater the likelihood that you are in a situation where you badly need help. In desperate situations your brain often gets stuck measuring various dangers against each other instead of acting. For instance, comparing whether it would be better to climb back out of a tiger cage and suffer intense ridicule from your friends for falling over the railing, or to lose a limb or two and hope the incident has been forgotten by the time you emerge from the hospital. Your brain is just a tool for weighing outcomes. To make up for your brain's failings you have useful instincts like *terror* and *all-encompassing panic* which help you make good decisions around tigers. But Preston still had a lot of lessons to learn about his brain. This was not even one of the most important ones.

So he settled his hands down onto the keyboard instead of calling for help. And right away another block of text faded in on his screen.

Excellent! Let's just jump right into the deep end of the pool and start learning Computer Programming! Here is what a computer program looks like!

And the browser window began to scroll. Row after densely packed row of unrecognizable shapes filled the screen. The shapes were not letters or numbers, at least not in any language he had ever seen. They did not seem to be organized into sentences or words or groups of any kind. They were many different colors. Some of them seemed to be moving. Each was about the size of Preston's thumb. There were blobs and three dimensional shapes and things that resembled graphs and other things that made him nauseous when he tried to look at them. A very fancy but recognizable number 7 scrolled past but by the time it disappeared off the top of the screen it had morphed into a gravy stain.

Eventually the scrolling shapes all scrolled completely away and were gone, and the instructions faded in once again.

That was a very powerful Computer Program used to make a day longer by slowing the rotation of a planet! It can be useful when you find yourself on a tight deadline or when you need just a few more hours in the sun to complete your splendid tan! It will be many hundreds of years before you are skilled enough to Program anything like that. But it is nice to have something to strive for!

Let's try creating our first Computer Program, shall we? You will be working in a language called Spynnlang. In this project you will create a template! When completed it will appear as an iOS application on your phone, and display an orange ball that you can control with your mind!

This template is your Skills Assessment. It will be used to determine your aptitudes in a number of conceptual domains so that coursework can better be designed to instruct you in Computer Programming! There may be some unbelievably horrible discomforts involved, or maybe not! Ready? Go!

The text faded out, and an image of two hands above a keyboard faded in. As Preston watched, the hands animated to demonstrate pressing a series of keys.

It looked like a typing program created by a madman. It was hard to tell what was even going on in some of the pictures. The animations seemed to indicate that while some keys were to be pressed very slowly, others should be pressed as fast as possible. At the same time, some single keys were to be pressed with two fingers at once. In one image the right hand was on the left side of the keyboard, while the left hand was underneath it on the right. One image showed the *T* and the *U* being pressed using the second knuckles of the left index finger and the ring finger while the right pinky reached between them from above and pressed the *G* key. Many of the contortions actually looked impossible.

It was all so startling and inexplicable that Preston sat back in his chair to stare. The moment his hands moved away from the keyboard he felt as though they had been seared in a pot of acid, and he whipped them back into position. He felt a line of sweat rolling down the side of his face. He wanted to wipe it off, but he did not dare lift his hand to his cheek. His breathing was coming in deep gulps. He felt as if he were about to cry.

At long last one of his useful but delayed instincts — *overwhelming panic* — reared up in his chest and started demanding action, and Preston decided that he really did need help. But by this time it was too late. His brain had frittered away his best chance to escape. When he tried to yell, his throat closed off and his eyes watered and he gasped. Something prevented him from calling out.

On the screen, large and bold, flashed a message.

Remember, Preston Oliver Nowak: Computer Programming is actually quite impossible! But you can do it! The Dark Folk will soon be rising, and Computer Programming is the only thing you can use to keep them at bay!

And then the pain started in his hands, and the only way to stop it was to follow the animations on the screen and bend his fingers in the most unnatural and excruciating ways.

There were eight different sequences he had to move through. They were called *Object, Body Type, Density, Friction, Bounce, Rotation, Gravity* and *Scale*. The first sequence, *Object*, was a simple-seeming series of key presses and finger positions made deeply frustrating by the variations in speed that had to be perfected. Slow, then fast, then *lightning* fast, then glacially slow, then repeat with new keys, then again with the left hand upside down. Each time he made a mistake, blazing fire surged from his nails up past every knuckle, turning each finger into a blowtorch of agony. Halfway through, he thought his heart would stop. His whole body was sopping wet with sweat; it was pouring into his eyes and blinding him.

Somehow he got all the way through the *Object* sequence, mostly through luck he was convinced. And when he typed the last key of the sequence with his upside-down left hand, he was rewarded with four rows of shapes, fading in on the screen. They were green and red, mold spots or snowflakes or steering wheels. It had taken him an hour. He paused, briefly relieved, until the pain erupted and pushed him on to the next sequence, *Body Type*.

And so it went, hour after hour, late into the night, the light from his screen a yellow blue glow in the darkness. Sequence after sequence, each contortion more challenging and painful than the last. *Density, Friction, Bounce.* As he completed those in turn, his screen scrolled with more and more of the Spynnlang icons. And he noticed as he went, despite the strain in his arms and the impossible twisting positions and the feats of concentration, that something was changing.

He began to feel as though he were floating just outside and above his body, and interacting with the keyboard from a distance, as if by remote control. He knew that some of the contortions he was subjecting his hands to must be excruciating, but from his increasing height he found it did not bother him. It almost felt like he was directing someone else's body. By the seventh sequence, *Gravity*, he knew that he could make his fingers do anything. He began to feel, as the instructions had stated, that Computer Programming was impossible — but that he, Preston Oliver Nowak, was doing it anyway.

Finally, in the early hours of the morning, with birds just beginning to sing outside his window, he finished the final set — *Scale*. Eight impossible puzzles, eight unbelievably complicated Spynnlang sequences, done. Pages and pages of inscrutable symbols and shapes logged on his screen. And now that it was over he found that he could drop his hands without the searing fire. He felt empty. Empty of pain, empty of thought, empty of everything.

The instruction text returned.

Congratulations, Preston Oliver Nowak! You have completed your Skills Assessment. Press the Enter key with your right index knuckle while your left hand performs step four of the Object sequence. This will deploy your template application to its destination.

He felt mindless. Like a drone. He curled his right index finger and tapped the Enter key, while his left hand, almost without thinking, went through a complex series. A quick twist on the Shift keys, a few double taps with his index knuckle and sequences of eight keys pressed at the same time, then seven, six, five, four, three, two and a last, single key. *H*. For a moment there was silence. And then, from his desk cubby, a chime.

Excellent work. You have deployed your template. Now perform the final phase of the Skills Assessment: Usability Testing.

Another chime — it was his phone in the cubby. When he reached for it he saw that his hands were shaking. And not just his hands. His arms. In fact his entire body was beginning to tremble. He fumbled the phone onto the desk just before it slipped from his fingers to the floor, then tapped it to life with an unsteady swipe. A new application was waiting on his home screen, right next to the Calendar app: a blue app icon with a tiny orange circle, called Spynncaster.

Another jittery stab from his finger launched the app. And there, positioned in the middle of an empty black screen, an orange circle hung motionless.

But suddenly there were two circles, their edges blurred, orbiting awkwardly around each other. It took Preston a moment to realize that this was actually a result of his eyes crossing. Then the entire room rolled backward, very dramatically, and he felt sick to his stomach. Another moment passed before he saw that his head had rolled forward so it was facing downward on his chest. His neck muscles were weak as Jell-O. He forced them to lift his chin up and point his face at his desk.

His vision cleared for a moment. There was something he needed to do, he thought. A last thing. What was it?

Ah. He remembered.

Usability test.

You were supposed to be able to move the circle around the screen with your mind. He went back and forth over that thought, dully. Could that be right? Some part of him, some deep down part of him, protested. Things do not get moved around on computers or phones using minds. Moving objects required a mouse. Or a keyboard. Or a finger. That was true. The idea gained some strength inside him. It was hard to argue with. How do you interact with a device using your mind? *Move*, he thought at the ball. But nothing happened. Because that's not the way computers worked. Hello.

As a gamer Preston was distinctive in only one particular way. While it was true that he had fast reflexes, there were plenty of others who were faster. He had quite a lot of stamina, but not an extraordinary amount. His eye hand coordination was well developed, but not that far above average. Many of his friends had these same attributes. But the one thing that set Preston apart as a gamer was that he liked to read the instructions. It was the first thing he did whenever he installed a new game. And after everyone else had maxed out their skills on any given game so they could not twitch any faster or aim any steadier, *then* Preston would slowly begin to gain on them. There are always secrets in the documentation. Preston had learned how to find them.

But in the case of the Spynncaster app, there were no instructions. The only written information at all had been the text on the main Spynnlang webpage. Of course, there was the Spynnlang programming itself, the blobs and icons, but that was no help. That was eight sequences of brain-frying gibberish.

Then he thought about it. Maybe that wasn't true. Eight sequences. Each of them had a name. *Object, Body Type, Density, Friction, Bounce, Rotation, Gravity* and *Scale*. From his experience picking details out of badly written translations of Asian-language instructions, he had developed an intuition about what information was important. And right now something was saying that these eight names were important.

Settings! Some of them were settings that appeared in physics-based games. Yes. *Gravity*, for instance. Or *Bounce*. Even *Density* and *Friction* were physics settings that could be changed in certain games. What if Spynncaster was a physics game? If the orange ball was an *Object*, then it might be affected by *Gravity*. It seemed right. But how did that help him?

His head fell forward again, and this time it stayed there for three minutes before he found the strength to tilt it back up. His body kept trying to slide off the chair and down onto the floor. He needed to lie on his bed. His hands felt as if they were encased in clay; he couldn't make them grip, so he slid the phone to the edge of the desk and pressed it up between his palms, holding them as if he was praying. He tried to stand. He could not.

Somewhere he found the leverage to inch his rolling chair to the edge of his bed. His head kept dropping. Waves of dizziness were making his stomach heave. He managed to topple sideways and land on top of his covers, and with the last of his strength he pulled his legs up after him.

Blood beat through his body. It was the most curious sensation he had ever experienced. His legs and arms throbbed with each pump of his heart. He must be twitching like a garden hose, he felt: a hose someone kept filling, draining, filling, draining. On the bed, just within his field of vision, he could see the phone where it had landed. The orange circle faded in, faded out, with each surge of his blood.

He could not turn his head. He wanted to hold the phone, but he could not raise his arms, so he inched his face closer, and closer still. There was something magnetic and beautiful about his orange circle. It did not glitter or sparkle, but somehow it looked like a jewel. It radiated an invisible corona, as if, just behind it, the most valuable diamond in the world lay shimmering. Just lying there beside it, and knowing it was his, that he was the one who had created it, made him so happy. So happy. Now he just wanted to sleep for a thousand years.

But first, move the circle. Physics. *Gravity*. Where was the gravity? The gravity was missing. The gravity should pull the ball down. Now he understood. He just needed to turn on the gravity.

He closed his eyes. One of the Spynnlang shapes appeared in his mind and he understood that it was *Gravity*. The orange ball appeared above it. He imagined *Gravity* pulling the ball down. When he opened his eyes, the ball on his phone was moving. It dropped. It simply dropped from the middle of the screen to the bottom. It bounced a few times, rolled into a corner, and was still. Usability Test — *check*.

Outside his window he heard the drip irrigation system come on. Every morning at 7:00 AM he heard the same wheeze, and then the sound of water through the pipes like an alarm. His father was very proud of this system. The fact that his father had never really planted anything in the area that he had drip-irrigated did not seem to bother him.

And just like clockwork, his mother came into his room to get him up for school.

"Okay, Pres, seven o'clock. Up and at 'em, let's... Pres?" He was facing away from her, lying on his side, but he could tell from her voice that something was wrong. He heard her hurry to the bed.

"Pres? You're shaking. Are you sick?"

He wanted to tell her about everything that had happened. How happy he was. But he could not make his tongue move. She rolled him over and felt his head. He was surprised to see the fear on her face. There was really nothing to be afraid of. He had just accomplished something stupendous. It was an unbelievable feat. He was a Computer Programmer.

"Pres? Preston, say something! Preston!"

His mother turned and yelled for this father out the bedroom door.

Preston glanced one more time at his phone, and the amazing mind-controlled orange ball he had created.

"That is the most incredible technology I have ever heard of," he thought.

And then he dropped into a deep and lasting coma

THREE

Comas make people look one of two ways. You either appear absolutely peaceful, or you look shocked and horrified. It all depends on whether you are in the coma or outside of it.

If it's your coma then your expression will be tranquil, like a tourist on a tropical island, maybe relaxing on a beach near a shaved ice vendor, maybe resting after collecting starfish. You will look unbuttoned and trouble free. But anyone discovering you will look terrified, as if you have been bitten in half by a shark and pitched up out of the water at low tide. At first they will prod you gingerly, then they are likely to call your name and scream that someone needs to get an ambulance. It is probable that some of them will cry. You will drool nonchalantly and look serene. But inside your coma, it might not feel at all like an island vacation.

In Preston's case he found himself on top of a very tall hill, with steeply sloping sides that curved out far below him to become the surface of a vast and spreading plain. At the very far edges of this plain he could see a forest, ringing his hilltop like a distant buttress.

"The Dark Folk come," said a female voice behind him on his right, which was his first clue that his hilltop was not actually his.

The Dark Folk, Preston thought. *Where have I heard that before?*

"We must Synch," said a deeper voice, behind him on his left.

He looked over his shoulder. Three hooded, robed figures shared the hilltop with him: a woman in a purple robe, a short man in a monks robe, and a taller thin man in a deep, luxurious hood. They all faced outwards in separate directions, squared off on the points of a compass. Each of them held a glowing orange ball of energy suspended in their right hand. Preston looked down and saw that in his own right hand he held his phone. On it was his app, Spynncaster, and the flat orange ball which he had been controlling with his mind.

The man on his left took his left hand. The woman on his right took his right, and the phone he had held floated politely upwards to give her room, then hung there. Preston looked behind him to see that all four of them were now joined in an outward facing circle, and their orange energy balls were all floating near their clasped hands. Preston looked back at his phone, levitating where he joined hands with the woman in the purple robe. It was a neat trick.

And then, from out of the distant forest, a gibbering, nightmarish horde began to roar toward them, pouring in from all sides. The hoard was composed of green skinned monsters, shaped enough like human beings that each had two legs and two arms and (for the most part) one head, but a startling degree of variety was present other than that. Some were the size of elephants, and some the size of third graders. Their joints rotated in many unusual directions. The arms of some were immensely long and dragged the ground as they ran, while the tiny arms of others seemed permanently to be reaching into the air. All of them were screaming, however. They shared that trait. And from their expressions, it was clear to Preston that they all shared the additional trait of wanting to rip him to pieces.

He started to feel very nervous.

At this point, the people who have been in comas before might laugh and shake their heads. It is possible that one of these people might want to offer Preston some advice. Oh Preston, one of them might say, don't be nervous. *Just relax.* These are only the sorts of funny things *all* people see in comas. *Just relax,* because soon you will wake up and go back to sixth grade, and later in life you will tell this terrifying story to your grandchildren and they will have nightmares for many months afterwards and wish that you had never come to visit, but you won't even care. You will already be gone, collecting beaded necklaces on a Mardi Gras cruise vacation. *Just relax.*

Clearly this advice would be odd, and probably useless. But in addition to being odd and useless advice, it would also be very bad advice, for two reasons. For one, you must always try to leave your grandchildren with the impression that you are lovable, harmless, and a bit dimwitted, so they will feel bad for you and come clean your garage when you ask for help. Garages do not clean themselves, and they grow more resistant to self-cleaning as they become more tightly packed with stacks of newspapers and boxes of National Geographics magazines.

Secondly, and more importantly, the advice to *just relax* is a very poor strategy. It is almost never the right move to *just relax.* Whatever activity you find yourself in the midst of—a baseball game, a swim, a coma, basically anything other than falling asleep—you can increase your odds of success dramatically in several simple ways. You can *just concentrate,* for instance, or *just try harder,* or even *just panic.* But when someone tells you that your problems will be solved if you will only *just relax,* it almost always means that they do not understand your problems, and you should ignore them.

Fortunately for Preston he had no one around giving him advice, because he was in a coma, and so when the screaming hoard emerged from the forest and began running directly towards him with murder in their eyes, he choose getting nervous and worried over getting comfortable and relaxed.

"The Dark Folk are coming!" yelled the woman in the purple

robe, again. Preston was gratified to hear that she sounded nervous as well. It helped convince him that he had made the right choice.

"They come! We must *Synch*!" bellowed one of the others.

A wind was rising, and the woman's hair was blowing out behind her. She raised her arms into the air, and Preston's phone rose as she pulled his right hand high. The figure on his left raised his hand too, and his globe floated upwards, and then all four of them were standing with their arms in the air and their orange energy balls (or phone) floating above them.

Preston hoped none of these people expected him to know what was going on.

"*Synch*!" cried the purple woman.

"*Synch*!" cried monk robe.

"*Synch*!" cried deep hood.

"*Yeah*," cried Preston. "*Synch*!" because it was obviously his turn. There was a flash, and a blue glow appeared above them, and then they all let go of each other's hands and the others began to move their fingers in disturbing and seemingly impossible ways. Preston recognized the things they were doing with their fingers. It was Spynnlang, the programming language, but performed without a keyboard.

Deep hood was first to finish his Spynnlang sequence. His hands stopped for an instant, and then his orange globe fired off. It flew fast, like a model rocket shot straight out, and struck the first of the onrushing creatures, who all became stuck together. The creatures behind the stuck together creatures ran into them, and then they stuck together also. The hoard was slowed and the stickiness spread through an entire sector. Preston began to feel a little better about his chances of not being ripped to pieces. Not so much better that he relaxed. But marginally better.

"Shield!" yelled the purple woman on his left. She was talking to him. "We need a Shield *now*!"

The creatures were getting closer on the other side of the hill from the stuck together section, and Preston could see that, as they ran, they were making awkward, chest-high shoving gestures. Each time they did it, tiny white sparks flew out. Most sparks landed with no effect, but in some cases there were effects. Very strange ones.

Where one spark landed a small aquarium appeared. It quickly tipped over to spill root beer and kelp and multicolored turtles onto the ground. Another spark landed and a tornado grew from an acorn, then roared toward his position on the hill. He saw beautiful wedding dresses drop from the sky and turn into stalks of corn. Another white spark landed and a fireball followed the tornado, speeding right at Preston.

"SHIELD!" bellowed monk robe. He was talking to Preston just like the purple robed woman.

The purple robed woman finished her Spynnlang, and cast her globe into the onrushing army where it exploded with a devastating green fire. The was an electrical SNAP, and another orange ball dropped from the blue glow above her.

"We need a SHIELD," bellowed monk robe a third time, looking right at Preston. "We need it now!"

Another bead of light landed, and a series of red brick walls rose between his hilltop and the army, fifty feet high and topped with tiny umbrellas. Preston wondered if some of the creatures were trying to slow their own advance — until he saw that they were not affected by walls, nor slowed by umbrellas. They ran up one side, bodies turned parallel to the ground, faces to the sky, and then ran down the other, facing straight at the earth. And on they came.

Monk robe turned to Preston. "Without a Shield we will perish. Why do you wait?"

"I'm really, really sorry," Preston told him, "I don't know how to do a Shield."

And then two events occurred at one time. There is almost never a happy outcome when more than one thing happens at a time. If they are good things, you are sure to miss one of them, and if they are bad things then you are probably going to get run over by a car or burn yourself on a toaster. And these two things were very bad.

From one direction, on Preston's left, flew a streak of molten, dripping lightning. It flashed across the field one way, then came back another way, like a snake seeking a smell, and then struck like a spear at the hilltop. It buried itself in monk robe's back. He arched up, off the ground, and fell to his side. Smoke rose from his body.

From the other direction came an old woman, a human woman, wearing a plaid skirt and a business jacket, with plate mail gauntlets on her hands. She emerged from the hoard and began to sprint toward them, much faster than the rest. It was Olympic caliber sprinting, Preston thought. Despite her obvious age she was covering the ground between them as quickly as the lightning.

Preston pointed. His two remaining companions were bent over their fallen comrade. "Who's *that*?" he asked. They looked where he was pointing.

"It cannot be her," breathed the purple woman when she saw.

"It is! The Crone!" Deep hood cried in despair.

"No! It *cannot* be!" said the purple woman. "The Dark Crone was banished!"

And then the Crone was on the hillside below them, and then she was beside him. It was like a stage illusion, one second there, the next second here.

The two others backed away, but the Crone only had eyes for Preston. She was old, but her clothes and makeup were color-coordinated and formfitting. Her skin was lightly wrinkled. If Preston's mom had seen her she would have sniffed and said, "Well, *she's* made a few trips to the Botox kiosk." The Crone wore blush and tasteful pale lipstick. Her hair was bobbed. She stood away from the three of them and ran her gauntleted hands over her tailored jacket.

"Do you like it?" she asked, looking down at her clothes. "I dressed for the occasion."

The creatures were almost upon them. No one on the hilltop moved.

"So," said the Crone, peering at Preston. "This is the Einstein Object."

When she said it, realization surged through Preston. Yes! That was him! He was the Einstein Object. It was a very unusual feeling. He had always thought of himself as Preston Oliver Nowak. That's what it said on his Boy Scout name tag at the Jamboree. That's what his mother said when she was mad at him. But that, he now saw, had been wrong all along. He was The Einstein Object.

While he was having these thoughts about the nature of his identity, and wondering if he would need to change the information on his PlayStation Plus account, a massive black grand piano arched up into the air from the army rushing toward them, tumbling and spinning. So unexpected was it, they could only watch as it swept toward the hilltop, landed with a thud, and crushed deep hood beneath it. Preston saw that the purple woman was frozen motionless, terrified. Then he realized that she was actually just frozen. Something from the horde had struck her and turned her to ice.

Preston was hit in the leg by a crystal chandelier, and he lurched forward and fell down onto one knee. It was like being in some kind of crazy cartoon. He had never seen so many unexpected objects flying through the air. In the sky above, giant soaring cows breathed fire. A diamond filing cabinet whizzed past his head. It was utter chaos.

He settled onto the ground, unable to stand. His phone was clutched in his hand, and the Crone leaned close to it. Orange light from the app lit up her face. "Soon this will be mine," she said, no longer even looking at Preston.

And of all the things that had happened, this was the one threat he could not stand. Not his phone. "No!" he cried, and pushed her away.

His hand struck her shoulder. She flinched, surprised, bringing her mailed fist up to bat his arm. She hit his elbow, and his hand bounced toward her face.

She blinked.

His palm struck her softly powdered cheek.

And there was an instant transformation.

Suddenly, standing before him in place of a coifed, conventional elderly woman — albeit an extremely swift one wearing pieces of armor — Preston saw a creature. Green skin. Loose, sick white hair falling out in strands. Long double-jointed arms that hung to the ground. She wore rags that might once have been a gown. The only thing left of the elderly human were her thick, plated gloves. These slipped from her root-like fingers to clatter at her feet.

Despite his shock, anger propelled him. "You can't have my iPhone!" Preston cried. "I just got it! I waited twelve years for this phone!" He was not giving it up now. Oh no. Not even if he had to fight a horde of demons from hell.

The Crone stepped close to him. She bent, reached out, and wrapped his neck in both sets of tapering fingers. Suddenly he found himself wishing she still wanted the phone. She pulled his face close to hers, very close. He saw ragged black teeth and a purple tongue.

"Oh yes, I *will* have it." She was squeezing, cutting off his air. He pounded her arms, but she might have been made of stone for all the effect he had. He felt himself losing consciousness. "For I have returned. And everything I had, I will have again. And more!"

Behind her, green creatures poured up over the lip of the hill in a mass, wave after wave, jabbering and lurching everywhere. They left a space around the Crone, where she bent low over Preston's body. She pulled his forehead in so that it touched hers, and she slowly wrung his throat like a towel.

"You will give me back what your family stole," she spat wickedly. "And then I will destroy you. And your family. The world will be mine and my Dark Folk will dance on your graves!"

"You're... ch... ch... " Preston tried to say.

"Choking you, yes, " she squeezed harder, "because you are the Einstein Object. You have a destiny to fulfill. And I," harder she twisted, "will be there," harder still, "to take it from you and rule! It's only fair. *Now WAKE UP!*"

His heart stopped beating then. His eyes bulged and closed. And her Dark Folk did dance. And then he woke from his coma, and discovered that three full months of sixth grade had vanished from his life.

CHAPTER

FOUR

In reality, people do not suddenly wake out of comas and begin discovering things, like how long they have been asleep or who the president is now. Waking up from a coma can be a long and difficult process. Quite often you are *almost* awake for several weeks, which people sometimes do not even notice, so you have a chance to listen to them talk about your aunt's secret smoking habit and learn 5 Steps to Delicious Pastry from cooking shows on the hospital TV. You are almost certain to have been put into a hospital room for the duration of your coma. It is just the way things are done.

Preston's coma ended fairly suddenly, though, and it was only about thirty seconds before someone noticed. The first thing he saw when his eyes fluttered open were multicolored lights. Sometimes seeing multicolored lights coming out of a coma means that your optic nerves have exploded while you were unconscious, but in this case the lights were coming from a tiny plastic Christmas tree set up beside him on a table.

"What was that?" he heard a voice say. Footsteps flew toward him. A body appeared between Preston and the plastic tree, and a head on top of the body bent down close to him. The head had a face, with eyes full of tears. His mom.

"Oh god, he's back!" she said. "Preston, honey, you're back!"

Back, he thought. From someplace else. What just happened?

He tried to talk but he could hardly make a sound. His dad appeared, and bent down very close.

"What, kiddo? Are you trying to say something?"

He was. He was trying to say something very important.

"Where's?" he grunted.

"Where's what?"

"My?"

"Your what, Pres? Where's your what?"

"Phone?" Preston whispered.

"You want your phone," his dad said, shaking his head and smiling. Then he stood up and told everyone in the room, "He comes out of his coma and the first thing he wants is his phone!"

Everyone in the room laughed, and they all sounded so happy and relieved that he could hardly hold it against them, but he did not have any idea what was so funny. It was a serious question. He was awake, he was apparently in a hospital room, his family and some doctors and some nurses were all crowded around him. He had no idea what any of that meant. And it didn't even matter. None of that mattered. He kept croaking, "... Phone?" and everyone kept smiling and cheering. And then someone lifted up his hand from under the hospital sheet, and there was his phone, clutched in his fingers. His white, rigid fingers.

"They couldn't get your hand open," his mom told him. "They were going to try to pry the phone out, but they were afraid they would break your fingers. You've been holding it like that for three months."

"Three months?" he asked. His voice was getting stronger already, after a few sips of water. "Three months?"

"Yes, honey, you've been unconscious for three months. We're so glad you came back to us!"

Soon the doctors, who were unable to provide any explanation for Preston's coma but were determined that he would not exhaust himself and suffer another one so soon after recovering from the first, made everyone leave the room. They wanted Preston to get some rest. His mom and dad took turns just sitting in the corner reading and staring at him, wearing goofy smiles.

Preston fell asleep that night still clutching his phone, and trying to sort a few things out in his mind. Like, why had he fallen into a coma in the first place? And what were the strange, half images floating through his head, of a hilltop and green hands reaching for him?

But most importantly he wanted to understand why, after being unplugged and held locked in his grip for more than three months, his phone had come instantly to life, with a completely full charge, the minute he had turned it on? And what was the small, trickling tingle of energy that seemed to be flowing from his hand into his iPhone?

After five more days of tests and physical therapy, Preston's mom and dad bundled him up in the car and home they went. The house was decorated in the full Nowak Christmas regalia. It was like a giant spatula had been dipped in glittering Christmas Sauce and spread upon the surface of every room. A bounty of wreaths, large and small, decorated doors inside and out. Lights framed windows. The mantel and shelves fired off exuberant winks of green and red and white cheer. The tree in the corner was so loaded with baubles it was just barely recognizable as a former plant.

But something was missing. Before going to bed that night he surveyed his pile of opened presents, most of them video games. He closed his eyes and then slowly opened them so the lights on the tree, and the Santas ho-hoing on the shelves, and the wreaths and scraps of wrapping paper could work their magic and fill him with joy and a desire to play. But he just... didn't care. He went to sleep that night wondering whether he had suffered the Coma that

Destroyed Christmas Forever. There was a hole in him. What could possibly fill it now?

THE WHEEZE of the drip irrigation system lodging its morning protest woke him up. All night long he had been dreaming of an orange ball hanging in front of him, so he was not at first surprised to see an orange ball when he opened his eyes.

The telltale squealing outside grew louder as water forced its way deep into the pipes. The view of his room grew distinct as he came fully awake. And there sat the disk from his dream, suspended in his hand: flat, solid, orange.

Urging him to do something.

He remembered the dream — this orange circle, hanging in front of him. Nothing else. The whole night, just one dream: this ball, prompting him silently to act. It had been like a staring contest with a traffic light. He had waited for the light to change, to *do* something. And it, in turn, had been compelling him to act.

And now it was in his bed. He was lying on his side, with his open hand up near his face, and the circle floated there in his palm, the size of a quarter, just an inch above the flesh of his hand. There was a familiar pinching coming from that palm.

He blinked, and then he was amazed to see his phone fade into view around the disk. For a second he could see his fingers *through* the screen, and then it was solid. And loaded on the phone was Spynncaster, his app, with the orange circle suspended in the center of a black screen, commanding him to do something. Something he did not want to do.

He closed his hand and felt the metal and plastic. It had been there the entire time. Of course it had, he had gone to sleep with it. He must still be waking up from his dream.

He pushed his covers down, and creaked and levered himself up to sit on his mattress. It was not easy, but five days ago it would have been impossible. He looked down at the device in his lap. It had been with him, either in his hand or in a pocket, ever since he had taken it from his mother in the hospital. Fully charged, though never plugged in. He had been avoiding the implications of this. He had been trying not to think about any of it, his not-remembered-but-still-present dreams, the memories of programming.

But now this orange circle had followed him out of a dream, trying to persuade him to act. He knew what the ball wanted. He knew it as surely as he knew his name. He knew it, but he refused to do it.

The doctors had warned him there might be lingering effects. Sometimes people have difficulty telling reality from dreams after a coma. "I'm not crazy," he said, shaking his head.

The orange ball stared back at him. *Do it,* the disk seemed to be saying. "No," he said. "No." But the same compulsion that made him maintain skin contact with the phone, that made him nervous if it was out of his sight, that kept telling him there was an invisible strand of energy feeding the battery from his own body, was now telling him to do one simple thing. It was strong. Too strong. He resisted another second, then his resistance crumbled.

"Down," he whispered to the orange ball, and thought about Gravity being located at the bottom of the screen.

The circle sank.

He yelped, jerking back in shock.

BING, went the computer on his desk, chiming to life.

The two machines were still connected. It really was the most amazing technology. Some sort of advanced networking processes, he thought. But reading his thoughts? How was that even possible? He tried again. "Up," he thought, without even whispering, and located Gravity at the top of the screen. The ball fell upward, bouncing to a stop on the app's "ceiling."

He slipped from the edge of the bed. Five days ago walking from his bed to his desk would have been impossible. Today it was just very, very wobbly, and when he got there he was happy to sit down. On his screen was the Spynnlang Welcome Page.

Congratulations, Preston Oliver Nowak! You successfully completed your Skills Assessment! That wasn't so hard, was it? Your exciting career as a Computer Programmer is about to begin! Steal treasure buried for eons! Sack impregnable fortresses! Bend foreign Princes to your will! Start your Coursework today!

Once again he read the fine print, which indicated that if his heart continued to beat it would be taken as agreement to the terms and conditions stipulated, and that if he was not Preston Oliver Nowak he should call down a cloud of locusts to eat his eyes from their sockets and then devour the computer. He clicked the link to proceed to the Coursework page.

There were four simple, numbered hyperlinks on the page, and nothing else. The first one said *Casting*. The other three blurred when he tried to look at them. He clicked the *Casting* link.

Preston Oliver Nowak, your Computer Programming Course has been organized into Four Exciting Sections! Remember, Computer Programming is basically impossible for anyone who is not named Preston Oliver Nowak! So if you work through these lessons and encounter absurdly insurmountable obstacles, remember — it's still easier for you than it would be for anyone else!

Review the material below. It may appear that there are tens of millions of pages to learn, but you are probably just counting wrong! Learn at your own pace. But hurry! Go as fast as you possibly can! Because the Dark Folk are rising, and you of all people don't have to be told what that's going to be like!

And then an unexpected thing happened in his mind, near the back, in a dark corner he hadn't realized existed. For just the briefest moment it was as if a door opened, and while it was open he could see into a movie theater where the climactic scene of a horrible battle was being played. There were explosions. Enormous balls of light. Crying voices and thundering crashes, and gunshots and the clang of swords and strains of distant music.

The door opened wider and he could see heaving bodies, surging up a hill — green bodies. Terrifying bodies. Some of them wore chain mail. Some wore ball gowns. Some wore swimsuits or were dressed like construction workers or like nuns or wore nothing but rags and filth. They were screaming, these creatures, digging into the mud of a hillside they rushed to climb, and blood and fire and smoke was everywhere — and he knew they were coming for *him*. These are the Dark Folk, he thought. These are the creatures that are rising! They were coming for him. He had to run, he needed to *RUN —*

And then the door in his mind slammed shut.

It was several moments before he could catch his breath. As calm returned, as the immediacy of the vision faded, he tried to under-stand — this had to be some sort of dream, didn't it? Something left over from his coma, as the doctors had said might happen? It had felt real, but it couldn't be. Dark Folk? He closed his eyes and took a deep breath. Just let it pass, he told himself. Concentrate on what is right in front of you.

Which meant his computer. There was nothing more certain to be real than images on a computer screen, as far as Preston was concerned. Before him on the monitor were pages and pages of diagrams and Spynnlang symbols. He rolled his chair closer to the desk. He cracked his knuckles. This was real.

And then he started following along with the Casting coursework.

An hour later his father opened the door and came in. Typically Preston would have heard him, but he had been so engrossed in his studies that he had not noticed Preston Sr. coming down the hall.

"You're up!" his dad said. "Good job!"

"Yeah, I wanted to do a few things."

"Love that," he said, coming up behind Preston and looking at his screen. "What are you working on?"

"Computer programming coursework. Casting section."

"Ok, Casting, I see. Programming. Uh-huh. How's it going?"

"There are absurdly insurmountable obstacles."

"Oooh, I see," said his father, not seeing at all.

"But I'm going to figure it out, Dad. I feel like I can do this."

"That's right, Pres. That's the attitude." He peered closer at the monitor, filled with Spynnlang. "So that's computer programming. Wow. Never seen it before up close." He watched Preston typing, straining his fingers through his sets at unnatural angles. He grimaced. "Okay. Hey. Are you sure you're supposed to do it like that?"

Preston nodded. Then he turned, still stiff, and looked up at his dad. "I have to." He was coming to a realization, a profound realization, even as he spoke. "I know what I want to do, Dad. I know what I am. I'm a Computer Programmer."

His dad looked at him as if waiting for the punch line. Preston looked back. Something deep and permanent was passing between them, somewhere beneath these words.

"Wow. How about that? Well that's... whatever you want to do, I'm sure you can do it. Your mother's going to bring you some breakfast. I'm going to go open the store." Preston turned back to his monitor and keyboard. He could see his father's reflection in the glass. Preston Sr. seemed to be searching for a way to say something.

"You know, Pres, the store will always be there, if you decide that programming isn't for you. Your grandfather gave it to me. I want to give it to you. It's an honorable profession. Everybody needs shoes." Preston nodded. He knew that. Of course.

"Okay then. Well, I love you, kiddo. I'm glad to have you home. Let's make sure we do your therapy and get you back on your feet."

Preston gave his father a thumbs-up without turning around, and kept on typing.

THE WEEKS PASSED, and Preston steadily grew stronger. One afternoon several of his classmates came over. There was a sticky, nervous feeling in the room. At first they skirted around the issue, then one of them blurted it out — what had it been like to be in a coma? Preston admitted it had been like nothing. Not even sleeping. Just a blank. It was not a satisfying answer. He asked them about school. What was there to say? School was school. Similar in many ways to a coma. There were strange silences in the room. He could tell he was not acting like the old Preston. They wanted to play video games, do the things they thought were normal. He told them to go ahead. While they plugged in his uncharged controllers and popped in his still unwrapped Christmas cartridges, he just watched. Then, when they were completely engrossed, he went around gathering their phones.

"I just want to update my information in your contacts," he told them. They gave him a few odd looks, but were engrossed in their competition and happy to have Preston out of the room.

The truth was, the only reason he had invited them over at all was because he wanted to use their phones as a test. Because try as hard as he might, he had stopped making progress with Spynnlang. In fact, he had begun to doubt that it was real.

He had worked his way through the positions in the Casting section. Though the illustrations he was following were so contorted that sometimes at the end of an hour he felt like he had put his fingers into a blender, he was doing it. He was dedicating himself relentlessly, following every instruction to the letter. But it was just not gelling in his mind. He couldn't make sense of it. What *was* Casting? What did it do? How did you *use* any of it to make software?

But an idea had occurred to him. There was one Spynnlang sequence he remembered how to use — the sequence he had performed that first night to make his app appear on the phone. If this language was real, he ought to be able to deploy the app again. All he needed was a phone to test it on. Or even better, he had reasoned, several phones. So he had invited his friends, and collected their phones. And now it was all or nothing. Succeed at this, make Spynnlang *do* something, or go back to his old life.

He lined the devices up on his desk. Four phones, silent and empty. He closed his eyes and visualized the key press sequences and the gestures he had used to load his own phone. It was crystal clear to him. So clear. In fact, he saw how he could make just the slightest adjustment to the script and deploy to all the phones at one time.

He positioned his hands. He held a picture of the phones in his mind, and then he leaned forward. A quick twist on the Shift keys, a few double taps with his index knuckle and then the new element, a back tap with four fingers in a row. Four phones, four fingers. Then eight keys depressed at the same time, then seven, six, five, four, three, two and a last, single key. H. He held it down with his left thumb for two seconds, then let it go.

All or nothing, he thought. He was willing to walk away from this project, if he was not going to be able to take even a small step forward. For a moment he stared at the Spynnlang script he had created on the screen, and waited for something to happen. And then, one after the other, the phones started to vibrate.

A smile of relief spread across his face. It was real.

After five seconds the phones stopped. He was reaching for one of them when it started to ring — they all began to ring. Then the screens woke up and started flashing on and off, and he could see an orange ball briefly outlined on each one. All the devices began vibrating again, violently, without stopping, and ringing at the same time and screaming all their notification sounds at full volume. It was bedlam; it was so loud that the video games in the living room could not mask it, and suddenly four boys tumbled into his bedroom.

The phones had now begun to crackle and snap with heat. Preston backed away from his desk in horror. Crackles are not the noise any cell phone owner wants to hear coming from his device, and Preston could see the dismay growing on his friends' faces. He shared it, but there was nothing he could do. Not now. Helplessly they watched as their glass screens burst loose from their phone casings, and streamers of hot blue smoke spun up to the ceiling while flares of superheated gas hissed from inside the phones like tiny jets of dragon's breath. At last the ringing died. The phones gave a series of strangled, gurgling chimes, and then were silent.

The boys turned, slowly, and looked at Preston.

He held out his hands. Boy, was that weird, his gesture said, what in the world could have caused *that*?

His friends left soon afterward, stunned, holding their decimated electronics in their hands, and they did not come back. Preston could not blame them. It was not clear to them exactly what had happened, but it was apparent to all that Preston was the culprit. He felt absolutely terrible, but there was nothing he could do.

That night he had the dream again. He seemed to be standing, or floating, in deepest space. Stars, like minute pinpricks in a black blanket, could just be seen in a field some immense distance away. He was alone, except for an orange circle, the size of a deck of cards, that hung in front of him. The circle had a message. A very important message. But he woke up with no idea what the message was.

THE NEXT MORNING he took a walk with his mother. It was the farthest he had gone since returning from the hospital, all the way to the park. When they returned to the house he found that he was tired, but not exhausted. Almost recovered, he realized.

His mom sat him down at the kitchen table and quizzed him about his energy and the clarity of his thinking and his appetite, and before long he understood where she was headed with her questions. Apparently it was time for him to go back to school.

"You'll have a little catching up to do," she told him. "But think of it as an opportunity. Get a fresh start. I think you should try some new activities."

That was not a welcome suggestion. He remembered her saying the same thing, in the same tone of voice, the time she had attempted to sign him up for the school square dancing group. In fact, she seemed to feel that one of her chief responsibilities as a parent was combing bulletin boards and online forums to discover "new activities" to test his capacity for discomfort and feeling awkward. Horseback riding. Expressionist painting. Bluejay birdhouse carpentry. He steeled himself for whatever she had in mind now.

"What kind of new activities?" he asked slowly.

"Well. You've been in your room doing all that mysterious programming. How about trying the Programming Club? I picked this up at school."

She pushed a photocopy on a yellow piece of paper across the table to him. On it was a blotchy black-and-white illustration. A computer screen with happy eyes sat atop a desk, where a drawer stuck out like a tongue. The drawer-mouth spewed printing in a cartoon font:

Hi kids. Come join Einstein Elementary School's Programming Club. Meet new friends and build your skills. Learn Javascript, HTML, and Object Oriented Programming principals. Exchange ideas with some of Albert Einstein Elementary's friendliest students. Meets Thursdays in the library. Everyone is welcome.

He pushed the paper back to her like a prescription for the plague. He shook his head.

"Mom. That's for geeks."

"Geeks are people too," she told him severely. "Don't be rude."

He took a breath, and pictured it all in his mind. Back to school. Starting over. It did not feel like he could possibly be ready. But on the other hand, was there anything left to keep him away?

"I guess I have to go back to school," he said, watching her expression carefully in case there was a chance he was wrong. But there was no chance. "Fine. But there's no way I'm joining any *Programming Club*."

CHAPTER
FIVE

Pasadena's Albert Einstein Elementary had been christened with great optimism in 1950 and hailed as the first of a wave of "functional and beautiful" elementary schools for the Pasadena School District. In fact, it turned out to be the last school the district built for another twenty years. By Preston's time only glass-half-full type people would have described it as "functional" and not even its enthusiastic Principal, Mrs. Vargas, could bring herself to call it "beautiful." She referred to it as "beloved," and occasionally "hallowed," but that was as far as she was willing to push things.

It was Mrs. Vargas herself who was now escorting Preston back onto the grounds of the campus. She looked exactly the same as she had four months earlier, but apparently he looked completely different, because Mrs. Vargas seemed to have forgotten that Preston had ever been a student there.

"Welcome to Albert Einstein Elementary, Preston," she enthused as she pushed a discarded juice box aside with her foot and headed them out of the office and across the school yard toward his old

46

classroom. "We are very excited to have you. We know you are going to just *love* our school."

"I've been going here since kindergarten," he reminded her.

"Oh?" she said without listening. "How *very* nice! That must have been *wonderful* for you. Be careful of that banana peel."

They hurried past the library, which was the newest building on the campus. Its architecture was distinctly different from the rest of the school, but at least the paint was all one color. The other buildings, the gym and the cafeteria and the L-shaped, two story block of classrooms, had been patched and stuccoed through the years in ways that had nothing to do with aesthetics and everything to do with using the last drop of paint in every precious bucket.

"Now, we've never had a student on campus in a coma before," Mrs. Vargas continued in a distracted tone, the big, polished beads on her bracelets and necklaces clacking noisily as they walked. He was having trouble keeping up.

"I'm not in a coma," Preston told her.

"Yes, of course. But you were in a coma. Weren't you?"

"Yes."

"For quite a time, yes? Five years?"

"Three months."

"Still. So you are a very special student, and we hope to use you to convince the school district to give us extra funding so that we can accommodate other coma sufferers like you. And also make the toilets flush more effectively."

"I don't want any special — " he began, but was interrupted.

"Oh, tish-tosh!" She stopped and bent down to him. She smiled. She had a wide mouth and dark lipstick, and the effect was dramatic enough that it tended to make the youngest students cry the first few times they witnessed it. "Our school cares deeply about all those with disabilities, it's right there on our website, and we want to use those disabilities to raise money to provide them with all the help they need, to, ah, overcome the disabilities. That we care deeply about." And then she was off again. "Hurry up now."

"Can we rest a minute, my legs — "

"None of that, young man! Your disability is not an excuse for sloth — it is a badge of honor! Be proud of your coma. We are! Let's get you to math."

He followed as quickly as he could. He was getting stronger every day, but keeping pace with Mrs. Vargas could be challenging even for Coach Mark, who could do four hundred jumping jacks between the end of snack and the start of third period. They swept past the tetherball poles, past the Reading Garden with the mural of Albert Einstein where the nerdy kids sat at lunch, and finally up the stairs and into his old classroom.

"Children," Mrs. Vargas announced as she opened the door and dragged Preston inside with her, "we have a new student." She looked at the teacher, Mr. Nichols, and mouthed the word *COMA*, pointing not very secretively at Preston, then turned back to the class. "This is Preston. Everyone say 'Hello Preston, welcome to our school.'"

There was a general sense of confusion. He recognized everyone in the class, and they all recognized him. But at last several of the most obedient sixth graders said, "Hello Preston, welcome to our school," and Mrs. Vargas smiled, patted Preston on the back, and jangled swiftly out of the room. There was a moment of silence.

"Welcome back, Preston," sighed Mr. Nichols. "We're just getting started on an algebra test. You can sit in the back and we'll figure out how to get you caught up."

"I'll take the test," he said, shrugging as if to say, *why wouldn't I?* All Preston wanted was to blend in. And so he sat in the last row, started on the algebra test he had not studied for, and did his best to disappear, while Mr. Nichols called out the names of several students who could not seem to resist the urge to turn and gawk.

During lunch it was clear that word had spread — Preston had become the subject of rumors. Drug overdose. Contagious jungle fever. Police beating. His old friends, still upset at the destruction of their phones and confused by Preston's disinterest in video games, steered clear. It was true that he walked slower, was still a little thin, and did not have the energy to play handball or dodgeball yet, but he had no scars. No speech impediment. All his limbs were visibly attached to his body. Something clung to him however, faint but obvious to everyone. He stood in a corner of the yard, in the shade of a tall eucalyptus tree, and he saw it — coma. He was now the coma boy. How long this was going to last, he did not know.

He watched the outcasts sitting in the Reading Garden, where Albert Einstein's chipped eyes gazed down from the tile mosaic. In the past Preston had felt a little sorry for this group, the unknowns, outside the main current of life at the school. But at least they had found each other. Preston did not know what he had expected on returning to school, but it was not this. Would he end up in the Reading Garden? Or would even *those* kids avoid him?

He had returned to school on a Monday, and by Wednesday he was plotting ways to get himself back out of school. About the only thing that had gone well was his algebra test, which he had unexpectedly passed with a score of one hundred. Mr. Nichols had written *MATH STAR!* in big red letters on the top of the paper. Preston had not even recognized his own writing on the paper. Was this even his life? What was happening to him?

He had complained to his mother, had even suggested that he was afraid that his coma was going to reoccur unless he was allowed to return home and remain there for the rest of the school year. He complained of tiredness. Lack of appetite. Excessive thirst. He lobbed as many symptom as he could think of into her patient arms, and watched as each was caught, examined, and discovered to be insufficient. And then he made his one real, tactical error. On top of every other excuse he could think of, he accidentally told her the truth.

"My old friends are all ignoring me," he blurted, "and I can't find anybody new to hang out with."

He knew at once that his fate was sealed. Instantly, as if she had been waiting for this, patiently watching for him to make this single, specific blunder, she smiled. She reached to the kitchen counter and produced the yellow, photo copied flier.

"You could try the Programming Club," she told him, handing him the paper.

"Mom." He examining the paper with a sinking feeling. "That's just, incredibly, you know... *lame.*"

"Pres, listen to me." She took his chin and turned it toward her. "You've been through a very difficult experience. It's going to take time, but things will get back to normal. But you might have to stretch yourself a little bit. Make some new discoveries about yourself. You are my boy. I know you're not happy. I think you need some new... activities." He could tell she had been about to say *new friends.* She understood his situation. She nodded at the flier.

"Can you really afford to pass up this opportunity? These kids might be just like you. They meet tomorrow."

"But my coma... " he started. She raised an eyebrow in a way that clearly said, *don't even bother.* So he nodded. Programming Club it was.

AFTER SCHOOL ENDED the next day, he stood outside the library, building up the nerve to open the door. Meeting new people had never been his strong suit. And the idea that the Programming Club kids might, as his mom had proposed, be just like him was not a reassuring thought. If it was true then his situation was even worse than he had imagined. But he had to give it a try, just so he could tell his mother he did not like it.

He swung the door open and stood in the doorway. At a table with rows of computers sat three kids Preston had a hazy memory of having seen before, each one at a monitor. A portable whiteboard had been wheeled up behind their table, and a woman stood before it pointing to a diagram. When Preston came into the room everyone turned to look. He held up the yellow flier. For a moment he thought his voice had failed him. Nothing came out. The people in the room watched, waiting. Then he managed to speak.

"Is this Programming Club?" he asked.

The woman, who wore slim jeans, a long-sleeved turtleneck shirt and tight-fitting black gloves, smiled.

"This is us," she said, pointing to the three kids and gesturing to include herself. "In all our dubious glory."

"*You* all may be dubiously glorious," said one of the kids, "but my light shines for all to see." He posed with his finger to his cheek. He wore red sunglasses with studs sparkling around the rims. Now Preston realized where he had seen these kids. They were the ones who ate lunch in the Reading Garden.

With a certain foreboding he heard the door click shut behind him.

"Come, come in," said the woman. "I'm Ms. Fredrick. Just call me Sally." She was young, and somehow both classically graceful and nerdily awkward at the same time, as if she had spent years shuttling between ballet classes and Minecraft gaming conventions. There was also something about her that seemed much older than her years. Maybe it was just the way she spoke, which was lilting and cultured like a person from a black-and-white movie.

"Over here," she called gently. "We don't bite."

"Speak for yourself," said one of the other three kids, a girl in a black hoodie, leaning forward on her elbows and tapping her fingers on the table. Even from here he could see that the nails on the fingers had been chewed back mercilessly. Preston tried not to stare, but she obviously did not care where he looked. She stared back at him, appraising him from behind strategic black bangs. Her eyes were lined with thick mascara. She looked like a video game assassin.

"Jacey, please," said Ms. Fredrick, with a quick, exasperated murmur. To Preston she said, "Honestly, come join us. You make me a little nervous lingering over there." With a deep breath he moved up to the table and stood, holding his backpack.

"Yes, introductions!" said Ms. Fredrick. "This Is Jacey. Who apparently bites, though I've yet to see it. This is Regan." She pointed to the boy with the sunglasses, who performed a small bow with his head and his hand. It appeared surprisingly courtly, Preston thought.

"And this gentleman at the end of the table is Matias," she finished, indicating a very heavy boy with close-cropped hair, a fleshy face, and a blank — or unbelievably patient — expression. He had both his hands folded in front of him on the table and sat stiffly, moving very little.

"He's our own little Buddha," said Regan.

"Hardly. Buddha wasn't on the spectrum," scoffed Jacey.

"Jacey," warned Ms. Fredrick.

"How do you know Buddha wasn't autistic?" Matias asked Jacey suddenly. He didn't move his hands from the table or shift in his seat, but there was something very active in his eyes. It was hard for Preston to read him. He was either the most understated prankster in the history of the world or he was dangerously crazy.

"Because autism is a creation of the American Medical Association," Jacey said, fingers clenching, "without any definitive biological markers. Defined exclusively by symptoms. Buddha was not autistic because autism only came into existence in 1943 when they gave a bunch of random symptoms a name."

"That's purely semantic," Matias said mildly, staring straight ahead. "The syndrome would exist regardless of whether it had formally been codified, so Buddha — "

"Hey guys," said Regan, "I think we're scaring what's-his-name." He gestured with an eloquent thumb at Preston. "By the way," he said to Preston, "what's your name?"

"Preston," he blurted.

"Hello Preston," Ms. Fredrick said. "Pull up a chair." She indicated a spot at the table in front of another monitor, and Preston dropped his pack and slid into it, feeling very conspicuous. Out of the corner of his eye he could see all three of the kids watching him.

"We were just having a bit of a theoretical discussion when you arrived," she said. She turned around and looked at the whiteboard.

At the top were the letters *OOP*, and below that a diagram showed a large circle with branching lines connecting rows of smaller and smaller circles below it. Ms. Fredrick tapped the largest circle at the top, which was labeled DOG.

"OOP, or Object Oriented Programming. You are familiar with the concept, Preston?"

"Well, not exactly... " he said.

"Not to worry. Object Oriented Programming uses the concept of Objects to take the real world and model it in software." She traced down from the large DOG circle through the smaller and smaller circles, each linked by lines to the object above.

"In OOP there are Parent Objects and there are Child Objects. If the Parent is a DOG, all Child Objects of DOG inherit all the traits in DOG, such as Four Legged, Tailed, Tendency to Bite Mailmen. That is called *Inheritance*. That's clear, yes Preston?"

He felt his head nod, which was puzzling because he had no idea what she was talking about. Ms. Fredrick seemed to sense his confusion. She pointed back at the board and said, "Child Objects are created with everything the Parent Object gives them through a process called *Inheritance*. Sort of like a factory that makes toys from a mold."

Jacey suddenly groaned. "Seriously? Inheritance? Are we in kindergarten? Are we regressing to basic Object Oriented Programming? This is *stupid!*"

Ms. Fredrick turned back from the board and fixed Jacey with a glare. "Jacey Stathold. Two months ago you challenged me to a contest, do you recall?" Jacey stopped talking and sat stony faced. "The winner was to set the subject and the schedule for these meetings for the duration of the year. I was very willing to abide by the outcome of our match. Do you remember the outcome?"

Jacey set her jaw and crossed her arms. She nodded.

"That's right. You were unable to penetrate the firewall shielding my extremely simple server, while I rather easily disabled your scripts and at the same time gained access to the Facebook account which you have not revealed to your parents. Is that correct?"

Jacey shrugged, slumping lower in her chair. "I don't know how you did it. But I'm going to figure it out… "

Ms. Fredrick smiled. "Yes you are. That is the entire point. But until you grow as accomplished as I am, or your pouting and negativity convinces me to abandon my post altogether, I will be here, determining the subject matter for these meetings and offering you new opportunities to learn."

Regan observed this exchange with amusement, Matias did not seem to notice it very much at all, and Preston was confused but fascinated. Watching other people get in trouble was one of the great pleasures of sixth-grade life. In an environment like this, where he was so new he could not possibly be regarded as a co-conspirator or accomplice, gawking was even safer. Despite that, when Jacey pointed her mascara rimmed scowl at him, he pretended he had not noticed anything that had been said.

"So," Ms. Fredrick continued, "the question — the *theoretical* question — that we were addressing when Preston came in was this: is Reality actually structured the way Object Oriented Programming suggests, where things can be organized in a hierarchy of Objects, each Child inheriting from its Parent?" Ms. Fredrick turned her back to them and examined the whiteboard, totally engrossed in the thought she was proposing, "And if reality *is* structured that way — what if you had a magic wand and could create Objects in the physical world? Would you then be able to program Reality itself?"

She turned and faced them. "Well?"

"Unlikely," said Matias.

"Seriously?" sighed Jacey, in exaggerated disdain. "Uh, no."

"That would be chaos," said Regan. "Vastly entertaining. But no."

Ms. Fredrick turned to Preston. He felt surprise and excitement. *Yes, TOTALLY*, he wanted to say — *that sounds like the best explanation for a bunch of stuff that already happened to me.* But he did not say that.

"I guess that seems, you know, crazy," he managed. "Programming reality. What kind of technology would that be?"

At that moment Ms. Fredrick's phone rang. She reached into her purse with her carefully gloved hand, and checked the caller. "Oh!" she said. "I do have to take this. I'll be right back." She held the phone up to her ear and moved away from the table toward the librarian's office. The kids watched her go. Then three sets of eyes pivoted slowly to Preston.

Jacey snapped her fingers. "I remember you. You're the new coma kid. Right?"

Preston nodded uncomfortably. He was not sure he wanted to be identified as the Coma Kid, but it did not appear he had much choice.

"I'm not new, though. I've been here since — "

"Is it true you took those phones from those kids and set them on fire?" she interrupted.

"No," Preston said. The only thing he had less desire to talk about than his coma was the incident with the cellphones.

Jacey arched her brows. "Everybody says you did it."

"That's not what happened, I was — "

Matias broke in. "What languages do you know?"

"Just English," Preston said. "A little Spanish — "

"Programming languages," Matias said. "If you have high-level Python I have a project — "

"I have high-level Python," said Jacey. "Why ask him?"

"You said you were busy," said Matias. Jacey thought for a moment.

"I am," she decided.

"I don't know Python," Preston said.

"Ok, so what's your stack? LAMP? WISA?" asked Jacey. "How's your Objective C? How's your Java?"

"I don't know those. Mostly I'm just doing Spynnlang," said Preston. "I've been getting into it pretty deep the last month or so."

This created a momentary silence. Then Regan spoke. "Deeply into what, again?" he asked. "Spang?"

"No, Spynnlang," Preston said. "I'm not an expert or anything. Actually I'm kind of hitting a wall. But I made this." He took out his phone and showed them Spynncaster. "I programmed this; it was the first project. The Skills Assessment on the welcome page, you probably know it, I guess." He passed the phone around, a black screen with an orange ball hanging in the middle of it. Each of the others took it, touched the motionless ball, tilted the phone. Nothing happened. They handed it back to Preston.

"What the hell is that?" asked Jacey. "A screenshot? What's it supposed to do?"

"This," Preston said, and in his mind he shifted Gravity so that it pulled the ball to the bottom of the screen. Then he set Gravity to Nowhere, so the ball was free floating, as if it hung in space, and he pushed it with his mind, flicking it so it bounced from one side of the screen to the other.

"Up," he said, pushing the ball up. "Left, right, loop de loop. See?" he asked. "I'm moving the ball with… " *my mind,* he thought, but did not say out loud. A reasonable voice inside was telling him to slow down. So instead, he set the phone on the table and turned on the computer he sat in front of. He typed in the Spynnlang Welcome URL and quickly clicked through to the Casting coursework section.

"Here," he turned the monitor to show them the Spynnlang icons. "This is as far as I've gotten. You guys probably know way more about it than me, but… " Something in the way they were looking at the work he had done was gratifying. Could it be that he was even more advanced than they were? Was all the hard work and misfortune of the last four months finally starting to pay off?

"This is a joke, right?" said Jacey.

"I do not understand that," Matias intoned. He went back to his seat. "That is not a programming language."

"Who are you trying to fool, anyway?" Jacey sat on the table, leaning in close to Preston. "Let me ask you a question — do you know what a loop is? Or a variable? Or a conditional?" Preston had heard these words before, but he didn't know what they meant. He shook his head. "Do you know anything?"

"Hey," Regan stepped in between Preston and Jacey. "Down Jacey. Bad Jacey. Sit."

"No, look," she insisted, "if he wants to be a programmer, then this is his first lesson. You either know what you're talking about or you don't. He doesn't." She sat back in her seat. "You don't impress us, your work doesn't matter to us, we don't want you here."

Regan flared. "Jacey, I swear, if you and Matias drive off another perfectly — " But Preston interrupted him.

"Great, ok, I get it," Preston said, anger flaring. He turned off the computer and put his phone in his pocket. "You people are all just Reading Garden nerds anyway! I don't care if I'm in your idiotic club!" He grabbed his backpack from the floor and stalked toward the door. Because it was still difficult for him to stand straight up and start walking without a pause and a stretch, he hoped his legs were not going to collapse beneath him and strip away his last shreds of pride. Fortunately he made it to the door. He pushed through and closed it behind him. He walked a few yards away, and then he could tell that his legs were about to go, so he sat and leaned his back against the wall.

Perfect, he thought. Not even the nerds were interested in having him around.

The library door opened, and Regan stepped out. He scanned the lunch area and the corridors, then saw Preston sitting just a few yards away on the ground. He let the door close behind him, then came to lean against the wall near Preston's pack. It was a moment before he spoke.

"Reading Garden nerds. That was pithy. With a touch of cruel intent. Bravo. May I sit?"

"It's a free walkway," Preston sighed. The day could hardly get any worse. And he was not feeling ready to walk again. Regan sat, and was quiet for a moment.

"You know what is ironic about this school being called Albert

Einstein Elementary?" Regan asked then, staring out at the basket-ball hoops through his sparkling red sunglasses. Preston ignored him.

Regan continued, answering his own question. "Genius is not valued here."

"I never said I was a genius."

"Clearly I wasn't talking about you."

"Look, what do you want?" Preston demanded. "I'm leaving your club, you should be happy."

Regan shrugged. "But I'm not. Every time an applicant attempts to join the programming club, those two in there" he pointed irri-tably back into the library "run them off. I had hopes for you. I thought you might be different."

"Different than what?"

"You aren't trying to impress us. Not pretending to know things you don't. Not trying to win points. You are who you are, in your own limited fashion. An innocent."

This was too much for Preston. "Look, who do you think you are? Nobody cares about your stupid programming club. Why would anyone want to try to impress *you?*"

"Oh, Preston." Regan looked skyward as if he was searching for words. He sighed. "You do not understand the hierarchy in this school. So listen, and I will explain." Regan cut the air in from of him into several layers, and pointed to the lowest one. "First, you have the deeply mentally challenged, the students with the special classes. Then above that, you have the average students, such as yourself, mentally challenged but functional. Above those, here, you have the garden variety 'gifted' and 'highly gifted' sorts, the poor souls tortured by the knowledge that they are above average, but not truly extraordinary. And then at the top are Jacey, Matias and myself. Jacey and Matias have run all the 'gifted' group off. They show up with their pesky hacks and their URL shorteners and try to impress us — Jacey herself actually *wrote* many of the scripts they have downloaded to try to pass off as their own. It's so very tiresome. And then here you wander in. Like a fresh breeze. Only to be snuffed out by Jacey's pique. I think I've mixed my metaphor."

Preston sat up away from the wall and really examined Regan for the first time. Curly head of brown hair. Skinny. Weird habit of pursing his lips and gesturing with his palms facing upward. "So, do you always talk like this?" Preston asked.

"Yes," said Regan, with deep satisfaction.

"How old are you?"

"I am thirteen hard won years of age. And you?"

"Twelve. So you're saying... you're some kind of *boy genius*?"

"Oh, marvelous! Yes, I am a boy genius! And Jacey is a mad genius — by which I mean a psychotically angry genius. Unwell, really."

"What about Matias?" Preston asked, playing along.

"Ah, Matias. He is an inscrutable genius. A fat, inscrutable genius. You may tell him I said so. You will not be able to determine whether he likes that description or not. He is too inscrutable."

Preston leaned back against the wall. It was all a bit much. "So if you're all so smart, how come you're going to this school?"

"A variety of reasons. I choose not to reveal my own. You may ask Jacey and Matias yourself, though Jacey will shriek at you and Matias may crush you in a killing embrace. He is deceptively strong."

Preston laughed. It felt good.

"I have a question for you," Regan said. Preston waited. "The app you showed us. I was watching as your ball moved around the screen. It was not touch control. Not gyroscopic. How were you controlling it?"

Preston waited a moment, then decided. "With my mind," he said.

"Oh, coma boy," said Regan, staring in slow surprise and then smiling, "you are funny! Well, this *is* a gift. You are still water running deep." Preston did not know whether to be insulted or complimented. He was saved from having to make a choice when Ms. Fredrick stuck her head out the door.

"Boys, come in. I have wonderful news!"

Regan stood up. He offered Preston his hand. Preston took it without thinking, and found himself following Regan back into the library. Ms. Fredrick was standing by the whiteboard again. She was almost jumping up and down with excitement.

"The phone call I took just now was a confirmation. Our programming club has been accepted into the Code Portal Hackathon!"

This meant nothing to Preston, but Regan, Jacey and even Matias began an instant onslaught of questions. Apparently the Code Portal was a very big deal, some sort of programming competition. At last Ms. Fredrick got them calmed down.

"So, as I said. Short notice. Today is Thursday, the first round of the Hackathon is this Saturday. We will have to drive to Anaheim, but I can provide transportation." She turned to Preston, who was standing a little apart from the others. "Will you be joining us, Preston? Will you attend as part of the Einstein Programming Club?" Jacey rolled her eyes. Matias seemed not to notice there was a question on the table. Regan cocked an eyebrow at Preston and waited.

Preston didn't give it a second thought. "I'm in," he said, surprising himself.

"Wonderful!" she cried. "It's such a pleasure to see a new face Preston! And I'm excited to bring you up to speed on Object Oriented Programming. We've covered Objects. Next week we will look at Getters and Setters. And I will see you all on Saturday."

CHAPTER

SIX

At first, of course, Preston's parents said no. This is what any parent whose child has recently emerged from months of unconsciousness will say when the child wants to run off on a sudden field trip. But Preston had made the proposal with a day and a half to spare, time enough to listen to their protests, challenge every objection with a rational response, and leverage their affection by strategically mumbling that he was, "just not hungry for dinner." He even played the coma card, using a faint voice to refer to himself as the victim of a "tragedy," which had forever "scarred him," and left him nothing, nothing at all, except "going to Code Portal with these kids I just met." And in the end his parents relented. Permission slips were signed.

And so Saturday morning, he stood with Jacey, Regan and Matias on the sidewalk in front of the school while his mother watched from the car a few parking spots away. He could have walked, but she wanted to see him off. Jacey wore a black hoodie and boots with buckles. Matias wore the same brown shirt and brown pants he always seemed to have on, and Regan had on bellbottoms and a red silk shirt to go with a new and larger pair of sunglasses. When

Preston's mother saw him, she cackled. "Are you kids going to a disco?" she asked.

Soon a huge black Suburban came gliding up to the curb, and Ms. Fredrick rolled down the tinted black passenger window. "Greetings, travelers! Your carriage awaits," she called. Sitting behind the steering wheel, in her gloves and sleek turtleneck, she looked tiny, like a Lego figure that had been dropped into a giant truck from another line of toys.

She unlocked the rear door. "I will warn you up front," she said as they peered in, "I both love, and am ashamed of, my car. I went to the dealership for a minnow and I left with a whale. Apparently I have no defenses against salesmen. But you must admit, it is perfect for road trips!"

Preston gave his mother a last wave and climbed into the SUV. It was silent and dark inside. He settled himself into a deep leather seat. Ms. Fredrick's eyes in the rearview mirror blinked back from what seemed like a football field away. There was a TV facing him, built into the back of the driver's seat. Every surface was taut with luxurious black leather or soft, seductive fabric. Mysterious buttons beckoned from the arm rest. By pressing them he could make his seat perform amazing tricks, tilting and raising and — could it be true — massaging? In the row behind him he could hear Jacey and Matias exchanging equally astonished comments, their voices vibrating as their chairs worked magic fingers up and down their spines. Regan, sitting in the seat beside Preston, scanned the interior without interest, then buckled himself in.

"No hot tub," was his only comment.

The trip to Anaheim took about an hour. Preston was full of questions.

"So this is a contest, right?" he asked. "I think I've heard of hackathons."

"Oh super. He's heard of hackathons," said Jacey from behind him. "Our victory is assured."

Ms. Fredrick's voice came to them over hidden speakers, as if she were sitting right in among them. "That's right, Preston. All hackathons are different. But, as a general rule, they are opportunities for programmers to come together, share code and opinions, and advance their craft."

"But Code Portal is just a *little bit more*," said Jacey. "Like, one hundred thousand dollars in prize money more." There was excitement in her voice. It was smoothed over, pushed down, denied full release, but it was there. Preston realized that this trip was, for Jacey, more than just an opportunity to meet other programmers. Obviously she wanted to win this prize.

"Code Portal is a special event," Ms. Fredrick said, "and the prize is certainly a compelling incentive. One hundred thousand dollars and an iPad Pro. But you four are in the Junior Category, as you know, so you are not eligible for the financial prize at all. You will be competing for an iPad Mini."

Behind him Preston heard Jacey mutter something and laugh. Matias chuckled. Regan spun swiftly to face back between the seats and put his finger to his lips. "The audio is great in this car, Sally," he said softly to Ms. Fredrick, though he was facing away from the driver's seat. "Are there microphones?"

"Yes," came her embarrassed voice over the speakers. "It's such a large vehicle that in order to talk to the passengers in the third row the driver is provided with this speaker and microphones. So no plotting against me!"

Regan turned back and settled into his seat. He gave Preston a wink and held his finger to his lips again. Preston frowned at him, but Regan just closed his eyes and seemed to sleep.

"So how does the competition work?" Preston said to Ms. Fredrick, though he was watching Regan and feeling irritated. He knew he had no right to expect to be included in the club's secrets, not yet at least. But that did not make it easier to be excluded.

"When the event begins," she said, "you are given a theme, such as World Peace, or Genetics, or Space Travel, and you have a set amount of time to complete an application — in the case of Code

Portal a mobile application — that illustrates the theme. There are three stages. Today is the first. And then two more, over the following two weeks, with teams eliminated each week. Though again, not for the Junior Category. Just a single round for you."

"And anyone can go?" he asked.

"Oh no. Teams must be invited to compete. That's why it is such an honor. Even in the Junior category the team members must each have an extensive GitHub presence. Only the best of the best!"

"What's GitHub?" Preston asked, regretting it instantly.

"Oh. My. *God.*" Jacey spoke from behind. Then no more. Apparently no more was needed to make her point.

"Think of GitHub as an online platform where developers exchange code and work on open source projects together," said Ms. Fredrick. "You may not realize it yet, but your teammates have quite an online reputation." Preston thought he heard a touch of pride, or *something*, in her voice. "Yes, they are quite the little crew indeed."

The rest of the trip seemed to pass in an instant for Preston. He had come south this way less than a year before when his family had visited Disneyland. He was surprised to see that the exit off the freeway they finally took was the same one that funneled cars to the Disney parking lots. They were close to the Magic Kingdom, it seemed.

Code Portal turned out to be in a large hotel directly adjacent to the park. Preston tried not to feel intimidated as they left the parking structure and walked down manicured paths, around fountains, and toward the dramatic, arching hotel entrance. Ms. Fredrick seemed supremely confident, goosing them on from behind like a sheep dog. She propelled them through the wide entry, held open by uniformed valets, and then they were inside.

Guests swirled. Preston looked up, trying to find the ceiling, but he could not. The lobby was many stories high and encased in glass. Hotel room balconies overlooked them. Descending from somewhere above were massive pipes and tubes, purportedly the work of a famous artist. A pond with ducks was ringed by seats. It was like being inside an upside-down fishbowl that had been lowered down on top of a mall. Restaurants and jewelry stores and clothing outlets beckoned. He saw a Verizon store, and then a Sprint store, and he felt tormented by those legions of functional phones that were not his to use.

"This way," called Ms. Fredrick, leading them toward an impressive banner. It stretched above sets of double doors leading into a massive conference room. The words *Code Portal* were emblazoned on the banner, and as they came closer they saw many smaller placards which all bore the *Code Portal* branding. A hum of voices rose in volume as they drew closer to the entrance to the hall. Ms. Fredrick stopped at a desk and checked them in, and they each were given a name tag to hang around their necks.

Preston's feeling of intimidation was growing. This was a coding competition, but he only knew a tiny bit of Spynnlang, and even that had become a struggle. He didn't have any of the skills anyone would need for a hackathon. He didn't even have a GitHub account. With a sinking feeling he began to wonder if he was going to be called up on a stage and told to write computer code. Was he about to be held up for ridicule in front of a huge crowd of people like Jacey?

Regan gave him a nudge with his elbow. "Ok," he said. His voice cracked with energy. "Hold onto your hat. Such a pity you don't have a hat. Perhaps we should have team hats? In any case, this is where things start getting fun!" And something in the undiluted pleasure lighting up Regan's face gave Preston back a semblance of calm. If he stuck with the team, everything would be fine.

They swept through the doors and into the hall, and were greeted by pandemonium. The noise in the conference room made the lobby seem like a library. At least a thousand people stood and sat in desks arranged in rows, rows which spanned the room the way mounds of tilled soil span a plowed field. Computers stood crowded on every surface. Cables ran in massive, root like tangles through the room, tucked beneath the rows of desks.

"That way," said Ms. Fredrick, pointing them toward the far side of the arena. She had a peculiar, pained expression as she looked around the crowded space, as if something about the place made her uncomfortable. She stayed near the wall as they trooped their way around the perimeter, and she took care to side step the people who walked into her path.

"What's up with Ms. Fredrick?" Preston asked Regan.

"Sally does not like crowds," Regan explained. "In fact, she does not like to be touched. You notice her gloves?" Of course Preston had. He had been waiting for an opportunity to ask about them. "And the turtlenecks she always wears. She only joined us four months ago, you know. It was a while before she felt comfortable enough to tell us. She has a blood condition, and she bruises very easily. And, let us be frank, she is at least as brilliant as Jacey, Matias, or I. And that comes with certain, shall we say, peculiarities?" He pointed to his temple and made a looping gesture. "Speaking purely from personal experience, you understand."

"She's crazy?" Preston asked.

"No," Regan shrugged. "But she is utterly brilliant. She is accomplished at certain exotic programming languages that even Jacey has not mastered, which is virtually unheard of. Jacey knows them all. However, brilliance has its price. Poor little genius."

After that Preston watched more closely, and he saw it was true. Ms. Fredrick avoided being touched by people. She was graceful to an amazing degree as she slid and stalked among the attendees, but it was clear that the strain of being here was taking a toll.

"Stop," she instructed them. She pointed. "Here we part. There is your section, the Junior Category participants. I will keep an eye on you from the periphery. Now I leave you to your destiny!" She smiled at her attempt at humor, but it was a strain. She actually looked older, her skin drawn and her eyes lined. She turned and exited swiftly out one of the side doors and into the less crowded lobby. And they were on their own.

"Ok. Let's go kick some ass," Jacey said, and led them forward.

They wove through the intervening rows and between the desks until they stood beside the placard saying *Junior Category Participants*, at the entrance to a roped off group of desks.

"Look at the babies," tisked Regan. The age range inside the roped off area was different from elsewhere in the room. Here the participants ranged from one or two years younger than the Einstein group to one or two years older. These were their peers.

Jacey headed in first, followed by Matias, Regan, and finally Preston, and it took only a moment for Preston to see that as they moved through the younger crowd they caused a disturbance. Whenever they passed a table the kids would stop, whisper, and point. It caused Jacey to glare more furiously and pull her hoodie over her head, and of course Matias did not seem to notice, but Regan grew animated, smiling, passing his hand through the air in a lazy wave and nodding as if he were blessing people when he saw them. One of the kids got up and came forward tentatively, as if to greet them or ask for something, but he bumped into Matias — who continued without slowing or blinking — and was thrown to the side. Apparently the Einstein group was a very well-known band. Several of the other groups looked dejected and shook their heads. Were the Einsteins also feared? He felt many Junior eyes following him, probably wondering who he was and how he fit in.

"Our adoring public," said Regan, as they reached their desks and sat.

A mix of sounds from the massive room was washing over them, voices and music and laughter, chairs banging and tables scraping. Preston had to take a deep breath. The months he had lost to the coma had left him with an elevated sensitivity to noise.

"Look at this," Jacey scoffed, holding up a paper. The same paper could be seen on all the other desks in the Junior section. "Here's the Junior assignment: build an e-commerce website." Regan laughed, and even Matias chuckled. Jacey was furious.

"No, this is an insult. Who do they think we are?" Jacey demanded.

"They do not know who we are," said Regan.

"I propose that we introduce ourselves," said Matias.

Jacey continued to fume. "Look at this, they don't even keep it a secret. The theme for the main competition is going to be announced to everyone, but they think Juniors need extra help. Look, they list resources we can use! There's a server with a bunch of modules available, so all we have to do is wire them up. It's infuriating!"

"Jacey, dear," Regan said, putting his hand on her arm, "please focus. We do not have much time. We have to penetrate the local network before the competition starts. Remember? To activate an account? The *Plan*?" Jacey nodded, blinking rapidly and shaking out her hands.

"All I need is network access," Matias said, waiting for a moment when they were not being watched and then ducking under the table. "They'll expect any compromising contact to come on wireless, so that's what they will be defending against," came his muffled voice. "But I'll use these cables below the desk."

"Okay Mr. Literal," sighed Regan. "Will you be announcing each step of your plan as you go?"

"Guys," Preston asked quietly, "what's going on?"

"Right away, he's a distraction," protested Jacey.

Regan settled his chair a few inches closer to Preston's, and spoke in a low voice. "Preston. We are in the Junior category right now. But we do not plan to remain there. You see?" Preston did not see. He shook his head slowly. Jacey rose angrily.

"I have to get started. You explain things to brain death here, I'm going."

"Jacey, wait. He should go with you. Look at that table," Regan indicated a raised platform against a far wall where a microphone stood and administrative personnel hovered over desks. "You're going to need help."

Jacey looked, and after a minute she seemed to agree with Regan.

"Right. So you come," she said.

"No, I have to feed data to Matias, and I have to hack access to the bar code scripts." He turned back to Preston. "Here it is, Preston.

We are going to enter an app in the Main competition, not the Junior competition, because we plan to win the Main competition, and collect one hundred thousand dollars and an iPad Pro. However, we do not have an account in said Main competition, thus our plan — "

"Regan," Jacey seethed, "To. The. Point. I swear listening to you enjoy yourself talk makes me want to stab myself in the eye."

"Fair point. Okay, Preston. We must hack a new account. Jacey will steal a server hash. You will help her." He looked at Jacey. "How was that?"

"You still need practice." She grabbed Preston by the collar as she headed for the dais. "Come with me. Shut your mouth. Do every-thing I say."

Preston stumbled and followed her. They threaded their way toward the administrative platform as quickly as they could without drawing attention to themselves. Jacey was eyeing the setup care-fully as they got closer. When they were only one row away she dropped into an empty chair and pulled Preston down next to her. She reached into her pocket and pulled out two rubber bands, stretching them out and back compulsively.

"Ok, you see the guy on the end?" She tilted her head. "Green shirt."

"I see him," Preston said.

"He just took off his lanyard. See?"

"What's a lanyard?"

"Oh, Zeus save me. Lanyard. His, you know, the cord around his neck with the badge on it. See? He just put in on the table!"

Preston nodded.

"Ok. He's been going around scanning a bar code on that badge into every station when a new team gets seated. We need to steal that lanyard. Got it?"

Preston nodded again. And then he shook his head vigorously. "No! No, no. I mean, how are we supposed to do that?"

"I'll create a distraction, you grab the badge, we head back to Junior land." Preston was still shaking his head. Jacey looked like she was about to spit fire. She leaned in close to him and whispered viciously from within her hood, "Look, Regan thinks you can do this. So can you?"

"I guess... " he began. Apparently she took that for a yes, because she stood up and headed straight to the steps by the microphone. He took another deep breath, the only variety he had taken since entering the building, and went around the other side, headed for the man in the green shirt.

"Hello, excuse me please?" he heard a nasally voice say near the stage. He was so fixated on the table that he had not been watching Jacey, but the voice was coming from that direction. He turned, and saw that it was Jacey talking. But a dramatically different Jacey. She had used the rubber bands to raise her hair out of her eyes and pull it into two pig tails on either side of her head. She had taken off the black hoody and tied it high around her waist, revealing a bright purple Pokemon shirt underneath, and had pulled her pants up so her socks showed.

It was a complete transformation.

"Oh, excuse me," she said, waving a limp hand at the stage. "Oh, excuse me! Oh, can you help me?"

All three of the administrators on the stage were looking at her. Preston moved closer, angling to get around the last desk and within reach of the stage.

"Umm, I lost my little Algernon, he ran up there," Jacey whimpered. She worked in some wheezing for good measure, as if afflicted by asthma. Preston thought she might be overdoing it. But it was still very impressive. "Have you see my little Algernon?"

The group shook their heads. Jacey frowned. "He's a big, big rat, like this big." She held her hands apart to indicate the dimensions of a small toaster oven. "He ran right up under your table."

That got their attention. They jumped up from their chairs looking at their feet, just as Preston arrived at the edge of the stage in striking distance of his target. Which is also exactly the moment the green-shirted man grabbed his lanyard and hung it back around his neck.

Preston froze. There was no way he could get the badge. He looked at Jacey. He could swear that she caught him out of the corner of her eye, but she did not look at him. She was pointing under the table.

"There he is!" she squealed. "Just like his *picture*. I can show you a *picture* of him. If you help me catch him we can take a *picture* together. Take a *PICTURE*."

She shot him a single meaningful glare as she was pointing and yelling. And it hit him. Picture. The man in the green shirt was standing right in front of him. They needed the bar code, not the actual badge. Preston pulled out his phone, and flipped up the camera. As casually as he was able, which was in reality not that casually, he aimed and fired six quick shots of the man's chest, and then the man ducked under the table, searching for a giant, escaped rat.

Preston backed away. He had done everything he could. He wanted to escape; he felt his heart pounding and the weakness in his legs was hitting him. He turned and stumbled back, through the crowd that had gathered, ducking and weaving until he arrived in the Junior section and collapsed in a chair.

"What in the name — what happened up there?" Regan demanded. Preston was out of breath. He slumped with his head down. "Did you get the lanyard?"

"No," Preston gulped, "he put it on. Right at the last second. Is Jacey here?"

At that moment Jacey sauntered up, as if nothing in the world had happened. Her hoody was back on. Her hair was in her eyes. It was the old Jacey. Preston could not help gawking. She was an illusionist.

"So did you get it?" she asked Preston.

"No," Regan told her. Preston could see deep disappointment on his face. It was a flash of something real, something Preston had not seen yet. Preston thought Regan looked thirteen years old for the first time since they had met. "No lanyard," Regan said. "That was our chance."

Matias clambered up from beneath the table. "I got a splitter into the ethernet cable. We are... what is happening?"

"They did not get the badge," Regan told him. Matias nodded, still unflappable.

Jacey pointed to Preston. "I hope you're a little Ansel Adams," she said. "Well?" Preston pulled out his phone, unlocked it, and handed it to her.

"You look," he told her. "I wouldn't recognize it if I saw it." Regan started to ask a question, but Jacey held up a finger and it stopped him. She swiped and thumbed through the shots. Her face grew grimmer. She came to the sixth and final photo. She stared at it. Then she held up the phone, facing the other three.

"Bingo," she said. On the screen was a perfectly framed barcode against a blurred green background.

"Yes!" Regan exulted softly. "I found the scanner page. Not even hashed up. This is child's play. So, boys and girls." He took the phone, showed them the picture. "The big moment." He held the screen carefully up to the camera on the monitor in front of him. The barcode stabilized in a webpage on the screen. A beep sounded. "Account Activated," appeared in a green popup. "Welcome to Code Portal. Enter Team Name."

He turned back to Preston. "And we are in," he said. "Very nice work, coma boy." He performed the same step on the computers in front of Jacey, Matias, and finally the one in front of Preston's seat. They all entered *Einstein Programming* as the team name.

"What am I going to do with this, though?" Preston asked Regan, looking at the screen.

"Gaze at it in profound satisfaction," Regan suggested. "You earned it."

Jacey narrowed her eyes speculatively, examining Preston.

"Well," she said, "your photography sucks. But you're not a total idiot."

"You have just received Jacey's highest compliment," Regan told him. "Be very proud."

"ATTENTION," called an amplified voice over the huge sound system. This was followed by the entirely unnecessary sound of a thumb tapping the microphone. "HELLO? CAN YOU HEAR ME?"

All eyes turned to the stage, and the speaker motioned for the sound to be turned down slightly.

"Welcome to Code Portal!" he called. The crowd cheered. He delivered a short speech about the importance of coding as a tool to change the world. He thanked the sponsors who had made the event possible. And then he paused.

"And now, the theme of the inaugural Code Portal Hackathon, the theme you've all been waiting for... is... Play Ball!"

For two seconds there was absolute silence as the phrase sank in, and then a muted buzz seemed to seal the room from the outside world, spreading over the crowd like oil over water, as each group bent inward to begin furiously planning. The Einstein team did the same.

"Ok, quickly people," Regan urged. "Play ball. Ideas?"

"Baseball simulation," Matias proposed.

Jacey shot it down. "Everyone will do that."

"Well," said Regan, "that seems like what they want. How can we do it differently?"

"Fully unified shaders for the models. Pixel and vertex shaders on 3D scaffolding," Matias suggested. Preston struggled to make sense of what they were saying. And then he stopped struggling, and gave up. These were real programmers talking. It was out of his league.

"I can do that," Regan said. "I can blow that up."

"It's not enough," Jacey said. "Look at the teams in this room. There's a team here from Nvidia, for god sake, you don't think they can do unified shaders?"

"What then?" said Regan.

Jacey shook her head. "We need an angle. How can we make baseball different?" They stared at each other. None of them had any bright ideas.

"Baseball in outer space," blurted Preston. "Baseball on the moon. Mars. Let the player choose his own planet."

The team stopped thinking and turned to him. Regan stared, mouth a thoughtful pucker, brows raised. He nodded. "Now there is an idea."

"The ball would fly forever in outer space," Matias observed. "And on the right planetoid, you might be able to hit it all the way around the surface."

"We would need some pretty tight physics modeling," Jacey said.

"I'm proficient with that math," Matias rumbled, "and if we presume no atmosphere we won't need to model drag. It'll be complex, but doable."

"Ok then. Consider it settled," Regan said. "I get the modeling. Hello, unified shaders. Matias to the physics. Jacey darling, someone will have to do the more pedestrian work of pounding out an account management framework and implementing a rules system for gameplay. I'm afraid that must fall to you."

Jacey snorted. "Fine. For a hundred thousand dollars? I'd eat my own disgusting Pokemon shirt."

"Will you be able to finish all that in eight hours?" Preston asked Regan.

"We don't need to finish, simply get enough of it working so we move on to the next round. Now, Preston, you will need to leave us alone. There is work to be done."

Around them the other Junior category participants had begun working, but as Jacey, Regan, and Matias turned to their consoles Preston was able to see a very distinct difference in their approach. The Einstein team seemed to slip easily into something like a trance. They reached for their keyboards and the rest of their bodies stopped moving. It was instant. Occasionally they would mutter to each other, or lean and look at another's screen and point, but only with the greatest efficiency of motion. Preston realized that he was watching something very rare. This was genius, motivated and focused, totally in its element. They were like a pride of hunting animals, perfectly coordinated, and each a matchless machine in its own right.

By contrast the other Junior participants, though purportedly the most talented of their peer group, squirmed, chatted, and left to get soda. Some of the Junior teams even got up as a group and ate lunch from backpacks they had brought. Preston himself was forced to stand and stretch, but his teammates were focused on their screens like air traffic controllers in the middle of tornado season, and they did not move. After several hours the endless sitting was too much, and Preston had to stand and walk the perimeter of the room.

Near enough to the Junior section to keep an eye on them he found Ms. Fredrick. She was sitting in a corner, barricaded subtly behind another chair. She saw him and waved.

"Well, Preston, what do you think of Code Portal so far?"

"It's great," he said. Though in fact he was feeling a little disconnected, wondering again what he was doing here. "I'm just walking around." His mood was not hard to guess.

"No worries, Preston, it won't take long for you to fit in here. Regan mentioned that you already have an application built. True?"

"Yeah. It... doesn't do much. I'm kind of stuck," he admitted.

"May I see it?"

"I guess." He pulled out his phone and loaded Spynncaster. He held the screen out to her. "Like I said it's not... "

A frozen look came over Ms. Fredrick's face. For just a second she seemed to stop, absolutely motionless, as she gazed at the phone. She reached out a single, delicate finger, as if she wanted to tap the screen, then drew her hand back. Her eyes flicked up at him. In them he saw desire, and at the same time, fear. Preston thought about her anxiety over being touched and felt a wave of sympathy.

"Well," she said, "it's a start. Keep it up! What are your plans for it?"

"There's an online course. I'm stuck at a certain section though." He thought about the month he had spent trying everything he could think of to conquer the first step in the Spynnlang coursework. "Really, I guess I'm about to give up."

"Oh no," she admonished, concerned and sincere. "You must never quit. Do you want to be a computer programmer?"

"Yeah, I do! It's just... " Something unexpected forced its way up inside of him. It was hot frustration, born of trial and error without success.

"I'm just tired of failing!" he burst out. It was true. His frustration had turned to fury as the weeks had passed. He wanted to succeed so badly, but it was too hard!

"If you want it, then look deep inside, Preston Oliver Nowak. Your anger is trying to tell you something."

He nodded noncommittally. Then he frowned. "How do you know my middle name?"

She stared at him. Her eyes were gravity wells, and he could not look away. "It is written above your heart," she said. She pointed at his chest. He looked down and saw his name tag where it hung around his neck. *Preston Oliver Nowak* read the bold black letters. He rolled his eyes. It figured. His mom had filled out the online registration form. She seemed to love torturing him by using all his names on every official form. Again, he thanked his dead grandfather. I'm glad I never met him, he thought. I might have had to hit him in the nose.

He said goodbye to Ms. Fredrick and continued around the room. Far from comforting him, her advice to look deep within had made him feel worse. Because when he looked there, he did not see anything. Nothing except failure. Failure and anger.

Preston considered what he had to work with. From his Computer Programming coursework, all he had learned so far was *Casting*. He grasped the way to form all the convoluted postures to produce the icons, but he just could not see how to make it all work together. Sometimes there was a glimmer, but essential insight just slid away every time he reached for it. Something basic was missing. He was afraid he might not be smart enough.

He came to a thick round pillar on the far side of the room, one of the deep structural supports that held the building up. And he found his phone in his hand. Frustration rose again, and with it the impulse to hurl his device against the concrete column. Without a conscious thought that made it happen, he felt his arm draw itself back, behind his ear, trembling with tension. He shifted to fire it forward, shatter it into a thousand pieces. Then he looked back at his hand and discovered that the phone was not there. Once again, all he held was a quarter sized orange disk. Waiting to be thrown. To be flung. To be... cast.

And it came to him. The code that underlay the Casting section was a framework allowing him to *cast* the ball. To cast it *out of the phone.* He had been struggling to see how the pieces were to be used within the bounds of his device, which is why it had made no sense. It was as if he had been reading the instructions for piloting an airplane and trying to apply them to driving a train; he was being told to go up, down, left and right — directions that train tracks did not go. But now he saw it, and he wondered how he had ever missed it. Spynnlang had methods to breach those boundaries, and extend itself in all those directions. He was not driving a train. He was piloting a jet.

He was frozen there, in front of the concrete support, in the pose of an Olympic javelin thrower, and after a moment he saw that he was attracting attention. Even in this arena of hyper focus and idio-syncrasy, he realized, people will still stare at you if you faced a wall long enough, grunting and pretending to throw your cell phone. He broke the pose. He put his phone away. And then he slunk back to his desk in the Junior Section.

Nothing had changed with the team. He stood behind Regan, far enough back not to disturb him, and watched as he built and tested an amazingly lifelike set of three-dimensional player models. Jacey was pounding at her keys as though she wanted to beat them down through the table so they spilled out at her feet. He had never seen anyone type that fast. Code, indecipherable to him, filled the pages like leaves shooting out in front of a blower.

Matias worked at a more methodical pace. In fact, every few minutes he stopped, stared at the screen, then squirted out a few more lines. His work was mainly numerical, long strings of mathematical symbols and equations.

These were the physics modeling algorithms, Preston assumed, based on what he had heard earlier. He found himself drawn gradually closer to Matias's screen. It was strange, but he found himself extracting bits and pieces of meaning up out of the formula there. He found that he could not look away. How could he be understanding this? He had almost failed pre-algebra. He felt lightheaded, as though his brain were inexplicably being fed extra oxygen, or denied oxygen altogether. The balance of the math was breathtaking. The way the mass of one object bent space and interacted with the mass of another object, and then there, right there, underlying it all like an intoxicating melody, was the universal gravitation constant.

Yes, the universal gravitation constant — where, he saw, something was amiss. It should not be that low. Preston realized that Matias had made a mistake. He looked again to be sure. It was as obvious to him as a dead fly in a bowl of soup. It was going to cost them time down the line — Matias would be able to work his way back and fix it, but the time he wasted would be time they did not have.

"Look," he said, putting this hand on Matias's shoulder and bending down to peer at his screen. "There's a problem here, in the constant. Let me. It's quick... "

Matias seemed so surprised to be interrupted that his normally immovable frame shifted easily to the side when Preston pushed his hands off the keyboard. Preston did some fast number sorting in his mind, and pinned down the solution. Matias had G, the gravitational constant, as *6.673 x 1^{-11} Nm^2/kg$^{2[4]}$*, which was wrong. It only took a couple of key strokes to rectify. Then he stood back. Matias scrutinized the new formula.

"That is correct," Matias said. He turned and fixed Preston with a puzzled stare, though as usual he did not meet Preston's eyes, but concentrated on his cheeks or forehead.

"Go," said Preston. "The clock's ticking."

Matias nodded and returned to his work. And then a curtain seemed to fall in Preston's mind, so that when he looked back at Matias's screen he had no idea what any of it meant. Where a second before it had been clear and beautiful, now it was nothing more than strings of symbols and numbers mashed together, making his head hurt. He felt cold, as if he had stepped from a heated house into a cold October night. Sweat broke out on his face and neck; his body felt clammy. He took several tentative steps back, and sat at his own desk. What was happening to him?

His thoughts were interrupted by a loud chime.

"TWO-HOUR WARNING," came the announcement. "YOU HAVE TWO HOURS TO BRING YOUR CODE TO A SUITABLY PRESENTABLE CONDITION AND SUBMIT IT."

"How are we doing?" Regan asked Jacey from the corner of his mouth.

"Burning through this," said Jacey. "I'll be ready."

"Matias?" he asked.

Matias did not answer. Regan looked at him, then Jacey did too. They discovered that Matias was staring in Preston's direction.

"Matias?" said Jacey. "You good?"

Matias nodded at last. "Yes. I'm feeling surprise. It won't affect my work."

Regan snorted. "Okaaay," he said. "Matias is *feeling surprise*." His laughter faded as he turned back to his keyboard, head down, gaze settling into unblinking focus.

Preston looked at his own computer. He was abruptly filled with images of Spynnlang, new insights growing out of his realization about the Casting method. He reached for his keyboard and brought up the coursework URL. When he closed his eyes for just a moment, an image of a hand, cupping a glowing orange ball and then hurling it into the dark, came to him. He opened his eyes, and began to type.

It was slow going. If he pushed himself and went from one posture to another quickly, he knew he would attract attention. No one was looking his way, no one was giving him a second thought right now, and he wanted to keep it that way. So he had to disguise the Spynnlang input, and extend the time he took between the individual postures. He supposed, if anyone did see him, it might look like he was doing a series of elaborate finger stretches. If such things as finger stretches existed.

He hoped they did.

It seemed as though Preston had just begun typing when another chime sounded. "FIFTEEN MINUTES," said the announcer's voice.

For the last thirty minutes or so Jacey, Matias, and Regan had been hurrying back and forth between desks, taking turns inserting and editing files on a flash drive. It seemed that they were in the final phase of committing all their work to a single code base. They were moving fast, and running low on time.

"It's done, Regan. Run it. Run it!" Jacey was almost shouting. But it went unnoticed, because at tables all around them the same frantic scene was playing out.

"We need the — " Regan insisted, standing at his desk and gesturing spastically.

"NO! We don't. Regan, shut up and do it. Build it. NOW!"

Regan huffed a few quick breaths like a sprinter at the starting blocks, then reached down and keyed a sequence. A long trail of code began flashing up from the bottom of the screen.

"No bugs, no bugs," Jacey was muttering under her breath. "No bugs please please please... "

The scrolling stopped, replaced by two simple words: *BUILD SUCCESSFUL.*

"YES!' she exclaimed. "Fourteen minutes to spare. We are god-like!"

Regan sat at his console. "Submitting it to the admin server now. Wait, what are we going to call it?"

They looked at Preston. It had been his idea, they seemed to be saying. So he should name it.

"Outer Space Ball," he suggested.

They nodded. They were worn out, weak, but jubilant, and they crowded around Regan's desk as he went through the final few steps to send their project off, along Matias's hacked network connection, to the Code Portal servers.

While they did this, Preston looked at his own work. He had completed the Casting section of the coursework, and had deployed his updated app to his phone. He was filled with relief. Finally, finally, after all his work: progress. Maybe he was a Computer Programmer after all.

He flipped back to the Code Portal Team page. *Submit Project*, blinked a simple link in the header. Curious, he clicked it.

"Drop Compiled Binary Here," read the text within a dotted rectangle. Beneath that was a *Submit* button. Preston felt himself filled with clarity, the way he had been when viewing Matias's gravitational calculations. It was so very obvious to him what he should do, and what would happen. A pleasant warmth suffused his whole body, and he felt like he was floating on a cloud of summer air. He dragged his file, the compiled binary for the updated Spynncaster application, to within the dotted rectangle, and dropped it. The *Submit* button blinked.

He was about to click it when he noticed another link near the bottom of the page: *Submission Instructions*. Even in his heightened, altered mental state, even feeling as if he knew things that he had no right to know, he could not bring himself to proceed without reading the documentation. It was a fundamental part of who he was. He clicked the *Instructions* link.

This showed him a form with additional required information. He filled it quickly: app description, team name, development methods.

Then he clicked *Submit.* And his warm glow faded.

He was absolutely, utterly drained.

The rest of the team gave a cheer. They had completed their own submission. They turned to Preston.

"Hey, Preston, you OK?" Regan sat on Preston's desk and looked in his eyes. "You look a little bleary."

"I'm good," Preston said. "I should probably eat."

"Yeah, we all should," Regan said. "We should eat a celebratory feast!" He stood, and held his arms wide. "Ladies and gentlemen, shall we adjourn?"

"I think we just kicked serious ass," Jacey announced. "Tell me I'm wrong. Did we just kick serious ass?"

Regan put his arm over her shoulders. "Very serious," he told her.

And they swept from the auditorium like victorious gladiators.

Later, as they rode home, and the excitement in the car had faded to a dull throb one step from exhaustion, Ms. Fredrick's voice floated back over the speakers.

"Well, people, I'm sorry you didn't win the Junior competition. Frankly I'm surprised. But there is always next year."

"When do we know who advances to the next round in the Primary Category?" asked Regan.

"On Monday, I believe."

"Well, it will be interesting to watch that list," he said. Jacey chortled.

"Preston," came Ms. Fredrick's voice, "did you have a productive experience?"

"I guess. I figured some stuff out. Sort of felt like I was in the way most of the time," he said sleepily. His elevated mental state had leached away and left him nothing but weariness. He wanted badly to slide into his bed and sleep.

"He assisted with physics modeling," said Matias abruptly. "It was unexpected."

"I didn't really do anything," Preston insisted.

"You found a computational error."

"Just a typo."

"It was a surprising insight. A deep insight few could have made."

Regan examined Preston carefully. "Physics, is it?" he said, softly. "Very interesting, coma boy. Still water indeed, running deeper and deeper." Preston gave a half smile and shrugged.

"Just a lucky guess," he said, then yawned and closed his eyes. But while they remained closed until the car returned to the school, he did not sleep a single minute of the trip. Because he knew he had not been lucky with that calculation. He had a strong feeling that it hadn't actually even been him *doing* it. Which led to another strong feeling that he might be going crazy.

That night he again had the dream, where he hung in space and faced a blank, flat orange circle. The circle was bigger now. It was the size of a refrigerator. And it still had a message. But now, Preston thought, it seemed to be losing its patience with him. It was pulsing, and surging back and forth: toward him, then away. He had the sense that it was trying to pull something out of his brain. Or pull something open. A door? Maybe. His brain, however, remained stubbornly closed. And when he woke up he found that he was still very tired.

CHAPTER

SEVEN

The next Monday during lunch period, Preston was forced to make a choice. Lunch periods are typically not the best time for making choices. Your blood sugar is low, you are pressed for time, your yogurt is very likely getting warm. But Preston was tired of eating alone. His coma had changed his reputation at the school, from *Preston is normal and totally invisible* to *comas are weird and so is Preston*. So the decision he had to make was this: if he walked over and asked to sit with Jacey, Matias, and Regan in the Reading Garden, and they *refused*, would it be worse than spending another day eating by himself in the corner of the lunch area?

Mrs. Vargas had not helped his reputation at all. She had actually declared today to be Coma Awareness Day at Albert Einstein Elementary. She had made an announcement over the school speakers, and had put a large piece of poster board featuring his picture up at the entrance to the campus. On top of his picture had been the words *COMA: Who Will Be Next?* And under that it read *Help Preston fight childhood coma syndrome! Please donate to the school coma fund today. All money will go toward making the campus more coma friendly, and also to dealing with the toilet situation.* She had gone so far as to ask him to sing "The Star Spangled Banner" during first recess, but he simulated a case of laryngitis and she dropped the idea.

In some ways, then, he had very little to lose. He had already become a bit of a leper. He examined the scene in the Reading Garden and meandered gradually closer, still trying to decide what he would do. Like all his old friends, Preston had assumed that only outcasts and misfits lurked on the benches beneath the Einstein mural. When he considered it now he was not even sure how they had gotten that impression. When you really watched what was going on in front of those benches, it seemed to operate more like a royal court than a reject containment zone. Even now Preston saw a boy with a model rocket approach Jacey meekly, only to be dismissed by Regan. "Begone, rocketeer. Do not trouble our meal with your missiles and your gunpowder." The boy looked confused and shuffled away.

All too quickly Preston had crossed the distance from the lunch area to the garden, and stood uncomfortably at its edge. Really, calling it a garden was demeaning to horticulture. It was just a ten-by-ten-foot section of packed earth bordered by six inches of concrete, with two stone benches and a black-and-white mural on the wall. Once each spring the janitor spilled a handful of seeds onto the ground which the entire school then neglected to water for the rest of the year, so the only plants growing there were varieties requiring neglect to thrive.

Preston rustled his bag softly to get their attention. Regan had his legs crossed and was drawing on a juice box through a straw, with enormous, blue, star shaped sunglasses perched on his nose. Jacey hunched forward over a paper bag of popcorn. Matias cut a tuna sandwich into fastidious cubes and ate them one by one with a plastic fork.

Preston tried to look as if he wanted to sit with them, but at the same time look as if he had just accidentally happened by with his lunch without noticing that they were present. Which meant that he only managed to look nervous and baffled. After a moment, without saying anything, without even looking at him, Regan shifted down the bench, displacing Jacey and Matias an equal amount, and patted the newly exposed surface beside him. Then he returned to sipping his drink, surveying the school the way a prince surveys his kingdom.

"Do you think," he wondered to no one and to everyone, "that they will create a Programming Garden to honor us here one day?"

Preston sat and took out his lunch. The feeling of fitting in again was quietly overwhelming.

"Yeah," Jacey said. "But Vargas will make us pay for it ourselves."

And then there was a screech over the school speakers. "Will the following students please come to the principal's office: Jacey Stathold, Matias Dias, Regan Franklin, and Preston Nowak."

Preston's stomach dropped. This is the normal response of any student whose name has just been called over the school speakers. To Preston's knowledge, no good had ever come from any such summons. But Regan stood calmly, and set his juice box on the bench, and looked at his watch. The other two rose as well, though Jacey seemed jittery with eagerness. Matias, typically, was expressionless.

"I believe Matias has won our little pool," Regan said.

"There must have been traffic," Jacey snapped. "She's late."

"My calculations suggested travel was not a variable," said Matias. "The math was clear."

"What if this isn't Sally?" Jacey said. "We might be in trouble."

"The likelihood is infinitesimal," Matias assured her.

They stepped away from the benches and walked quickly toward the office. Preston could not understand it. No one ever walked quickly toward the office.

"Preston, come," Regan called over his shoulder. Preston followed. Quickly.

They were ushered through a waist-high swinging door with a glower and a finger crook from Mr. Swinton, the office clerk charged with filing tardy paperwork and with scowling. They passed the empty nurse's station where scraped and sickened children helped themselves to Band-Aids and cold packs in the absence of qualified nursing personnel. And then they came into view of Mrs. Vargas's open office door. As they moved closer they could see her sitting behind her disheveled desk, talking to someone out of sight. And at last, like windup toys that have come to the end of their springs, they slowed and stopped. Not even Regan's astonishing self-confidence could waft them directly into that sanctum without an invitation.

Mrs. Vargas noticed them.

"Come in, children," she said with great enthusiasm. "I believe you know Ms. Fredrick?"

They wedged themselves into whatever space they could find in the office not otherwise taken with bundles of auction forms, boxes of cookies, and towers of cellophane wrapped fund raising baskets, and saw that the other person in the office was, in fact, their programming counselor. Mrs. Vargas gestured for them to sit in chairs which did not exist, while she herself stood.

"On behalf of the hallowed institution of Albert Einstein Elementary School, I would like to congratulate you, the members of our illustrious programming club — it's called the programming club, Ms. Fredrick? Yes? — I would like to congratulate you all on your victory at the Code Portal Hackatronic."

"Hackathon," corrected Ms. Fredrick.

"You may all choose a small fund raising basket."

As far as Preston could tell, there were no small baskets.

"What can all of this mean?" Regan declared, eyes wide with innocent wonder. "Has there been some mixup? We were entered into the Junior Category, but sadly we did not win."

"Perhaps it was because you did not submit a project in the Junior Category," said Ms. Fredrick, with an equal amount of wide eyed wonder. "Shall we adjourn to the library and discuss this miraculous event?"

Mrs. Vargas watched this exchange with growing alarm.

"I'm sorry," she began, "are you saying that the children *didn't* win? Because if that's the case I can't allow them to leave with a basket."

"Oh, they won," said Ms. Fredrick. "But I do not think they deserve a basket. Do you, children?" She eyed them. Severely. All four of them shook their heads. Mrs. Vargas looked relieved.

"Well, isn't that lovely! A group of students who put the funding needs of the school ahead of their own childish desires. In that case you are all excused."

And with that they trooped out of the office, past the Mr. Swinton's glower, and back through the lunch area to the library, where Ms. Fredrick swung open the door. She flipped on the overhead lights and went to stand in front of the whiteboard, which stood where they had left it, still covered with object oriented programming diagrams. She slapped a folder onto the desk and stood facing them. The rest of the club came in after her. Preston noticed that they seemed uncertain, as if they had expected a different reaction.

"Well?" She said, after staring silently for several seconds. "What do you have to say for yourselves?"

"Well," Regan began. But, very uncharacteristically, he had nothing else to offer.

"Did you or did you not hack yourselves a Main Category account, and submit a Round One project into the Main Competition?"

"Well," Jacey ventured. "It is called a *hack*-athon —"

"Do you know," said Ms. Fredrick, "how much trouble you could have gotten into? Not to mention the disciplinary measures that might have fallen upon the school district and upon me personally? Did you think about any of that?"

Preston, watching Regan, Jacey and Matias, was pretty sure they had not thought about any of that.

"But the Junior Category sucked," Jacey protested. "Those kids are newbs, they couldn't make an ecommerce website in eight hours without a library of modules —"

"I am aware of the caliber of your competition, Jacey. But it is no excuse for putting the reputations — the careers — of other people at risk." She stared angrily at them. "I have more than half a mind to decline your invitation into Round Two. Your *ill gotten* invitation."

At that a chorus of pleading arose. "Please, Sally!" Regan begged. "It was the only choice we had. Why is it fair that our age should be the single criteria used to determine our capacity?"

"You can't do this!" Jacey howled. "You can't!"

"Oh, yes I can, Jacey," Ms. Fredrick responded, in a voice that had grown very cold. A moment passed, and even Matias's breath was shallow as he waited for the ax to fall. "But in the interest of providing an ongoing environment of learning and discovery, I will overlook it this one time. Congratulations. You have progressed to Round Two of the Code Portal Hackathon."

They cheered, Preston included. After a moment Ms. Fredrick smiled too, won over by the atmosphere of revelry. She settled them down.

"All right now, all right. The next round is this Saturday. When we see each other at the club meeting on Thursday we can finalize our travel plans. So. As I am now a co-conspirator, I ought to know the details. Tell me about your app, this... " she opened her folder and pulled out a paper to consult, "Let's see... Spynncaster."

"You mean... Outer Space Ball. Right?" Jacey asked.

"No," Ms. Fredrick shook her head and read, "the Einstein Programming Team has been accepted into Round Two to continue developing their application, Spynncaster. Oh... " She paused and read further. "Oh, here. You apparently *also* submitted an entry named Outer Space Ball?"

"No, we only submitted one entry," Regan said.

Ms. Fredrick frowned. "It says here that Outer Space Ball was rejected because of missing metadata."

"*What?*" demanded Jacey. "What metadata?"

"Apparently there were, let's see... there were submission instructions which required additional application specific data. Team members, development stack, experience, methodology, etc."

She watched them, puzzled. "I don't understand. You obviously provided the metadata for your Spynncaster application."

"We didn't submit a Spynncaster application!" Jacey yelled.

"Um," Preston mumbled. "That was... " he stopped when they looked at him.

"What?" Jacey snarled.

"I submitted that. Spynncaster. That was my app. You all saw it, last week... " Again he slowed and stopped. Ms. Fredrick's expression was strangely neutral. Everyone else wore looks of anger or confusion. Preston wished he had kept quiet.

"That thing?" Jacey spat. "That thing with the orange ball?"

"Yeah, but I updated it — "

"Are you *kidding* me?"

"Obviously we failed to follow the instructions completely," Matias intoned. "In the future we will exercise more caution. This has been a learning experience — "

"But our app was *awesome*," Jacey moaned, sinking into her chair. "We could have won the whole competition. How could this happen?"

Ms. Fredrick crossed her arms and looked satisfied. "Well. How very interesting this all is. The newest member of our club has saved your chances, through the simple expedient of following the instructions! It is rather fitting, considering the circumstances. Don't you think?"

"Saved our chances?" Jacey continued to moan. "Saved our chances? Have you seen his so called *app*? We can't win anything with that. It's not even... it's... "

Ms. Fredrick looked at her watch. "Oh goodness, I have to fly." She put her papers back into the folder while she surveyed her club. "I will let you collect yourselves. Talk it through and tell me what you decide. I will see you on Thursday. Please make sure the lights are off and the door is closed when you leave the library. Perhaps you can snatch victory from the jaws of defeat, if you look at this in the right way." She checked her watch again, and hurried out.

Regan sat beside Jacey. "It's okay, Jace. Think this through. We still have a chance."

"No we don't! Are you kidding? Did you see — how did his stupid app even get accepted?"

Matias stepped close to Preston and met, and held, Preston's gaze. None of them had ever seen anything like that happen. Matias took great care never to hold anyone's gaze for more than a millisecond.

"I saw your application," he told Preston. "It was simplistic and useless. If you have managed to submit it and it's been accepted, then there is something here that I don't understand. Explain. Now."

Preston backed a step away, and Matias followed him, intent. He even began to reach out to grab Preston by the shoulders, and then Regan jumped up and moved Matias back gently.

"Ok people. People," he said, "listen. This is not the situation we wanted, but all is not lost. As Sally pointed out. Jacey? Darling? Can we have your attention here for a moment?" Regan got them all focused on him, and then he turned to Preston.

"Preston, you obviously piggybacked on our hack, which was very clever of you, and very devious as well. We will forgive you these transgressions. But first — what the *hell?* What is this Spynncaster application? What does it *do?*"

Preston sank gradually into a seat. Matias sat across from him. Jacey slumped in a chair to his right, Regan on his left. They waited.

"It's a game," Preston began. Which was a simple enough statement, but it surprised him anyway, for he had never before been able to verbalize what Spynncaster was. A template, the coursework page called it. Part of his Skills Assessment. These things he had known. But only now, pressed by the intensity of his friends at this table, was he able, somehow, to sift through what he had learned, dig into what he had dreamed, smell the lingering traces of events from his three unconscious months, and pull up this information. A game. Which was not right. Not exactly. But it was close. So he kept drawing information up, and as it rose a string of other insights were pulled up with it. He could almost see them. They held him motionless. It went on for just a few seconds too long for Jacey's taste.

"Hey. Coma Kid. What's going on?" she demanded, and pounded the table. He shook himself clear of the visions so he could speak.

"It's a game. It centers around an energy called Spynn."

"What kind of energy?" Matias demanded. "Gravitational? Chemical? Kinetic or Potential energy?"

"Magical," said Preston.

Regan shrugged. "That is a well-established game trope," he said. "We could work with that. Continue."

It was actually difficult for Preston to talk. With the visions crowded so densely around him now, his own thoughts had fewer places to go. He raised his hand and batted the air in front of him. Regan and Jacey glanced at each other, frowns deepening.

"Spynn is," Preston said, struggling for clarity, "it's from a world where battles... no, that's not right. Not a world. A universe. Battles are fought there, by people called Spynncasters. Spynncaster! That's the app!" he cried. It was like finding a gold coin under his pillow. A gift straight from the underworld. Jacey and Regan were looking more and more concerned. Matias looked interested.

"How do these Spynncasters harness this energy?" he asked. "In your game?"

"They use... they use programming. No, that's not right. Is it? They use gestures. They collect Spynn and shape it with programming — no, with spells. Spell? These gestures have names, and they Cast this energy at their enemies. Their enemies... " again he trailed off.

He knew who these enemies were — he had seen them behind a door in his mind, streaming up a hillside, clawing for his blood, straining to rend him and burn him. But that vision had no place in the *game*. There was a line where his game and the real world blurred back and forth into each other. It was very hard to understand. There was no way to talk about it.

"Uh, Preston," said Regan, "perhaps we should take a different tack. Could you show us your application? Give us an idea of how this, ah, *vision*, of yours, is implemented? Maybe we can figure out how to work on it. We might still be able to pull off this contest."

Preston drew his phone from his pocket and loaded the app, happy to have something concrete to do. He held it in front of him over the table. Matias rose quickly and stood behind Preston's chair, Regan followed, and Jacey came last, muttering and shaking her head.

Preston waited a moment, staring at the orange ball.

"I updated it," he said. "I used the Casting methods, and I made it interactive, so two people could play."

"How does it work?" Regan prompted, because Preston kept losing focus and drifting.

"Ok," he said. "This orange ball. I guess... that is a ball of Spynn."

"You guess?" asked Regan.

"I mean, yes. It is. It's a ball of Spynn energy." Another discovery. He felt as though he were sinking more and more certainly into a very new, very extraordinary world. A world where things had finally begun making sense.

"Wow," said Jacey. "Will you look at that. An orange ball. I've got to tell you Preston, this is blowing my little mind."

"How do you play?" Regan asked.

"Well, I can't show you that right now," Preston said. "Because no one else has the app running."

"How would you know who to play against?" Matias asked. "Is there a lobby system? How do you perform the data handshake? How would you establish a connection with another player?"

Preston squinted. "I would just know."

"Oh my god," Jacey said. "This is ridiculous. I'm leaving."

"I can put the app on your phones," Preston said. "Then we could all play. It would only take a few seconds."

Jacey stopped. "Oh really? You're going to get my phone logged into your Apple developer account and make me a beta tester, then deploy to me, and it's only going to take a few seconds? That takes an hour if you're lucky."

"I have an Android device," Matias said. "You'll also need to access your Google Play Developer Console."

"I don't have those accounts," Preston said. "What are they? Should I get one?"

Regan's voice was patient when he spoke, the way you might talk to someone you had just discovered was very sick, and possibly also holding a live hand grenade with the pin pulled.

"Well, Preston," he said carefully, "you know the account you used to get your current beta onto your own phone? That is the only way you can deploy an application to any iPhone. To Jacey's or mine or... "

Regan's words petered out as he watched Preston spin to the computer in front of him and quickly bring up the Spynnlang URL. He navigated to a blank input section, and without saying anything else he began the deployment sequence. His companions were a captive, disturbed audience. At one particularly gruesome finger manipulation Regan gasped. All or nothing, Preston thought, and decided to deploy to all three of the phones at once. He had come a long way since his failure in his room. Eight fingers, seven, six, five, four, three, two, one. Then "H" for two seconds. The Spynnlang symbols hung, mysterious, shifting, slightly stomach churning. Preston examined them to make sure they were correct, then sat back in his chair.

The phones in the pockets of Jacey, Matias and Regan all chimed at the same time. Preston was relieved that the sequence had worked, or seemed to have so far. He watched, feeling just the slightest anxiety, as his friends pulled their phones free and gazed with surprise at the screens.

"How... ?" said Jacey.

"You've deployed your application to each of our phones," observed Matias. "Without their UDIDs. Without an email or a text registration. Using a single framework to reach *both* the Android and the iOS devices." He left his mouth open for a moment in case any other words felt like coming out. "This is very, very... surprising."

Regan dropped gracefully into the chair beside Preston and gazed at the monitor full of Spynnlang that Preston had just produced. He pointed.

"What is that?" he asked.

"Spynnlang," Preston said. "That's how you... that's the programming language. It's specially created for making Spynncaster."

"Spynnlang," Regan repeated. Preston nodded. Regan closed his eyes, speaking carefully. "So you are creating this application, *Spynncaster*, which revolves around a *magical energy,*" and he paused when he said that, as though tasting the words, "called *Spynn*. And you are using a programming language that is entirely unknown to anyone in this room, called *Spynnlang*, to create this application?" Preston nodded. Regan pressed his palms into his forehead for a moment. "Do you have a dog named *Spynn* as well? Do you live on *Spynn* street?"

"I don't understand," Preston said.

"Let's play this freaking game," Jacey said. She held her phone out. "How do we start? Let's go, put up or shut up. I'm tired of this crap."

Preston stood up from the desk. He held his own phone in front of him. "Who should I play with?" he asked.

"Me," Jacey demanded. "You play with me."

Preston was suddenly nervous, and uncertain. He had never played his game before. He had only *discovered* that it was a game a few moments earlier. He felt a great weight, a pressure, and it was not just the pressure of the people in the room wondering if he was crazy, even though he had started to see they thought exactly that. He also felt pressure from the *world of Spynn*. Which made no sense. But he had a growing idea that the stakes riding on this demonstration were immeasurable. Fate of the world stakes. And he actually did not know how the game was supposed to work. Not exactly.

He summoned what courage he had. Which, he found, was not much. He held his phone toward Jacey and noticed that his hand was shaking, and he forced it to stop.

"There are a couple of ways to move the ball," he told her. "You can use your finger — I just added that method before I submitted it at Code Portal — or you can use your mind." He focused, and he shoved, and he sent the ball flying off his own phone and onto Jacey's, where it bounced against the bottom of her screen and lay still.

Jacey scoffed, and resting her finger on her own ball she pushed it off the top of her screen. It disappeared. But it did not reappear on Preston's screen.

"Your networking schema are faulty," said Matias.

"It's broken," Jacey said. "Bug one. I'm out."

"No," protested Preston. "You're just not doing it right."

"Classic programmer comeback. Always the user's fault. At least you have that part down," Jacey laughed bitterly.

"You have to, you know... " Preston was struggling to think of words to describe what needed to happen. The players needed to connect using their *knowing*. The players had to let the Spynn energy between them form a path, so the ball could travel.

But what was he saying? There was no Spynn energy between them, that was just a made-up energy used in the story for the app. Right? But if that was true, how was he doing whatever it was that he was doing? Because he knew he could make a ball fly off his phone onto any of the other three phones in the room, just by deciding, in his mind, on a destination. What was that, if not Spynn?

"Look, you guys, can we try something?" he asked. The other three looked back at him, unwilling to commit to anything he might propose before hearing it first. He was losing them, he saw. Another few minutes of this and they would write him off entirely as crazy. Coma crazy.

An image had come to him, an image of a group of four people, standing on a hilltop, focusing together with a shared intensity, a measured and powerful strength. He needed to make his friends understand the things that he could see. He needed them to take a leap of faith.

"Okay," he said. "Listen. I never said I was a great programmer. I'm not. That is totally obvious. You guys have the experience. You're actual, literal *geniuses*. But even you have things to learn. I mean, right? Like reading instructions. I may be a beginning programmer, I may know nothing about any of your protocols or your conditionals or any of it, but *I read the instructions.*" He forced them to listen to him, he refused to let their minds wander, to let them speculate about his sanity. He used the only thing he had left, force of will, to seize their attention and demand that they hear him out.

"I read the instructions," he continued. "That's all. I have intuitions about the way things work, and I am telling you, there is something very, very important here. It involves all of us. We have to work together. As a team." His mouth was dry, but he noticed that his hands were no longer shaking. It was now or never.

"Regan," he said, "take my hand."

Preston walked to the center of the room and held his left hand out to Regan. This was it. He did not plead or cajole. He had spent all the emotional and interpersonal capital he had on this one chance. Regan would either agree to the risk, or not. It was all on the table now.

Long moments passed. The three geniuses around him stood without moving. The air seemed to snap with the force of Preston's regard as he looked from person to person, and back to Regan. And then Regan moved. Toward him.

There was a regality to this advance. He was not mocking. He had committed, and was all in. He held out his hand, and Preston raised his own palm up into Regan's downward facing palm, his phone clamped between them with Spynncaster loaded and waiting.

He held out his other hand, to Jacey. And now the dam was broken. The progress was easier. She flowed forward into the circle that was being built, and held out her own hand, palm up with her phone in it, and he reached out and placed his hand on top of hers.

And then Matias joined, behind him, holding Jacey's and Regan's hands, so they formed a ring facing outward, and within each join of their palms lay a phone with a circle of Spynn facing the sky. Preston raised his arms, and they all followed suit. He closed his eyes and he was *there*, on a hilltop, someplace he had been before though he could not think of the time or the reason, and around him were his companions, Jacey and Matias and Regan. A wind came up. The fabric of their garments swirled at their waists.

And then Preston cried out, "Synch!"

A moment later, Regan echoed him. "Synch!"

Then Jacey, "Synch!"

"Synch!" bellowed Matias.

And there was a loud crack and above them heat, and Preston's eyes flew open in the suddenly darkened library and there shimmered a faint, almost invisible blue ring of energy above them. It was there but not there, near the rafters, circling high beyond the stacks of books.

And then, from their joined palms, four orange circles rose. Two-dimensional, thin as sheets of paper, but solid and real. These circles began revolving around them, passing from hand to hand to hand, faster and faster until they were a blur. Preston glanced to his left, and saw Regan, his sunglasses glittering, his head thrown back, his mouth open, exultant. To the right he saw Jacey, her hair blowing behind her, her fiery eyes fixated on a point far distant, the blue and orange light playing over her features like lightning and ice flung down on a star. And behind him he heard Matias bellowing, thundering like a bull, his voice rising in a challenge to bring the heavens to the ground, to shake the foundations of the world.

"Now it has begun," Preston said in the pounding maelstrom of whirling Spynn. *And soon the Dark Folk come,* he thought to himself, and he was as certain of this as he had ever been of anything. *And we don't know enough, and I'm afraid we can never be ready in time.*

CHAPTER

EIGHT

fter that they all went to Social Studies. Because, really, what else were they going to do? There are some habits that are killed only with the very greatest difficulty, and if you are the kind of person who self-identifies as the "on time" type, you must almost be tied to a post or accidentally sent to another country in the storage compartment of an airplane to be made to miss an appointment. One thing that the Einstein Programming Club members all shared was a discomfort with the idea of being late to Social Studies. Or anything else.

But for his part Preston might as well have been trapped in the depressurized metal underbelly of a jet for all the attention he was able to pay to the significance of Hammurabi's Code. He got through the rest of the day in what could charitably be described as a "daze," but was actually just a few small steps above the coma he had risen from four months earlier. He did not see any of the club members through the rest of the day, as they attended special classes that were carefully prepared to be painful and boring for people with advanced intellectual ability, but when school ended, Regan, Matias, and Jacey all collected in a huddle in the Reading Garden. Preston saw them from the music room, and he waited as the rest of the student body swirled out the gates and off the campus grounds like water out the drain of a tub. Then he walked toward the Garden to greet them.

They watched him, exchanging small comments with each other but dropping into silence when he was close enough to hear. He ambled uncertainly to a stop in front of the bench, and the three of them gazed up, leaning close together like a trio of wary birds.

"Preston," said Regan, eyeing him carefully.

"Hey, Preston," said Jacey, glancing warily at Preston's hands.

"Hello Preston," said Matias, his eyes on Preston's chin.

"Hey guys," he said.

Regan cleared his throat. He stood. He straightened his sleeves and cleared his throat again, then he bowed slightly.

"I have been appointed to speak for the group," he said. "Given the events that occurred earlier today, events that were of a certain nature... events which... events not typically seen in school libraries. Given those events, we have drawn up a number of questions we would like you to address." He gazed at Preston as though expecting to be interrupted. "If that would be acceptable?"

"I'll tell you everything I know, but it's not much," Preston said.

"Fine." Regan was holding a piece of paper, and he glanced at it quickly before continuing. "So. Question one. Are you now, or have you ever been, the subject of a secret government experiment to create a telepathic human mutant?"

Preston wanted to laugh, but the three faces in front of him were watching him seriously. So he shook his head. "No I have never been in one of those programs," he said. Regan checked his paper.

"Very good. Question two. Are you an alien life form visiting this planet, or are you under the tele-operative control of beings residing on another planet or beings who may have come to this planet millennia ago and have lain hidden underground until precisely this moment in human history?"

"Are you kidding?" Preston said after a pause.

"I am not," said Regan.

"Well, no, I'm not an alien," Preston told him.

"All right. Though you could still be one and not know it. Three," and Regan seemed to roll his eyes briefly before going on, "are you a traveler from the future or from an alternate dimension?"

"You guys — " Preston protested.

Regan held up his hand. "I know. That line of inquiry is preposterous." Regan threw a sideways glance at Matias. "*However*, in the interests of — "

"It is not preposterous," said Matias. "It has a higher statistical likelihood than your proposition that he's an underground alien."

"Not true! Alien life most certainly exists in the universe — "

"But hiding underground for millennia?" Matias interrupted. "It's absurd!"

"Time travelers and government mutants are absurd! Aliens are — "

Jacey slammed her palm on the bench. "Government programs researching mutant abilities — "

"Guys!" Preston yelled. "GUYS!"

They all froze and looked at him. "I'm not a mutant or an alien or — what was the other thing?"

"Inter-dimensional traveler," offered Matias.

"Yeah, not that," said Preston. "I'm just, you know, a normal human."

"You may think you are normal," Regan told him softly, "but normal humans do not do what you did today. This is inarguable."

There was nothing Preston could say to that. He knew it was true. The question was, if he was not normal, then what was he? Why was he filled with a growing sense that the world was rushing toward a precipice and far from merely being along for the ride, he might actually be the one pushing it toward the edge? Synching in the library earlier had made everything feel accelerated. If the Dark Folk were, in fact, coming, he was starting to feel that they were coming soon.

"I feel normal," he protested weekly. "It's confusing. All I did was make an app." After a second, he corrected himself. "A game."

"I hope you appreciate how convoluted this is," Regan said to him, exasperation bubbling up. "It is almost insufferably circular, like a snake eating its own tail. This game you made, which centers around an energy called Spynn, an energy which is manipulated by so called Spynncasters, somehow bleeding over into the library at Albert Einstein Elementary so that we," he gestured, "like the merest puppets, find ourselves manipulating a kind of energy outside the game *while we are playing* the game — which is honestly not very much of a game, Preston, I would like to go on record as saying — and now we are left wondering what is magical and what is technological, and... " Regan seemed to have run through his irritation. "It is all in very poor taste."

"I'm sorry," said Preston.

"You are forgiven," said Regan. "It is also the least boring thing that has ever happened at this school. So carry on."

"How did it begin?" Matias wondered. "We should get to first causes. You are confused. We are confused. So. Preston. When did all this start?"

Now the three of them were scrutinizing him. He felt a little like a bug in a test tube, captured by three strikingly brilliant but very grouchy scientific geniuses. He gave the question as much thought as he guessed he could get away with, and then answered.

"It started just before my coma," he said.

"That is useful," Matias told him. "What caused your coma?"

"No one knows," Preston said.

"That is less useful," he said, sounding grouchy.

"But I think programming Spynncaster caused it," Preston offered quickly.

"I see," Matias said. "So if your coma was caused by program- ming, then perhaps the first cause we're seeking lies there. When did you begin programming Spynncaster?"

"The same night I went into a coma. It was my birthday." He

reached into his pocket. "I got this new cell phone that day as a birthday present, and — "

"STOP!" shouted all three of them at the same time. Preston froze. They were each fixated on the cell phone Preston had taken out.

"That phone?" Regan asked, pointing carefully. "That one you have been using to brain launch orange Spynn bombs at your unsuspecting companions?"

Preston nodded. Regan leaned nearer the device, tilting his head and trying to see underneath it without getting too close.

"You received it as a gift," he asked, "then began creating Spynncaster, and then you fell unconscious?" Preston nodded again, now holding his phone out a little suspiciously, focused on it as intently as the others.

"And before you got this phone, had you ever programmed or thought about programming?" Matias asked.

"No," he said. "It all started then."

For the first time in hours, he saw the three of them begin to relax, just a touch. Jacey cracked the hint of a smile.

"You think my phone is responsible somehow?" Preston asked.

"That," boomed Matias, standing, "is a testable hypothesis. At last."

Jacey shook her hands in twitchy finger fans as she stood beside Matias. "Now we've got something to hack. A foot in the door, little coma chameleon. That's all we need."

"Preston," Regan said, standing himself. "We should probably go to your house now."

FIFTEEN MINUTES later the four of them burst through Preston's front door going as fast as he could get them to move, and found Preston's mother sitting on the couch reading a real estate magazine. Preston had hoped the speed and momentum of their entrance would sweep them past her without a check in. But she took her duties as gate-keeper very seriously.

When she saw them she smiled, and stood, and looked them each in the eye with irresistible enthusiasm. This was her Real Estate Agent persona. She could put it on and off at will. Preston had seen her do it dozens of times, showing houses to prospective buyers — become a perfect, smiling, greeting machine, and assume complete control. There was never a question she could not answer. She served effortless jokes so beautifully that buyers didn't even know why they were laughing, they just knew they loved it. It was generally agreed at her office that she could have sold every house in Pasadena if she had wanted. But if she was off doing that, she would protest to them, who was supposed to raise Preston? His *father*? And everyone would laugh, since they had all met Mr. Nowak.

Now it became apparent that even geniuses were vulnerable to her magnetic subtleties. She plied them with questions about school that they found themselves answering, only later wondering what had prompted them to reveal those particular secrets. She congratulated them on their victory at Code Portal when she heard, made them promise not to wear Preston out, offered to bring the four of them each a cupcake after the batch in the oven had cooled and been frosted, and generally held them spellbound on the living room rug until she had looked them over long enough to be confident of their characters and intentions. Then she waved them through, like a crossing guard at the border of a friendly, immensely powerful country.

It took a few minutes for the effects of Mrs. Nowak's interrogation to wear off. They drifted down the hallway to Preston's room, trying to remember what they had come there to do. But the pressure of the events in the library soon brought them back to their task.

"Plug your phone in," Matias commanded, pointing at Preston's iMac. Preston inserted the cable and then backed away, and Matias dropped into the seat.

"Password," he said, and Preston happily gave it to him. At last, someone was going to do something about his phone!

Jacey stood beside Matias, watching as he began to type, bending low to comment. Regan took a few minutes to look over Preston's room. He rifled through a few stacks of comedy and adventure books, and raised his eyebrows at the video game posters on all the walls.

"How long will it take?" Preston asked him, mostly to forestall any questions about the decorations or his taste in action figures. It was clear that Regan found the room amusing.

"Difficult to say," Regan shrugged. "Matias does not like to make mistakes. Sometimes it seems as though his methods are slow. He is like the ocean, however. Impossible to resist." Matias and Jacey were muttering together, nodding and pointing at the screen.

"I noticed at the hackathon that Matias was doing the cables," Preston said. "Is that what he's good at?"

"Doing the cables? Yes. He is good at doing cables," Regan said. He had become engrossed in the intricate construction and hidden hinges and levers of one of Preston's Lego models. He seemed delighted each time he discovered a new, tiny door. "In truth, we are all good at all of it. However, Matias has a particular aptitude for hardware, networks, and certain higher math. Jacey has languages and programming patterns." He flipped up a lever, revealing a secret laser bay, and chortled.

"What about you?" Preston asked.

"I? I fill in around the edges," Regan said. "When three-dimensional transforms are required, or mapping exotic geometries, I will typically take those tasks." He set the model aside and stood up. "I also have a facility with codes and cyphers, though there is not much practical call for code breaking these days. I consider my *primary* role to be contributing glamour and fabulous good taste to all our proceedings. Now. Shall we go check the status of your mother's cupcakes?"

An hour and several cupcakes later, Matias and Jacey finally turned away from the computer and handed Preston back his phone.

Jacey was frowning daggers at the device, suspicious of a crime but unable to convict the suspect. "We checked everything. Background processes, cracked OS, malware. The BIOS checks out. It's clean."

"In terms of the software and the hardware, it's an entirely normal phone," said Matias.

Preston was deeply disappointed. "How can that be?"

The air in the room had changed completely, from engaged and excited to disheartened and bleak in a matter of seconds. Even Matias seemed to have caught the darkened mood.

"I don't think the phone is the first cause we are seeking," he said. "There is nothing unusual about it."

"Nothing except that I can't use it to make *phone calls*," Preston complained. It was the same pattern he had been caught in for months, two steps forward and one step back. Only this felt like two steps back. Now he was just running in place. It took a moment for him to realize that the others were staring at him.

"Please elaborate," Regan said carefully. "*Why* are you unable to make phone calls using your phone?"

"Who knows?" Preston said. "From the first day I got it, my phone number's been *pending activation*." He curled disdainful quotes in the air. "My dad called a few times. I sent emails. It's hopeless."

"It has never worked at all?" Regan asked.

"I got one text. It was the text that had the Spynnlang URL."

"Oh my god. Why didn't you say this earlier?" Jacey stepped forward and snatched his phone back. From the way she glared at him, he understood that the suspect she now wanted to convict was him. She swiped the phone up and checked the provider settings. "AT&T" she said.

"Yes, it may be a provider issue," Matias mused. "We may have been approaching this from the wrong side."

Jacey nodded. "We need access to AT&T's system."

"So," Regan said, "is there a zero day available? Does anyone know? Do we have a backdoor?"

"There is always a backdoor," said Matias. "It's simply a matter of procuring a key."

The room had sucked back some of its air of anticipation. It didn't take Matias long to find someone online who could get them access to the cell provider's systems. Apparently, Preston discovered, there were forums online where access to almost anything could be found or bought. Matias was a known entity in this world. Since the access they were seeking was based on an extremely valuable exploit, it took several tense minutes of negotiation to reach a deal. But finally Matias had what he wanted.

"Ok, we're in," Matias said.

"Impressive," said Regan. He whistled. He seemed to enjoy the effect, and he did it again. "This is a government backdoor. This is priceless."

"I gave them greater value," Matias said, focused on characters scrolling down the screen. "I have an exploit to disable the control system for self-driving cars. They were pleased with the exchange." Regan and Jacey seemed to take this information in stride. Preston wondered if it was such a good idea to be giving strangers on the internet the ability to shut off people's cars. However, it was too late now.

"Read me the number," Matias said.

"323-213-7079" Matias typed as Jacey read from Preston's phone.

"Let us check the records. Where did this mysterious text originate?" Matias said, speaking to himself. He spent the next ten minutes fishing though database records and long strings of text.

"I don't understand," he said after a while. "There is no record of any text. Let me see the phone." Jacey handed it to him. He frowned.

"Look, the sender number is nothing but zeros. It must be a system error. Let me find the master account for Preston's number. There we will find our answers."

But as it turned out, their answers were not to be found when he had at last located the account for Preston's number.

"Here," Matias said finally, after forty-five minutes navigating the guts of AT&T's databases. He moved his mouse to indicate an entry. He leaned closer, puzzled. "Hmm, this must be... " His voice trailed off. He gestured for the phone and compared the numbers. Then he stepped back through several pages of code, and went through the same routing a second time. When he arrived at the identical entry he gazed at the screen for a long moment.

"I don't know what this means. I'll export it as a flat file. Is your printer on?" Preston nodded. He was getting a very odd feeling from Matias, who kept glancing back at him as the printer pushed out a sheet of paper. Matias lifted it and passed it from Jacey to Regan, silently.

"What is it?" Preston asked.

"Billing records," Matias said. "AT&T used to be Bell Systems. Bell Systems was the original phone system for the entire United States, and so it has legacy records going back decades. These are billing records for your phone number, dated from its issuance in 1963."

Now Jacey and Regan, glancing back and forth from the paper to Preston, were giving him the same uneasy looks as Matias.

"So that number has been around a long time. That's not unusual, right?" Preston said. "I mean, there are only so many numbers. They get reused. Someone moves. Cancels their account. The phone company gives that number to someone else... " Matias was shaking his head.

"No. Your number has been in continual use since 1963. It has been registered to one person the entire time, though twelve years ago it appears that the bills stopped being paid. The number remained linked to the account. Very odd."

"Whose account?" Preston said. Finally they were getting somewhere. There was some mix-up; clearly he had been given someone else's number. He could take this information to AT&T

and get it straightened out. He waited, but they did not say anything.

"What?" he said, growing irritated. "*What?*"

"Since 1963," Matias said slowly, "this number has been in continual use by... you. Preston Oliver Nowak."

"But that's impossible," Preston said, taking the paper.

"Not," said Matias speculatively, "if you are a time traveler."

"Oh my god," said Jacey. "He's not a time traveler Matias, shut up!" She turned to Preston. "I'm still saying mutant."

"Aliens waiting beneath the earth could easily have planted records, and then — " Regan began, and then Jacey and Matias and Regan were rehashing their earlier argument. Preston gazed without understanding at the printout. The billing address was some street in the city of Pasadena that he did not recognize. How was it possible?

And then it hit him.

"Guys," he said. The three were spiraling down into alien government interdimensional conspiracy theories, completely oblivious to him now. He tried to break in a few more times without success. Finally he opened his phone and loaded Spynncaster. He held the thought of all three of their phones in his mind, and *flicked* the orange ball away with a thought. Instantly, in each of their pockets, there came a loud chime. They stopped arguing, reached for their phones, and found an orange ball staring at them when they looked at their screens.

"Attention, geniuses," Preston said. "Hi, can I say something?"

They looked up, wordlessly. Getting that ball on their phones seemed to have brought the events of earlier in the day forcefully back to them, as he hoped it might. Regan looked a little shaken. Jacey scowled with tension. Matias was impassive. Preston took their silence as permission to continue. "There was someone else named Preston Oliver Nowak."

"Who?" Jacey asked.

"My grandfather," Preston said. "Preston Oliver Nowak the First.

Grandpa Nowak. I was named after him." He paused, trying to work out the implications. "He died a long time ago. I never met him. But he lived in Pasadena. He had a shoe store here. It's my dad's store now. Nowak Shoes."

"So," Regan ventured after a moment, "is this his number?"

"I don't know," said Preston.

Matias turned back to the computer and typed. Google results appeared. He clicked. "Here he is. 1942. Hmm. These entries are on a physics mailing list archive." He read further while they waited. "Your grandfather published physics papers in the 1940s? Is this true?"

"Not as far as I know," Preston told him.

Matias read more. "Yes. He was a physicist. These papers all deal with quantum mechanics. The bio is sketchy. But," he turned to face Preston, "during a period from 1938 to 1945 he published in scientific journals and was known as an expert in the field of quantum entanglement."

Preston shook his head. "I mean, as far as I know, he owned a bunch of shoe stores. There used to be Nowak Shoes all over the country, but now there's only this one in Pasadena. My dad never talks about him."

Matias pulled more information up as Preston talked. "It's the same person. Nowak Shoes. Preston Oliver Nowak."

Regan began to laugh. "Your grandfather was a polymath and a cobbler. It is simply too absurd. I hope this is true!"

"So what?" growled Jacey. "The phone number got assigned to Preston because he has the same name?"

Matias was shaking his head. "That doesn't seem to be true. As far as I can tell, the number doesn't exist *at all* anymore. Twelve years ago, it was removed from the exchanges entirely. The account — your grandfather's account, apparently — is still active but is not being billed. And the number... does *not* exist. You were not assigned that number by AT&T, Preston. That number is completely absent from any exchange or registry anywhere in the global telecommunication system."

"Then how come it's on my phone?"

There was silence. From the kitchen they could hear Preston's mother pulling pots and pans from the cupboards, and then they heard her voice calling, "Preston? Do you think your friends want to stay for dinner?"

"No, Mom," he called. Jacey stepped close to him, and took hold of the front of his shirt.

"Okay, here's what's going to happen," she snarled. "From now until the hackathon this weekend, you are going to teach us Spynnlang. This phone number is a dead end. But there's not a language on the planet that I can't learn in a week. I'm going to learn it. And we are going to win that competition." Her eyes got a fierce focus that was actually much more intimidating than the fact that she was squeezing the skin under his shirt. "Languages talk to you about the people who created them," she purred. "Starting tomorrow after school. Got it?"

Preston nodded. It was all he could do. Jacey let go of him. Regan patted him on the back.

"Do not worry, little coma boy. All will be revealed soon. We will see you tomorrow at school."

Matias looked at him, his eyes leveled in that off-putting stare that hit you just at your chin, never meeting your eyes. "Your grandfather was a mathematical genius," he said. "Perhaps that explains your insights into the higher maths."

And then Preston walked the three of them out of the house and watched as they hurried off together down the sidewalk. He was worried, despite Regan's assurance. Jacey had said that there was not a language on the planet that she couldn't learn in a week. But, Preston wondered, what if Spynnlang was not from this planet?

CHAPTER
NINE

After dinner that night Preston's mother left with some agents from her office to hear a presentation on the current styles in kitchen remodeling, and Preston helped his dad wash the dishes. He waited until they were drying and stacking the ice cream bowls, and then, as casually as he could manage, he shifted toward the question he had been holding in for hours. He disguised it as a challenge. His father would always rise to a challenge.

"Hey Dad, do you really think you never forget a number?"

"My mind is a steel trap," his father answered, clinking the porcelain onto the rack with exaggerated precision. "Every little thing filed in place. You want to test me?"

This was going to be easier than he expected, Preston thought. Still, better to build to it gradually. "Ok," he said. "How many soft-soled leather loafers did you have in inventory last week?"

"156," his father said promptly. "Give me a hard one."

"How tall is the Empire State Building?"

"One thousand four hundred fifty-four feet," he said, quickly. "Come on, how about something really hard?"

"Ok. What was Grandpa Nowak's old phone number?"

His father paused and gave him a look, then. But when he answered his voice was absolutely certain. "323-213-7079"

And there is was. The same number. The number that had belonged to his grandfather since 1963, and then mysteriously vanished from the global telecommunications system. It might not exist now, but it had existed then. It was confirmation of a sort to hear his father actually speak the numbers. But confirmation of what?

Preston waited a few minutes, and then while they were putting the glasses away he asked, "So, was Grandpa Nowak a physicist?"

From the corner of his eye he saw his father almost drop a water glass. He set it carefully up in the cupboard before wiping his hands and turning to Preston.

"Why the interest in Grandpa Nowak?" he asked.

"My friends and I were doing research for a project," Preston said. He was very pleased not to have to make anything up. "There was someone named Preston Oliver Nowak who published scientific papers in the 1940s. But Grandpa Nowak just ran shoe stores, right?" His father did not answer. He stared at a shelf of coffee mugs and continued wiping his hands for several moments, as though he was trying to wear the pattern off the dish towel. And then he sighed.

"Yes, your grandfather was a scientist," he said. "He was a lot of things." Mr. Nowak untied the apron from his neck, folded it, and put his hand on Preston's head. "All right, then. I guess it's time I told you a bit about my dad."

Preston's father sat him on the couch in the living room and left him there. Preston could hear him rummaging in the closet where his mom kept her extra coats and dresses, and then he returned with an old shoe box. He sat down facing Preston in his lounging chair, holding the box in his lap. He turned on the reading lamp. He adjusted his glasses. Finally he folded his hands and put them on top of the box.

"Your grandfather and I didn't have the same kind of relationship that you and I do, Pres," his dad said.

Outside a nightingale called, and from the distant freeway the speeding hiss of cars came threading into the living room, now louder, now softer. A lonely sound, a ghost sighing. In the pool of light from the lamp his father looked to Preston like he was smaller, though maybe it was just the shadows.

"You never talked about him, so I just wondered," Preston said. He was no longer thinking about Spynncaster at all. Suddenly this had become about him and his father.

"I didn't really know him, Pres." His father looked at the box in his lap. "This is all I really have of him. Some pictures." He drummed his fingers on the lid once, punctuation to his words.

"When I was growing up, he was always away. He had the shoe stores, you know. And he was always teaching one seminar or another at Caltech. I think we might have been considered rich. I was raised by nannies. And then he sold the stores and we moved into a small house. After that it was just the two of us, but we never talked. Not when I was growing up. He was... " Preston Sr. shook his head at his words as he was saying them, "I think he was crazy. I mean, at the end he was, for sure. But I think, all along, he must have been. Crazy. I didn't really understand, though. I was only a boy."

His dad curled his fingers under the lid of the box and lifted it, a little reluctantly it seemed to Preston. Then he got up and sat beside Preston on the couch. He lifted out a small stack of black and white photos, and a few newspaper clippings. He held one up.

'This is the earliest picture I have of him. 1933. He was sixteen." In the picture five men and a boy leaned together over a table filled with papers, glowing smiles at the camera in a way that people never seemed to do any more. Like it was an event. The skinny kid who must be sixteen-year-old Grandpa Nowak was on the end, in a vest and slacks. A pendant of some kind hung around his neck and almost brushed the desk, he leaned forward with such energy.

Something about the image caught Preston's attention, but it took him several seconds to see it — the man in the middle of the picture, the one the others were crowding in around. Wild gray hair.

Mustache. Familiar heavy eyebrows. If all that hair was white, he thought, if the man was twenty years older — he looked up at his dad with his finger on the man's chest.

"Is that — "

"Albert Einstein. Grandpa Nowak met him for the first time at Caltech, right down the street. Einstein taught there for a couple years, I guess. Grandpa was a student, the youngest physics student they ever had. Your grandpa used to talk about Einstein, especially when he started to go, you know... " Preston's dad trailed off, leaving the impression of volumes unspoken.

"What did he say?" Preston asked. "About Einstein?"

"Well. At the end he would talk about how he'd killed Einstein. Killed Albert Einstein. Can you imagine?"

"What? What did he mean?"

"This was after we had to move him into the elder care facility. He was just plain crazy, old and crazy, at that point. Fantasies and whatnot. He was tortured, I guess you would say. By a lot of different things." To distance himself from those memories Preston Sr. took out another picture. It was of an older man, obviously Grandpa Nowak, with a boy at his side.

"Is that you?" Preston asked, pointing at the boy.

"That's me. Cute little cuss, right? About your age."

The two of them were standing in front of a sheet or backdrop of some kind, dressed up in 1960s suits. And at first Preston thought that there was something out of focus about the picture, because he couldn't see his grandfather's hands. But then he realized that they were wrapped in black cloth.

"What's on his hands?" he asked.

"Your grandfather's hands were badly disfigured. He never gave me any details," his father said, "and I never asked, believe me, but I figured out from bits and pieces. When he was younger there had been — I don't know, an experiment? Something exploded. *Something* happened anyway, and his hands were badly injured. Very painful. Covered with scars. It was hard for him to move them. He would sit and write letters, or write in a journal, and I could see him forcing himself through the pain, and it took him ages, but he always finished. When he went out in public, he covered them up."

Preston looked at the face, lined and hollow eyed. It was not hard to imagine that face grimacing in pain.

"Poor Grandpa," he murmured.

Preston Sr. took out another photo. This was the only framed picture in the box, a palm sized silver casing. The picture showed Grandpa Nowak in a very fancy suit, and beside him a woman in a wedding dress.

"1959. My mom. Grandma Nowak." His father seemed to get sucked into this picture, and it was several moments before he continued. "Of course, I never met her. She died giving birth to me." He put his arm around Preston then, held him close. "You know, that kind of thing used to happen more often back then. Medicine wasn't as good. But I don't think my dad ever got over it."

"Did he talk about her a lot?"

"No, but this was the only picture he ever had framed. He had it in his room. Sometimes I would find him staring at it, and I could hear him sort of whispering, *it was supposed to be me.*" His father sighed and shook his head. "Like I said, tortured."

Preston murmured the words to himself, softly. *It should have been me.* It gave him a frigid shiver.

"No," said his dad. "Not like that. He always said, *it was supposed to be me.* Like someone was *supposed* to die that night, but it was supposed to be him, not his wife."

"How did they meet?" Preston asked. It seemed like a very adult thing to ask. It surprised him a little to be interested. But he was falling under the spell of all these old images, old people looking young, having lives and playing out events long past.

"They barely knew each other. I read a letter once, I wish I'd kept it, from 1958, where he is basically saying *Splendid to meet you, I would be pleased to see more of you.* Back in those days you had to be very formal. That was '58, then in '59 they're married. Then I'm born in '60 and she's gone."

Preston Sr. pulled a long folded paper from the bottom of the box. He unfolded it on the coffee table, and Preston saw that it was a map of the United States, with *Nowak Shoes, National Branches* emblazoned at the top on a curly banner style graphic. Scattered all across the country were stars marking branch locations.

"At its peak, Nowak shoes had eighty-eight locations all over the country," his dad said. There was a note of pride in his voice, leftover pride from a time when his store had spread from coast to coast. "Grandpa Nowak had a very unique approach to placing his stores. Most people put shoe stores in big cities, and he had plenty of those. But he put stores all over the place. He had a few stores that were the only building for miles around, out on some back road in Montana or Pennsylvania. But they made money. He had a gimmick."

Preston Sr. pointed to an illustration at the bottom of the map. It showed a woman standing beside a machine, with her foot resting in a little opening near the floor. She was pointing at a screen on top of the machine where the bones of her foot were displayed. She was smiling and looking at Preston as if to say *Look at this! Is this not the most amazing technology you have ever seen?*

Every Store a High-Tech Marvel, read the caption.

"What is that?" Preston asked.

"The Ped Meter. They were all the rage for many years. It was basically an X-ray machine that let you look at your foot bones in real time and get an exact idea of the shoe size you needed. Eventually people realized that sitting there and bombarding your foot with radiation was not a great idea. But every single Nowak Shoes had one. Other shoe stores jumped on the bandwagon before the government banned them, but Nowak Shoes was the first. I think Dad got the idea from his physics work. Radiation. Particles and whatnot."

Preston leafed through the rest of the photos. A few more pictures of Grandpa Nowak with Einstein, a few with other well-dressed or lab-coated strangers. From between two of those photos, a key on a leather cord slipped to the couch. The key was old, covered with a dark patina, and the cord was worn.

"He was wearing that when they... they found that as they were preparing his body. After he died."

"What does it unlock?"

"I never saw him use it." Somehow the key seemed familiar — and then he realized, it was the same key hanging off of sixteen year old Grandpa Nowak's neck in the picture with Einstein.

"So what happened?" Preston asked, setting the items aside. "You said he went into an old folks home?"

"Well, he got more and more... he was crazy, Pres. He was tortured by what he thought were failures. Your grandma dying. His delusions about Einstein. At a certain point he just wasn't able to care for himself, and your mom and I couldn't do it. So we moved him to a care facility. He was there until he died."

At the very bottom of the box was a folded and stamped paper. Preston took it out. At the top was the name, Preston Oliver Nowak, and the address of Canyon Elder Care. And then details about his grandfather's death. Preston looked it over, feeling a little chilled to be looking at a death certificate with his own name on it. At the bottom, the time and date of death was listed.

"Hey," he said, pointing to the final line. "Grandpa Nowak died on my birthday!"

His father nodded. "Yep. Strange, isn't it? I was at the hospital with your mom, so... " This was yet another bump in his father's road, and Preston could almost see his dad playing the memories in his mind. Preston felt bad for getting the whole conversation started. But how could he have known?

"We actually worked it out, your mom and me, one time," his dad said softly. "You were born on October 7th, at 3:31 PM. And your grandfather *died* on October 7th, at 3:31 PM. Exact same time. Now *that's* a coincidence for the record books, right?"

The chill Preston had felt looking at his grandfather's death certificate suddenly spread until he actually shivered. Something told him it was not a coincidence. No. His grandfather dying as he himself was being born was not a coincidence.

His father hugged him again, then handed Preston the box.

"I tell you what, since you're doing this research, why don't you take responsibility for this stuff? You can keep it, in fact. The Nowak legacy?"

"Thanks, Dad," he said. And he meant it. This felt like a treasure from his dad's past. From his own past too, he supposed. He put the pictures and papers away carefully. "I'll put it in my room."

"You know," his dad said as Preston stood, "your grandfather always wanted me to have a kid. It was the one thing he always said he wanted. A grandchild. He made me promise to name you after him. I'll tell you, your mother was none too happy." His dad smiled. "But she's happy with you now. Regardless of your name."

In his room, Preston took out the map. *Nowak Shoes, National Branches.* He took down the video game posters from the wall above his bed, and he put the map up in their place. He was not even sure why, but looking up at it, faded with age, 88 stars hung upon the roads and byways and innocent geography of a country long gone by, made him feel connected to something. At least he had this now, this past he had never known.

He lifted the key on the leather cord from the box, and hung it around his neck, under his shirt. It was cold and smooth. He was happy to have it, and all the other artifacts from Grandpa Nowak's life. Even if he still did not know what any of it meant.

WALKING BACK to his house from school with Jacey, Matias and Regan the next day, he went over everything his father had told him. Matias was particularly interested in the Ped Meter. Regan seemed fascinated by Grandpa Nowak's belief that he was supposed to have died instead of his wife.

"So romantic, so tragic," Regan said, and nothing else.

Jacey kept going back to the coincidence of his grandfather dying at the exact same moment that Preston was being born, and they all agreed that, with everything else they knew at this point, it was hard to view it as a coincidence. But no one had any theories about what it might mean.

Preston found his own thoughts returning over and over to his grandfather's association with Albert Einstein. Surely Grandpa Nowak had known how Einstein had actually died? Preston had looked it up. Einstein had passed away from a sudden brain aneurysm in 1955. How could you believe that you had caused an aneurysm in someone else's brain? Or had Grandpa Nowak believed that something different had killed Einstein? Believing either one definitely seemed crazy. A crazy old man, tortured, maimed, cursed with a series of tragic accidents.

The moment they got to Preston's room, however, all talk of the past ceased, and they were entirely business, although Regan did take a minute to examine the new *Nowak Shoes* poster on the wall. Then Jacey was cracking the whip.

"Ok," she said. "Let's see this thing you've been working on."

So Preston pulled up the Spynnlang coursework page with the *Casting* link. The second link down was now visible, although the third and fourth were still blurry. The second link read, *Embody Phenomena.* They read the text at the top of the page.

Congratulations, Preston Oliver Nowak! You have successfully completed the Casting coursework! You're not a Computer Programmer yet, but you are getting close! And then — look out! Settle planetary affairs to your liking! Snap a finger and watch the love of your life throw him or herself at your feet! Lift mountains with the merest flick of your tiny pinky finger! Computer Programmers rule the world!

This time the fine print insisted that if his skin remained attached to his body after reading to the end of the paragraph, it would be taken as his agreement to the terms and conditions stipulated, and that if he was not Preston Oliver Nowak he should throw himself in front of the first solar flare that was convenient, and take the computer with him. He clicked the link to take them to the *Embody Phenomena* page.

Preston Oliver Nowak, welcome to the Spynnlang — Embody Phenomena coursework! Since you have come this far, the work here will be a piece of cake for you — though of course, Computer Programming is basically impossible for anyone other than Preston Oliver Nowak!

In this section you will learn to control and embody all the Phenomena in the physical and metaphysical universe! This includes Thunder, Tooth Brushing, and anything else you can think of! Right now you are thinking, wow, that is a lot of Phenomena, how will my minuscule brain ever be able to encompass a domain that monumentally gigantic! Hahahaha, that is a very good question. Don't worry about it!

Review the material below while continuing to not worry about it, and after you complete this section you will be that much closer to becoming what everyone dreams of being, a Computer Programmer and Master of the Omniverses. Remember, take your time, but the Dark Folk are rising, they are closer than ever — so work as fast as you possibly can even if you make a bunch of mistakes!

"The Dark Folk are rising?" Matias muttered. "Curious phrase. Who are these Dark Folk?"

Within Preston's mind he felt a latch rise, and a door prepare to swing open. *No*, he thought. *I refuse. Not now. Not ever! I am not crazy!* A tide of sound and violence rose, pushing to break out. Memories too wild to be real sought the light. But he fought them back, he held the door shut, and after a moment they subsided. His friends did not seem to notice the struggle.

"Let's get this party started," Jacey said, pulling a chair up beside him. Preston cleared his throat and peered at the screen, getting his equilibrium back.

"It also always says that about being *impossible for anyone other than Preston Oliver Nowak*," he said. "Do you think — "

"Impossible my ass," Jacey flared. "Let's go."

So Preston began showing her the basics. He ran through the

sequence he used to deploy an app, and then began outlining the ways the various shapes were combined to make other, more complicated shapes. He could not explain why it functioned, or the logic behind it, but he knew how to make it work. Jacey followed everything he said, referencing the screen, watching his hands, making notes on pieces of paper. She asked questions and made him repeat certain sections over and over. Soon Matias and Regan, who had been watching closely at the beginning, lost track of what was being said, and went to wait quietly on the bed. But Jacey was in a focused trance.

And for his part Preston was finding it much, much easier to master this section than it had been to become adept at the Casting work. It all seemed to be making so much more sense now, the ways that the various pieces interrelated, the small adjustments that could be made in the fingering between certain associated phrases or commands to achieve dramatically different or magnified results.

He worked his way through a list of what were presented as Beginner Level Phenomena. These were listed in no order that he could see: Fog, Gravity, Insight, Adhesion, Orbit, Elasticity, Eating, Friendship, Dog Walking, Digestion, Shield, Earthquakes, Flight, and endlessly on. Yes, he thought as he moved through the positions, yes, this. Yes, that. Yes, yes, yes.

By the end of three hours he was filled with energy. Jacey, however, did not look well at all. She was blinking rapidly, there was a film of sweat on her forehead, and she kept chewing on her upper lip as she gazed at the screen.

"Ok," she said, "I think I might be getting it. I've never seen anything like this. But no problem. No prob." She was nodding. But Preston did not think it looked like a *no problem* nod. He had been as helpful as he could be, he thought. He wanted Jacey to get this, he wanted it badly.

"Let me give you the URL," he told her. "Look it over later, it will probably make sense after it sits for a while." She nodded some more, and took a deep breath.

"Yeah, no worries," she said. He expected her to stand, it was time for them to go, but instead she remained fixated on the screen, as though she could not look away. Regan had to help her stand.

"Ok, little bird," he said, lifting her from behind. He had to get Matias to help.

"This way," Regan said, pushing her along toward the bedroom door. "Let's give that big, beautiful, slightly ragey brain of yours a few minutes downtime. Ok?" Jacey seemed to hear that, and she shook her hands out in her typical Jacey spasm.

"Yeah, I just need a break. Let's get going. See you at school Preston." He walked them out, and waved as they headed down the street. He hoped she had been right, but to Preston Jacey looked like she needed more than a break.

That night, he once again dreamed that he and an orange ball, now as big across as a jumbo jet, were hanging alone in space. Just suspended there together, in the middle of a featureless void. He felt like an ant having a conversation with a whale. But this time he thought he could hear something. The circle had a message, and it finally seemed to have grown large enough to make the message heard. Even so it was a quiet message, so soft that it might not have been a sound, it might have been a thought. But at last it was clear.

Remember, the subsonic message came. A force was pulling against the door inside him again. Prying it open.

Remember. And endlessly it wore on through the night, the message and the prying.

The next day at lunch, sitting on the benches, Preston was even more troubled by Jacey's appearance. She looked exhausted. She looked like she had not slept the night before, and when he remembered that he had given her the coursework URL he thought he knew what might have kept her up. When lunch ended Preston held Regan back until Jacey was out of earshot — not that she seemed to be listening to much anyway.

"I'm worried about her," he said, pointing. But Regan only shrugged.

"This is a typical pattern for Jacey," he said. "It is a bit self-destructive, but we all have our quirks. Jacey does not simply solve problems, she devours them whole. Sometimes, once she consumes them, she finds they are difficult to digest. But before long she always... " Regan thought about it a moment. "I choose not to take this metaphor to its logical conclusion. But you get the idea. There is nothing to worry about. She is unspeakably brilliant. She will arrive at a solution. She always does."

Preston nodded, though watching Jacey walk back to class he was not nearly as certain as Regan. He *was* worried. In fact, ever since his father had shown him the shoebox full of pieces of Grandpa Nowak's life there had been a part of him that had been questioning whether they should be doing any of this. There was more going on than any of them could keep track of. It was big. Was it too big?

He wondered if they shouldn't be talking to someone about the things they were discovering. But every time he thought that, he thought of what would happen next, remembering the warning the doctors had given him, how people sometimes have trouble telling fantasy from reality after coming out of a coma. If he heard any of this from someone else he would not believe it himself. So he ignored the seed of fear twisting in his stomach. He did not see what option they had but to continue down the path they had started, and hope, as Jacey did, that they would arrive at a solution.

After school they gathered in his room again, and progressed further through the *Embody Phenomena* coursework. Preston found the going even easier, while Jacey seemed to be falling farther into a well of silence, lip biting, and black scowls. She had stopped asking him to repeat sequences, and was no longer making notes. He watched her stumble a little bit when it was time for them to go home, as they made their way through the house and outside onto the porch. Regan and Matias stepped down toward the street, but Preston took Jacey's hand.

She looked at him blankly.

"Look, maybe this was a bad idea," he told her quietly. "Maybe

you're not supposed to be doing this. Maybe Spynnlang is not for you
— "

She snatched her hand away and wheeled on him. Her eyes were threatening squints, her voice a tense hiss.

"Shut up! You don't know what you're talking about. You. Shut. UP!" Preston, shocked, nodded. Jacey blinked at him, a big, slow blink, lazy like butterfly wings. Her eyes were vaguely unfocused. Without saying anything else she turned and followed Matias and Regan. All Preston could do was watch.

The next day was Thursday, and after school they met in the library for Computer Club. At lunch Jacey had not even sat with them but instead had wandered the schoolyard aimlessly with her hood drawn over her head, watching her feet and moving her lips as she talked to herself. Even Regan seemed to be getting worried now. And sitting at the desk in front of Ms. Fredrick's whiteboard, Jacey looked even more drawn and exhausted, as if she had not slept or eaten. Or changed her clothes or bathed, for that matter. She was a tangled mess.

Ms. Fredrick did not seem to notice.

"Well, it is good to see you all!" She smiled and clapped. "Congratulations again on progressing to Stage Two of Code Portal. When I saw you on Monday there was some question about whether you would be proceeding at the hackathon. Have you made any decisions?"

Preston felt in his gut that to not continue what they had begun at the hackathon would be a grave mistake, though he could not explain why he felt this way. It was the sensation of rushing toward the edge of something, of running to keep in front of a cresting and destructive wave of — what? History? Fate? Fear? If they stopped, they would be crushed. He felt they must move forward or face disastrous consequences.

But when he considered his friends, he doubted his impulse. The stories his father had told him had left Preston feeling an unease that had only grown stronger over the last few days. There was danger here. He could feel it. Wild energies. Plans and schemes he could not see, but could feel. He sensed a whirlpool slowly spinning open beneath him. Could he ask any of them to step into that unpredictable tumult with him?

"Damn right we're going," Jacey croaked. All three of her friends jumped. This was the longest sentence she had spoken in two days. "This thing's not beating us. We're going. Understand?" She glowered at the other three kids until they nodded. Then she sank back down into her chair, her hood pulled farther over her head.

"Well, I am glad to hear that!" Ms. Fredrick said. "Jacey dear, are you feeling well? Yes? All right. Let's go a little farther in our Object Oriented Programming conversation, just to bring Preston up to speed on some of the essential ideas."

He expected Jacey to moan and complain, but she said nothing. Ms. Fredrick drew a big circle on the top of the whiteboard and labeled it BIRDS.

"Now, OOP is a system for structuring code that models the real world. It is the foundation of every modern programming language. Objective C, or Java, for example. Using OOP we create Objects and manipulate them. But what does that mean in practical terms? Let us look at the game Angry Birds. We might create a Parent Object and call it BIRDS, then give this Parent Object the ability to be lofted in a catapult, and give it weight and density so that it can knock down buildings when it lands. Yes?"

She turned to make sure they were following her, though of course she was only talking to Preston. And the truth was that the last thing Preston wanted to do right now was listen to a dry lecture about programming. There was so much else on his mind. He tried to look interested. His face must have betrayed him though, because Ms. Fredrick set down her pen and leaned on the table, facing him. And suddenly it seemed as though there was no one else in the room except the two of them. Her eyes commanded him. Preston had not realized how riveting she could be when she put a bit of energy into it. He felt pinned to his seat, as though he were in the grip of a truly overwhelming intelligence.

"Preston Oliver Nowak, though this material seems trivial to you, these are in fact the building blocks of software. If you are to become a truly accomplished programmer, you will need mastery of these concepts." He nodded. She seemed to require it. "And that applies regardless of the particular project you might be involved in at any given time," she added. "These ideas apply to *any* programming project." And with a final searing flash of her eyes, she demanded, "Do you understand?"

"Uh, I think so," he said. Though in fact he suspected that he was missing a substantial piece of her meaning. He glanced to the side, at Matias and Regan and Jacey, but they did not seem to think there was anything unusual about Ms. Fredrick's intensity. They looked bored. They already knew Object Oriented Programming.

"Fine," said Ms. Fredrick, taking up her pen again. "This will only take a moment of the time you so clearly would rather be spending in other ways."

She turned back to the board, and drew three smaller circles, labeling them BLACK BIRD, PINK BIRD and GREY BIRD.

"From the parent object BIRD we can create Child objects that share BIRD's love of the catapult and ability to knock down build-ings, but we can add specific new abilities." Under BLACK BIRD she wrote *explodes,* under PINK BIRD she wrote *bubble trap,* and under GREY BIRD she wrote *dive bomb.* Then she stepped back.

"Now these Child objects all have different abilities, but share the abilities of the parent. It is immensely efficient. So eloquent. This, as we covered last week, is called *Inheritance.*" For a moment she was lost in a reverie. Then she stepped back to the board. "There is one final thing for us to look at today, and then I think we should adjourn early because I fear that Jacey may not be well. This is important, Preston."

And she wrote two words in large letters on the board. *SETTERS* and *GETTERS.*

"When we want to find out what kind of BIRD object has just been flung through the air, we use a method called a Getter. A Getter, as you may imagine, *gets* information from an object. And if we want to change an object, we use a Setter. A Setter *sets* an object's properties. Every single deeply powerful programing language employs these methods. Java. Objective C. C#. Lisp. Visual Basic. All of them. And this, though some would quibble, is the way the universe is structured and maintained. Objects. Inheritance. Getters. Setters. The entire universe, and everything beyond it."

She turned and smiled. "The end! I will see you Saturday morning. Goodbye for now!" Then she lifted her bag and swept from the room, a paragon of disjointed grace. A moment later the four kids followed.

THE NEXT DAY WAS FRIDAY, and at lunch Preston learned that Jacey was not at school.

"She sent me a text," Regan said when Preston asked. "All she said was *working*." It was clear that Regan was now worried.

"What can we do?" asked Preston.

"I fear that the only person who can do anything for Jacey right now is Jacey," Regan tisked. "Which, though I love her dearly, is not a position I would want to be in. Because Jacey is not particularly stable." Matias rumbled assent. And for the hundredth time that week, Preston wondered what in the world he had gotten his friends into.

TEN

J acey joined them on the sidewalk Saturday morning as they waited to be picked up, and the relief the other three felt could almost be seen in the air, like sunshine breaking out from a bank of clouds. She was silent, she was thin, she had deep black circles around her eyes. But she was there.

The drive down to Anaheim was quiet, each of them deep in reflections of their own. Preston felt his own thoughts moving him in two very different directions. On the one hand the trepidation he had felt during the week had not left him. Instead it had grown, so that now one half of him was filled with a black unease that he could not give a name to.

However, the other half of him seemed filled with confidence. And anticipation. The *Embody Phenomena* coursework was complete, as far as he could tell. There was a seemingly limitless, scrolling list of individual Phenomena, each with a fingering sequence to memo-rize. But he had become so familiar with the basic patterns that now, without even looking in advance, he could work out sequences that would call forth Spynnlang icons representing — *Embodying* — new

Phenomena. He had no idea what would happen at Code Portal today, but at least this time he felt like he had some tools to use.

Stage Two was being held in the same hotel, but in a much smaller venue. Ms. Fredrick guided them in, and only people who knew of her discomfort being touched could really see how watchful she was, positioning herself to avoid bumping the guests and attendees they passed. Her expression was carefully neutral, but Preston could see her discomfort. Even fear? Once again his heart was moved by her bravery. Behind her confidence she seemed to be hiding something more than a little broken. A lifetime of jumping to the side might do that to you, he thought.

The room they were using was different, and once they entered they saw that attendance had dropped from over a thousand programmers to less than two hundred. Though the space was smaller, the accommodations were an upgrade. There was an attached break room, though no one seemed to be using it. Everyone here at this point was focused on only one thing. There was less noise. There was no longer a Junior Section. There was now a lot of space between the tables: the field had thinned.

Ms. Fredrick saw them off at the door, and went to find more defensible seating.

"So, how is this to work, exactly?" Regan said. They had barely spoken on the ride down. "If we are to extend the Spynnlang application using whatever new topic the moderators choose, we will be relying entirely on you, Preston, since none of the rest of us are proficient in Spynnlang." All three of them looked at Jacey, but she was completely oblivious.

Something had been bothering Preston about Jacey.

"How in the world did her parents even let her come?" he asked. "I mean, why is she not at a doctor or something?" If this had been him, his mom would have had him at a hospital days ago, and she would definitely not have let him out of the house on his own to go to a hackathon.

"Jacey's household is, shall we say, less organized than yours,"

Regan said. "We do not all have the luxury of two parents, three meals, and utilities that reliably produce water and electricity. She is actually far safer here with us than at her quote-unquote *home*."

"Is she homeless?" Preston asked. Regan laughed, but not in a way that meant that he thought anything was funny.

"No. Though she might as well be. She is invisible there. Except for those occasions when, tragically, she is not."

Jacey slumped in her chair, arms folded on her chest, eyes lidded and mostly closed, lips moving, though no sound could be heard. Her condition seemed suddenly to have grown worse.

"Look, I have an idea," Preston said, making a decision. "I think I might be able to help her. Something I saw in the *Embody Phenomena* coursework. I think it — "

But at that moment a voice cracked out over the speakers in the room.

"GREETINGS HACKERS!" boomed the voice. "IS THIS THING ON?"

What followed were congratulations for making the Stage Two cut, a reminder about the prize money, and profuse thanks to the event sponsors. Then, after an awkward attempt to build suspense that the speaker abandoned when it became obvious that no one was buying it, he made his final announcement.

"Here is what you've all come for — the Stage Two Theme. This year's Stage Two Theme is... *Materialize Actions!* Now, GET TO HACKING!"

There was a momentary silence, then all the teams in the room crowded into little groups and began to plan. The Einsteins did the same. Preston led them. He was filled with a strange and ferocious passion, almost glee. In his mind the whole Spynncaster app was clicking into place, pieces sliding seamlessly into position on top of other pieces. Features and functions were laid out in his vision like instructions in a huge Lego diagram.

"*Materialize Actions*," he told Matias and Regan. "This is, like, tailor made for Spynncaster! That basically means the same thing as

Embody Phenomena. You see?" A rush of ideas cascaded over him, as if he was standing in a waterfall. The impressions were coming like physical blows, so forcefully that he actually looked up at the ceiling to see if tiles were loose. Then he pulled Matias and Regan closer.

"Here's what we're going to build," he said. "The orange ball. It's a ball of Spynn. Right? And players pass it back and forth between them. But now we'll make it so the ball can be imbued with Phenomena. The *Actions* they want us to *Materialize* here will be Embodied Phenomena that burst into effect on the other player's device when the ball comes in." He had to make a real effort to slow his speech down so the others could understand him. And they were obviously having a hard time doing that right now. He tried again. "Like this. Let's say, take the *Earthquake* Phenomena. We create an easy interface to attach an *Earthquake* to the orange ball. And when you Cast it to your opponent, the screen can jumble and shake, so it's really hard to cast the ball back. Or we can cast *Fog*, which can hide the ball so you can't cast it back because you can't see it!"

"Why do you need to cast the ball back?" asked Matias. "What is the point of this game?" He sounded peeved. It made Preston happy to have gotten that much of a reaction out of Matias.

"Because," Preston cried, seeing it all so clearly, "the longer the ball is on the other person's screen, the more points they lose. Each start with 100 points. First person to lose all their points loses the game. So — keep the ball on the other player's phone!"

Now they understood. And they began to get into the spirit. Regan's face lifted with growing understanding.

"I take back what I said about this not being much of a game. It still lacks good taste and drama, but I like where it is going!"

"You want drama?" Preston said. "Listen. The people in the universe of the Spynncasters have been locked in an endless battle against a foe who is equally powerless to step away from the blood-shed. The Dark Folk!" He felt like he was channeling information from another realm. "For eons they have slaughtered each other, and all because of a single curse leveled by one incredibly powerful... Faerie."

Regan raised one eyebrow. "A Faerie? Really?"

"Yes. The Dark Folk are Faeries. She was defeated, and they banished her, but her curse remains." Preston was giddy. It all made so much sense. Where was he getting this? "And now they fight on, unable to end the butchery. They will fight on forever." Preston was filled with a feeling of loss, suddenly, of resentment against this Faerie, whoever she had been. It was very much as though he were thinking of something that had really happened.

"Ok, JRR Tolkien," Regan drawled. "But what does this have to do with the game? Remember? This is a game?"

"We need art. Can you do art? Can you do four different classes of Spynncasters?" Preston asked him.

"*Do* art? Yes, I can *do* art, although that is a very disrespectful way to refer to one of mankind's most exalted pursuits. It trivializes the very — "

"Ok, ok," Preston interrupted. He was beginning to sympathize with Jacey — Regan did like to hear himself talk. But thinking of Jacey made him remember something else. He turned to look behind him, where Jacey had folded even farther into herself, rocking on her chair.

"We can't leave her like this," Preston said. "Look, I don't think she was supposed to try to figure out Spynnlang. I think it might actually be hurting her. Her mind. I think, for whatever reason, I'm the only one that can do it right now."

"Right now?" Matias said. "What does that mean?"

"It means — I don't know! It doesn't matter. I think I know a way to help her."

"Serotonin Reuptake Inhibitors?" Regan suggested.

"No. I'm going to Cast an *Embodied Phenomena* on her."

This stopped both Matias and Regan from moving at all. Finally Regan held up a single index finger and waved it slowly, back and forth.

"I have absolutely no idea what you are saying," he told Preston. "It is not a circumstance I am familiar with. But if this is anything at all like what happened in the library, then, *no*. Permission denied."

"The *Embodied Phenomena* only exist in your game," Matias pointed out.

"No. They're more than that," Preston said, certain it was true.

Matias and Regan both began to protest, but Preston shut them down quickly.

"We don't have time," he told him, moving toward one of the terminals registered to the Einstein team. "I have the Phenomena course figured out. This whole thing is starting to make so much sense. This is a game, yes. But it's more than a game." He sat down and began twisting through a sequence on the keyboard. "This is real."

Matias sat beside Preston.

"Perhaps," he said, watching Preston pull and bend his fingers through gruesome postures with no effort at all, "it would be wiser to wait. I believe this is real, though fantastical. But that also makes it dangerous."

"Look at her, Matias. We can't wait."

The Phenomena he was Embodying was called *Insight*. The idea had actually come to him the night before as he finished the course-work for the section. It was not the simplest sequence on the page, but many were far more complex. He knew he could have created the Spynnlang icons representing it without consulting the diagrams, but he wanted to take no chances. He carefully followed along with the pictures on the screen.

Within just a few minutes he was done. He updated the app and deployed the new build to their phones. And then he opened the app and pointed the phone at Jacey.

"She has the app on her phone, that's why this will work," he said to no one in particular.

"Oh, of course," Regan said, with a sarcastic nod, "*that* makes perfect sense. Now I understand *everything*." He stopped. "Good lord. I sound like Jacey."

"Preston — " said Matias, just as Preston said, *"Insight,"* and launched the ball at Jacey's phone with a mental flick.

There was a flash. Someone from an adjoining table glanced toward them, but quickly looked away.

The effect on Jacey was instantaneous.

She sat up. She blinked once, and then her eyes lifted open. Wide open. She took a deep breath and let it out slowly, and then stood and looked around the room as if she had never seen a room before.

"What effect is this *Insight* Phenomena intended to have?" Matias asked warily.

"The recipient gains *Insight* into whatever the caster Embodied into the Phenomena. I gave her *insight* into Spynnlang." Preston was feeling a little wobbly all of a sudden. In fact, he realized, it was more than just a wobble. But he continued explaining to Matias, hoping the feeling would pass. "I think it will give her enough of an understanding that it can break her out of whatever loop she is falling into. Then... ahhhh... "

And he could no longer talk. His head gave a single, thunderous throb. He heard a sound like the testing tone theaters play to demonstrate the fine quality of their sound system. It started high, notes in a chord that bent and flexed together, at the very edge of his hearing. And then it plunged. Downward. And sickeningly, it took his mind with it. The chords dropped, octave after octave, until they seemed as if they would disappear through the crust of the planet.

Preston's head seemed to shrink. The strength left his limbs. He felt as if his life force were being unspooled from his body, pulled out of him through his phone, the way a cat pulls a thread and unravels a sweater. He tried to stop the flow, but he could not. He listed to the side, and fell against Matias. Other sounds in the room were growing distant, and echoing, and his eyesight was greying out.

"Preston?" Matias said.

Regan was at his side, looking at his face, calling him. "Preston! What's happening?"

And that is when Preston heard the voice in his head. It was a low voice, smooth and hollow, like a hundred ghosts all speaking in perfect synchrony. It was filled with urgency. No, not urgency. *Anger.* And from the way Regan and Matias jerked their faces up and around, they heard it too.

"*You fools!*" the voice said, "*What have you done? What have you done to the Object?*"

Matias and Regan swiveled desperately, but they could not find the speaker.

"*The Einstein Object — it falters! It will fail! You must ACT!*"

Then Regan saw something else. "Matias — Jacey! She's wandering off!"

Matias left Preston's side and sprinted away.

Regan shook his head to get the voice out, and Preston would have done the same but the thread unravelling his body had left him no strength to move it at all. He was sinking, down, through the floor, through the very bottom of the physical realm, down into dark nothingness. He was being drawn into an inky pool of oblivion, and at the bottom lay death. He saw this. He watched it come swiftly closer.

Matias returned with Jacey. Her eyes were wide and calm. She was taking everything in like a tourist on vacation.

"Wonderful," Regan said. "Such a fantastic plan, Preston. She's like Bambi. Jacey, can you hear me?"

She nodded.

"*Can you Synch?*" demanded the voice. "*Only moments remain before the Einstein Object is drained and fades. CAN YOU SYNCH?*"

"Regan, are you experiencing this... voice?" Matias asked, holding his head and swaying.

"I am."

"I believe we're being asked to perform the procedure from the library."

"No!" Regan said.

"You FOOLS — Synch now, or all is lost!"

"Regan, I don't think we have a choice. We must... Synch."

"Fine!" spat Regan. "But I will not be held responsible if our brains are liquefied." He reached for Matias's hand. "Let's do it."

"No! Are you mad? Somewhere private — QUICKLY!"

"Where are we supposed — wait, the break room!" Regan pointed frantically. Wordlessly Matias swept Preston up in his arms, and Regan ushered Jacey toward the break room door.

"Just a fainting spell, nothing to be alarmed about," Regan said to the developers as they hurried past.

The break room was a small space, and mercifully unoccupied. Coffee machines lined a counter against one wall, vending machines were pushed against another. The central area ringed by hotel lounge chairs was empty, and here Matias lowered Preston to the floor. Regan kneeled and pulled Jacey down. They were now gathered on the carpet around Preston's prone body. Regan opened Jacey's hand and put her phone in her palm.

Preston felt himself nearly black out, but fought back to consciousness. He knew that once he slipped away completely he would be lost. He had to save the last of his energy for a single, final word.

"You have mere seconds! DO IT NOW!"

"Jacey, can you hear me?" Regan cried. "Do you hear this voice, do you know what is happening?" She nodded. Matias propped Preston up, then he took his own phone out. Preston's phone was still gripped in his hand. Regan, holding his device in his open palm, sat with his back to the other three and interlaced his fingers with Jacey's. Back to back they sat, clasped with hands and phones, and Regan said, "Oh for the love of god. Synch!"

"Synch!" said Matias.

"Synch," lilted Jacey softly.

"Synch," whispered Preston, with the last of his strength.

A ring of blue light ruptured the air above them, swelling to fill the room and twining in swift circles near the ceiling. The air pressure in the room dropped. Their ears popped. The lights darkened. And then into their closed group, from *somewhere else*, came energy. Some other hand was feeding them Spynn. Forcing it into their circle. There was violence to this act, there was fury. But, through the others Synched to him, like water seeking the lowest point on a plain, this Spynn energy flowed to Preston.

He felt it hit him. His back arched high off the floor. His teeth ground together and a scream was drawn from his mouth. This thrust of power was brutal, but its aim was certain. It filled him. He felt himself rise back up from the dark abyss. Like a balloon inflating, the outlines of his consciousness took shape again. And just as his vision was clearing and the echoes were fading from his hearing, the thrust was withdrawn. The source retracted. And their Synch collapsed.

The four of them sat panting on the floor with their backs together.

At that moment, Ms. Fredrick shot into the room.

"Children? What is happening?" She stopped a few feet away and watched. Preston pulled his feet up to his chest, and then rolled forward onto his hands and knees. He groaned. His shoulders ached, his legs were rubber bands, but still it was a very different sensation then what he had felt only seconds before. A welcome sensation. And even as he examined himself, he could feel strength returning, so that a moment later he could stand.

"What, may I ask, are you doing?" Ms. Fredrick demanded. She was out of breath and was deeply unsettled, glancing around the break room in alarm.

"We were meditating," they heard Jacey say. They turned to look. She stared back, slouched against a lounge chair, drawing deep breaths. For the first time in a week she appeared normal, if you could ignore the bags under her eyes. "Meditating helps us focus," she said to Ms. Fredrick. "And sometimes we chant. And use laser lights... for effect. That's what it was. Up on the ceiling. If you saw any lights?"

"Well, I did not see lights," Ms. Fredrick said doubtfully. "But I saw you carry Preston in here, which was alarming to say the least! And I do see you now, wasting time on the floor. I would suggest you rise up and begin working on your project, if you are to have any hope of advancing." She gestured back out the door. "Those people are deeply focused and productive. None of *them* are napping!"

And then, careful as always, she stepped back through the door, though she stumbled when she turned, as if the pressure was getting to her. Preston collapsed in a chair and held his face in his hands.

"What the hell just happened?" Jacey asked.

"My fault," Preston said, his voice still little more than a gasp. "I cast an Embodied Phenomena. To break you out of your, your thing, you were in a loop, or... " he closed his eyes. "I guess I don't know what I'm doing after all."

"Whatever you did, let's talk about it later," she said. "Although, also, you know... thanks." She paused, looking for words, then gave him a grimace and turned away. "So people," she said, including the other two, "we do have a hackathon to win. Let's go!"

They stumbled back into the main room, where their absence had not been noted. The remaining teams were dead serious, and not to be distracted, and now the Einsteins had fallen behind by a substantial margin. So the rest of the day was spent in a blur of activity. Regan created art. Despite his apparent disdain for a genre that included Fairies, he created compelling portraits to represent the characters Preston described. Jacey and Matias mostly ran interference, shielding Preston from view so he could chord Spynnlang on the keyboard without drawing unwanted attention.

And then at last, just as time was up, the app was built and finished and they submitted it to the moderators. And afterward, when the Einsteins trooped in an exhausted line back out into the evening air, then back inside Ms. Fredrick's dark and welcoming car,

Ms. Fredrick seemed as exhausted as they did. But she put on a stoic face and got them loaded in and on the way.

They had done it. But in each of their eyes, there was now something new. Disbelief, perhaps. Definitely fear. It was fifteen minutes of surface streets before they were back on the freeway, and another ten minutes after that before any of them spoke.

"I understand it now," Jacey finally said. "You guys. Listen."

Preston and Regan turned and looked back at Jacey in the seat behind them. She searched for words for a minute, could not seem to find them, and then simply began speaking.

"I don't know how to say this exactly. But Spynnlang, it's not just an Object *Oriented* language. It is like an Object *Only* language." She looked at Preston. "I can't tell how much OOP you've been picking up, but look. In Object Oriented Programming you create Parent Objects, right? And then Child Objects Inherit properties from those Parents? And you can identify those Objects with Getters, and manipulate them with Setters?" Preston nodded, surprised that he really had retained a lot of the information about OOP.

"Ok," said Jacey, "Well the Objects in Spynnlang aren't just software constructions. I don't understand this, I got lost trying to wrap my brain around a concept like... I was lost until you pulled me out, Preston. These Objects you create and manipulate. They are not software — they are *real things*. Am I right?"

Preston had not thought through any of this, but now he nodded. What Jacey was saying was correct. Spynnlang icons were not mere digital references to objects in the real world. Now that Jacey was making him face it, he saw it clearly. The Spynnlang icons *were* the objects they represented. But revealed and available, somehow. Malleable. Combinable. Accessible at a deep level — accessible through Computer Programming.

"Another thing that I couldn't see," she went on. "I couldn't understand because,

because — there is this master Object everywhere in the code, and I couldn't pin it down. It's woven through all the other Objects. Linking them all together. It didn't make sense, but

now... " She blinked at Preston, understanding in her eyes. *"You're the master Object. I'm right, aren't I?"*

"The Einstein Object," said Matias. "The voice was speaking of you, it called you the Einstein Object."

Preston could only nod. The Einstein Object. It resonated. He knew it from somewhere. He couldn't tell if the rest of what Jacey was saying was correct. He didn't know if he was somehow woven through all the Spynnlang icons. But he knew that, while he was still Preston Oliver Nowak, he was also the Einstein Object. Whatever that could possibly mean.

"So look, I have a theory," Jacey was saying. "It's kind of freaky, but that Embodied Phenomena you cast was powerful, it juiced me, it made everything click. You know your phone? I think when you accepted the phone number for your account, I think that was a Getter. An OOP method to identify an object. I think that when you agreed to accept the number as Preston Oliver Nowak, it was identifying you. And then the text that came through later that day? Where the sender number was all zeros? I think that text was a Setter. I think you got activated, Preston. Just like any Object in an OOP language. The Getter found you, and the Setter reached out and turned you on."

The distant hum of the tires on the dark freeway was the only sound in the car for many more minutes, as the four of them tried to work though the meaning of all that Jacey had said.

Finally Matias spoke again. "If this is true, it must require tremendous energy," he said. "Spynn energy, in theory. To *create* and manipulate real world objects, even if only by reference... " He trailed off as he tried to imagine it. "But it would explain Preston's attack, or bout, at Code Portal today. When he cast this Embodied Phenomena on Jacey, he took a step out of the digital game realm of moving orange balls from phone to phone. He attempted to affect a real, physical object. A person. He didn't have sufficient energy to pay for this, and so he nearly paid with his life. The voice claimed... " and when he said this, they all shivered. None of them was ready to talk about the voice. "You were very near to death, Preston. I think that you should cast no more Embodied Phenomena until we have a clearer idea of the mechanics of this Spynnlang framework."

"I second that," Regan said, "because it is such a colossal understatement."

Jacey nodded. "We need more information."

"And there is also this," Regan said. "After all we have learned about Preston's grandfather, and his history with — and purported delusions of slaying — Albert Einstein, could it possibly be coincidence to hear Preston referred to as... the *Einstein Object*?"

Preston sank back into his seat while they continued to propose theories and discuss possibilities. The programming concepts they were throwing around made sense to him, but they represented someone else's abstraction of the world, not his. He was glad it seemed to give the rest of the group something to grab ahold of. If it helped them understand the things that were happening then he was all for it. Understanding was going to be essential if they were to get through this in one piece. But to Preston, these were still foreign ideas, Getters and Setters and Objects. Inheritance.

Running short of Spynn and almost dying, *that* he understood. He didn't know what he was supposed to do about it, however. The Embodied Phenomena were obviously meant to be used, so if the Spynn to do it did not come from him, where was it supposed to come from? He held his phone and felt the trickle charge. He understood what it was at last. His body was literally pushing Spynn into the phone, where it was being converted into electricity. Or maybe Spynn was already electricity. Or maybe electricity had always been Spynn?

The thing Preston's mind kept returning to, though, was not his being an Object, or finding Spynn to power this Programming Language, or how Einstein or Grandpa Nowak fit into all of it. No.

What Preston kept thinking about was the voice. What was that voice?

Appearing suddenly, in their *minds*. Where had it come from, and how had it known to find him? And why, *why* had it seemed so very familiar?

CHAPTER
ELEVEN

Sundays were typically puttering days for Preston's dad, and sweeping days for his mom. Often enough the puttering and the sweeping got tangled up with each other, and then there were semi-friendly standoffs over who could occupy the laundry room walkway, and whether that broken lightbulb had appeared on the floor before or after it had been swept. His mom almost always emerged in the stronger position from these negotiations, though whenever his father accidentally shorted a fuse and threw the whole house into shadow he proudly took the lead, wondering aloud how they would ever be able to get along without him if he was not there to throw the breakers — that he had shorted — back on.

The Sunday after the Stage Two event, the Nowak household had the additional complication of hosting an impromptu meeting of the Einstein Programming Club in Preston's room. Jacey, Matias, and Regan had come over in the afternoon after they had all received an email from Ms. Fredrick. It had read, "Returns are speedy because the field is so much smaller — and the Einstein Programming Team has advanced to Stage Three! This is the final stage of the competition, and a very great honor. Congratulations to you all. We will make our plans for next Saturday when we gather on Thursday afternoon. Yours, Sally Fredrick."

The four of them were in Preston's room. Just now they were wincing as a crash was heard somewhere deep in the house, then they frowned at the sound of Preston's father skipping quickly out the back door, then they cowered as they heard Preston's mother cry, "What in the *world*?"

It was hard to concentrate, but they had important decisions to make.

"You know what a hundred thousand dollars buys in Arkansas? A palace," Jacey said.

"Do not forget the iPad Pro, which would also be ours," Regan said. "You could sell that and buy a pony."

"If you invested that money," said Matias, "you could double it in five years."

"I don't have five years," Jacey snarled. "Let's all just go live in Arkansas. We could each have our own floor. We could start a web development company."

"Groan," groaned Regan. "I know, let us tie ourselves to train tracks and allow ourselves to be decapitated. The pain would be over faster."

"What if the train derailed before it reached you?" Matias asked.

"Fine Regan, what would you do?" asked Jacey.

"Purchase a submarine, the most versatile of nautical conveyances, filled with catalogs from Restoration Hardware, and sail beneath the seven seas spreading restrained yet forward-thinking design to disadvantaged coastal dwellers everywhere."

Jacey closed her eyes and shook her head.

"God, Regan, you kind of take the air out of the room, you know? I mean sometimes you're so..." Jacey could not find the words.

"Visionary?" Regan suggested.

Preston was listening and laughing, but most of his attention was taken up with the contents of his father's shoe box. He had taken the photos out and arranged them on the bed in what he thought must be chronological order. On a separate piece of paper he was making a timeline, and tagging it with events and artifacts that he was sure of.

So far he had Grandpa Nowak's birthday from the death certificate: 1918. And he had Grandpa Nowak and Einstein meeting at Caltech in 1934 when Nowak was 16. From the map on the wall, he had the date that Nowak Shoes had begun: 1942. He had worked forward about halfway toward the day he himself had been born, but he kept getting hung up at the point where Nowak Shoes had been closed by his grandfather for reasons unknown.

"Hey, what am I missing here?" Preston asked his friends. They dropped their banter, which had mostly been for Preston's benefit anyway, and came to the bed.

"Look," he showed them, "by 1960 Nowak Shoes had 88 stores, all over the country. My father was born in 1960. He told me they were rich for the first few years of his life. And then in 1968, here, the whole business gets sold except for the single store, and they lived in a little house in Pasadena, just the two of them. Total change of lifestyle. It doesn't make sense. Does it?"

Preston was frowning and shaking his head, staring at the timeline. The others watched him, but seemed puzzled at his puzzlement.

"What's the discrepancy, Preston?" Matias asked.

"Well, they were rich from the stores. And then Grandpa *sold* the stores. Right?" Still they did not see. "Where did the money go? From selling the stores? Why did Grandpa and my dad go from nannies and chauffeurs and rolling lawns to a one room bungalow on Altadena Ave?"

Now they saw.

"A cogent insight, Preston." Matias rumbled. "Perhaps there were debts?"

"Maybe he was a gambler," Jacey said.

"Medical bills?" Regan offered. "He had those hands... "

Just then soft feet padded back in through the rear of the house, froze, and took a sudden scurrying left down Preston's hallway. A second later his father slipped into the room, closing the door behind him as quietly as possible.

"Hey kids," he whispered, waving. He listened at the door, then turned back to smile. "Well, hah, look at you all. What are you up to here, huh? Wow, look at this." He tiptoed over to the chronology laid out on the bed covers.

"Making a nice collage, are you?" he asked. "A collage out of Grandpa Nowak's family heirlooms? Well good for you kids." He was completely distracted by the sound of whisking coming from the kitchen. Preston took the opportunity that had fallen into his lap.

"Dad, remember you said Grandpa Nowak sold all the shoe stores except for the flagship store here in town?"

"Of course I remember that."

"So, did Grandpa Nowak make any money from selling the business?"

"Oh yes. Millions. He sold them lock stock and barrel to a big loafer outfit from Chicago. They went bankrupt a few years later. Didn't have Dad's business sense, I guess."

"He made millions of dollars? So how come you two moved into that tiny house up on Altadena?"

"He gave it all away, that's why." His dad turned to face Preston now. His eyebrows were doing their dolphin leaps of bewilderment behind his glasses. "He was a funny, solitary guy, Pres. I don't really know why he did *any* of the things he did."

"Who did he give the money to?" Preston asked. His friends, particularly Jacey, wore expressions as bewildered as Mr. Nowak's. Voluntarily forfeiting millions of dollars and leaving yourself with almost nothing was very hard to for most people to understand.

"Well... " His dad took a thoughtful pause, pursing his lips. "He gave a bit of it to some school projects in the area. Little things. A fountain here, a garden there. But most of it, almost the whole thing, he donated to Caltech. They named a department after him. You knew this, right?"

This was NOT the time for Preston to demand his father explain how he would've known that, given that no one had ever even hinted that such information existed.

"A department," he remarked, calmly. "I don't think so. Is it still there?"

"Oh yes. They do scientific experiments. It's the PON Center for Quantum Studies. Preston Oliver Nowak. PON." They heard a door open in the front of the house and Preston's mom's voice call from the front porch, "Preston!" All of them understood that it was Preston Sr. who was being summoned. He shrugged and patted Preston on the head.

"Well son, it's been nice having this chat with you. Now I have to go take your mother to an expensive lunch and go buy a dresser mirror for her." He took a deep breath and left the room.

"Your dad is..." Jacey said.

"I know," Preston said, resignedly.

"He's hilarious!" she finished. "It must be awesome living with him."

Regan was already snapping on the iMac and loading up the Caltech website.

"Here is it," he said. "The PON Center for Quantum Studies." He read aloud:

"*The mission of the Center for Quantum Studies is to provide a world-wide focal point for students, researchers, governments, and industries to collaborate on advanced studies of quantum mechanics, including: quantum foundations, quantum entanglement, quantum computing and technology.*"

Jacey pointed to a link under the main banner, Special Events. It was blinking. Regan clicked it.

"*Join Founding Chairwoman and Caltech's own Dr. Felicia Toss in a Community Forum presentation. This master class style forum will cover basic and not so basic theories and applications for Quantum Mechanics in the modern age. Join us this Sunday at 2:00 PM in the Jorgensen Building conference room. Open to the public.*"

They looked at each other, eyes wide.

"Founding Chairwoman," said Preston. "Do you think that means founding, like she's been there since the department was created? Like maybe she knew my Grandpa?"

"How come we never get fliers about this stuff at school?" Jacey complained. "We can just make it if we leave now and ride down Fair Oaks!"

And so they exited the house, Preston calling out, "Going to Caltech, Dad!" as he sailed by. His father had other concerns, and there was some question as to whether he'd heard, but Preston did not repeat himself. He could not. As soon as they were out of the house they were on their bikes, pedaling like the wind down the newly broadened bike paths on Fair Oaks Avenue. Fifteen minutes later they were riding the tree-lined paths of the campus.

Jorgensen Building, read a sign with an arrow, and they leaned over and pedaled that way. Students were few on the paths on a Sunday, but those they did see were happy to dance to the side. It was a campus of bike lovers, apparently.

They threw the locks around their bikes when they arrived at the doors, and then, shifting gears from "madcap" all the way down to "church going," they moved inside. A foyer lined with pictures greeted them. Through a set of closed double doors they could hear a woman's voice speaking on a mic. But before they entered the main room, Preston passed his gaze down the rows of pictures, down to the oldest pictures, which were all in black and white. And there, at the very beginning of the row, was a picture of Grandpa Nowak. Preston pointed silently. The others nodded. Then they passed into the conference room.

The room was full, but there were two groups of seats where they might be able to sit together. Five or six in the very front row, and a similar number in the very back. Jacey, Regan and Preston instinctively turned to the seats in the rear, and it was a moment before they saw that Matias had not followed them. He was making his way blithely down to the very front, gaze held like a baby on a rattle by the speaker on stage, Dr. Felicia Toss.

"Ridiculous social emotional misfit," Regan whispered savagely, as they were forced to follow. "That's right Matias, just wander in *front* of everyone. Human shame is meaningless to you, senseless, inscrutable Buddha oddball... " and he continued muttering as they moved, ducking and apologizing, all the way to the front, and finally were seated to either side of Matias, not eight feet from the low stage.

Dr. Felicia Toss was a bespectacled woman in her seventies. She wore a loose white shirt tucked into comfortable slacks, and had her hair up in a bun. She did not look at Preston and his friends as they made their way to their seats. She was expounding with tremendous energy upon the mysteries of quantum mechanics, stepping back and forth between the blackboards behind her and the lectern that held her notes.

The subject matter was advertised to have been a broad cross-section of quantum mechanical thought in the current era, but Dr. Toss seemed to have a special fascination with quantum entanglement.

"I imagine most of the attendees here today are familiar with the subject," she said, "and if you are not, then please apply to Caltech for a refresher course." There was respectful laughter from the crowd, which she acknowledged with a smile. "Actually, since this is also a community forum, and we may have some novice physicists here, I will quickly touch on the basics of entanglement." She moved to the blackboard and drew a circle. She labeled it *Earth*. On the other side of the blackboard, she drew another circle, and labeled it, *Massively Far Away Place*, which drew another small chuckle. Then she returned to her lectern. Preston sensed that this was a bit of a spur of the moment addition, and wondered if it was for their benefit.

"Essentially," she said, "quantum entanglement states that by doing something to an entangled particle here on *Earth* — let us suppose you change the direction of an electron's spin — we then instantly change the spin of the electron's entangled partner in a *Massively Far Away Place*. The distance does not matter. These two particles are *instantly and continuously connected*. Whether they are two inches apart or a quintillion miles apart, they will reflect each other. Einstein called quantum entanglement 'Spooky action at a distance' and for many years he refused to acknowledge its existence. But he came around at last. Quantum entanglement is the closest thing we have in modern science to *magic*."

Dr. Toss considered her notes for the briefest moment, and then looked back out at the audience. "So much for simple explanations. We would be remiss to an extreme if we did not dig into the math from here. Entanglement can be a complicated business." And for just a moment, as though to say "sorry, I tried," she looked down at the four of them in the front row with a shrug and a smile. Then she turned back to the blackboard and began to diagram formulas.

Preston, to his surprise, found himself following every moment of the presentation. He felt as though he was standing to one side, as though he were watching someone else think and calculate inside him, someone process and make connections, in many cases leaping many steps ahead of the math on the blackboard. These were the most amazing concepts he had ever heard: wave function collapse, probabilistic outcomes, the way a thing can be in more than one place at a time, but only until you tried to determine where it was.

The hour ended with gracious applause, but Preston felt that he could have sat through days and days of the material. He had to make a very concerted effort to step back from the sidelines of his mind and take full possession of his thoughts. Dr. Toss had opened the floor to questions.

Matias was first with his hand up. Dr. Toss pointed to him. Matias's voice boomed out as if on a loud speaker.

"You stated that electrons are dislodged by the photoelectric effect if light reaches a threshold frequency. Presumably each photon is related to the photon frequency by the Planck constant. Could you diagram that mathematically?"

Dr. Toss nodded, and seemed delighted by the question. She returned to the board and wrote out the formula. Matias nodded. Preston did as well. Felicia Toss took questions for another thirty minutes, and Jacey and Regan each got called upon and presented truly well thought out queries. Finally she looked at her watch.

"Oh, our time is almost up. I have time for one more question." Preston, whose hand had been up for the last 20 minutes, raised it once more. He resisted the urge to wave it, or to jump up and down. In fact, he sat back in his chair this time. He relaxed his fingers, and cupped his hand. He tried to smile. He liked this woman; the least he could do was present her a smiling face in the crowd.

And magically, she looked down from her lectern and pointed at him.

"Yes, young man in the front. What is your question?"

Preston cleared his throat and found, as he often did in public settings, that his voice had grown very soft. Oh, for Matias's booming voice, he thought. But he forced as much air as he could up past his vocal cords.

"Um. I've enjoyed your presentation very, very much. Your understanding of the material is humbling." His friends were looking at him, and at each other. What was he doing? Preston, they must have been certain, could not have been following the details of the presentation. There were only three geniuses in the programming club, after all.

She nodded. "Thank you indeed. Your question?"

Preston suddenly changed his mind. "I was going to ask about the uncertainty principle and the trade-offs in accuracy between the measurement of momentum and position. But that doesn't really matter, I guess. My real question is... did you know my grandfather?"

"Hmm," she smiled. "A trick question. Well. Who was your grandfather?"

"Preston Oliver Nowak."

And there, for the first time in an hour and a half of juggling the most complicated concepts the human mind had ever conceived, he saw hesitation. And surprise.

"Well. That is a name I have not heard in many years. Yes. I knew your grandfather." And no more. She paused, then she looked out at the assembled scientists, students, faculty and elementary school children, and she bid them good afternoon. And the session was over. Dr. Toss picked up her notes and walked to the back of the stage. Preston hoped against hope that she would turn, that she would give a signal. He had so many questions now.

And then she slowed. She turned her body, looked over one slight shoulder, sighted him speculatively, and pointed a finger at him. She turned her palm down. Wait, it said. Then she left the stage.

The audience took its time leaving the room. His friends had not seen Dr. Toss's subtle directions, and they were a little dubious when he explained, but they waited willingly enough. Finally the room was empty. The doors in the back of the room closed as the last of the audience departed. Five minutes passed. Then ten. Fifteen. Jacey was getting ready to leave despite Preston's protests, when Dr. Toss reappeared on the stage. This time she held an old cloth bag with a worn leather handle.

Preston stood up, as did the others, but she motioned for them to sit. She was moving slowly now. During the presentation she had appeared much younger, but that now seemed to have been the result of strong stage presence combined with a love of the subject matter, for as she came toward them she looked like exactly what she was: a seventy-five-year-old woman carrying a very heavy bag.

"Sit," she said, "please." She reached the edge of the stage and lowered the bag, and then lowered herself so that she sat on the stage edge, her legs hanging over. She looked them over for a moment before she spoke.

"I am getting too old for this," she smiled. "So. Professor Nowak's grandson, and his three brilliant friends. I should have known." She looked closer. "You look like him, you know. Or you will, in thirty years. Now how can I help you? Presumably you have come for a reason?"

"I'm just... I have some questions about my grandfather," Preston's voice stumbled. Where to start? "Things my dad doesn't know, I guess. Would you mind?"

"Mind? No, I wouldn't mind. It's the least I can do." She gestured to the walls and ceiling around them. "His generosity made all this possible. How could I possibly refuse his grandson a conversation about his memory?" She was looking at him very closely, paying particular attention to his hands. Then she met his eyes again. "Perhaps you'll introduce me to your friends?"

Preston introduced them all, feeling awkward. She nodded once to each, as though confirming them in her mind. And then she said, "So, Preston the Third. Are you called that?"

"My grandparents on my mom's side do," he said, dubiously.

"Fine, I will as well. What can I tell you about your grandfather?"

And Preston found his mind blank. He could think of no specific questions. He knew there were things — important things — that needed to be asked. But now the time had come, and he could not remember them. He looked to his friends, but they seemed to be in a similar condition.

"Why don't I tell you how we met?" she said. "And a little about the work we did together? Would that help?" Preston nodded gratefully.

"Very well. I was twenty-two, and one of the few female physics students at Caltech at the time. This was 1962. Your grandfather must have been forty-four, forty-five. It had been only a year, I think, since he'd lost his wife. During the birth of your father, it must have been."

"That's right," Preston said.

"Yes," she said, lost for a moment in the colors of the past. "Yes. Your grandfather was a visiting professor. That is, no tenure. No official status. But such a deep understanding of the subject matter that the school basically let him teach seminars any time he liked. A pupil of Albert Einstein. A celebrity. And that is where I met him. He was brilliant, but his hands handicapped him. You know about his hands, of course? So he would select graduate students — I suppose now we would call them interns — to help him type his papers. He would teach us exercises. Typing exercises. He was quite an eccentric in some ways."

"I worked closely with him for a number of years. I liked him. I found him very sad. Some thought him insane, but I didn't. He suffered from delusions, I think. But you can't be insane and at the same time have the kind of clear and penetrating understanding of the physical world that he had. Here at the Center we have basically been working through a series of experiments that your grandfather designed in the 50s and 60s, long before there were instruments sensitive enough to perform them. His legacy lives on here in a very real way. His twin passions were quantum entanglement and dark energy. Tell me... do you know anything at all of dark energy?"

Preston swallowed. He looked at Matias, Jacey, and Regan, but they offered him nothing. They all understood that the question had been addressed specifically to Preston. So he loosened the focus that seemed to keep him locked into the center of his brain, stood to one side, and let the big thoughts come.

"Roughly 95 percent of the universe is either Dark energy or Dark matter," he began. Calculations floated past in his brain. He had to fight to keep from being drawn deeper into the math. "Neither one can be seen or experienced; we only know about their existence because of the way they affect the speed of the expansion of the universe. All other matter — everything ever observed with all of our instruments, stars, planets, everything everywhere — adds up to less than 5 percent of the universe. To my knowledge no satisfactory explanation has ever been offered to account for the overwhelming prevalence of Dark matter and Dark energy. It seems to contradict much of what we think we know about the origins of time and space."

Regan let out a small sound, like a happy puppy who has been introduced to a new toy. Jacey smirked. Matias watched him without surprise — or any other emotion for that matter.

Dr. Toss nodded. "Less than 5 percent. That is the current estimate. While Dark matter and energy make up more than 95 percent of the observable universe. Professor Nowak was convinced, however, that until approximately 1955, the balance between dark and what he called light matter was exactly equal."

"What happened in 1955?" Regan asked.

"He never offered details. This theory was absurd on its face, so he never published. But," she said, and here she turned her gaze back to Preston, "he thought this idea was *crucial*, and he returned to it often."

"I digress, however," she said. She took a breath, remembering where she was in her story. "Ah, yes. When he closed his stores he was tremendously generous. He endowed this entire department, and insisted that I be made Founding Chairwoman. I can tell you, there were some political battles over that. But he was persistent." She took another moment to think, then said, "That, I think, about covers it. He was a brilliant, brilliant man."

Somehow Preston was surprised. He had expected more, a revelation. Could this really be all there was?

"Do you remember anything else?" he asked. "Anything that might be important?" Even to his ears that sounded desperate.

Dr. Toss tilted her head quizzically. "What is important to one person may be a triviality to another. I've told you some very important things already. What are you curious about? *Specifically?*"

She put a special emphasis on the last word. She had more to tell them, he realized. She was offering him a test. She would tell him more, but only if he asked the right question. She had already told him something important, she said — could there be a clue there? What had she talked about? His father being born, yes, but that had been before she met Grandpa Nowak. Being a female physics student, but that was surely not it. Grandpa's hands? The injury? But that had also happened before they met. Dark energy? Maybe.

Something to do with the increasing speed of the expanding universe?

And then he saw it. The clue she had left. Surely it was a clue.

"You said he taught you... typing exercises." Beside him he felt Matias, Jacey, and Regan grow very still. Typing. Could it be?

"What were those like?" he asked, and waited, barely breathing.

"Ah, yes." She nodded, and her hand moved out to touch the bag beside her, the kind of gesture that a person does not realize they are making because they have done it so many times in the past. "Most strange, the exercises. Most... difficult. Are *you* an accomplished typist, Preston Jr.?" Her stare was frank. It was almost pleading, he thought. He lifted his hands off his lap, paused, then slowly extended and held them in front of his chest. Should he? Should he do it?

Then, watching her face the entire time, he slowly fingered a series of Spynnlang sequences. In some ways it felt more natural to do it without a keyboard.

Dr. Toss closed her eyes, and he saw, they all saw, moisture swell beneath her lids. She took a huge, shuddering breath, and then she looked at him again.

"Yes. The exercises. I have waited so long. So long, you see. And now you are here." She took a moment to collect herself, to steady her breathing.

"So. To your question — yes, there are some other things I remember. Now that I think of it." She smiled. "There were certain students your grandfather chose. The smart ones. The ones who could already type well. He started us off with simple correspondence. I was so proud, you see. He was such a genius. A student of Einstein himself! But very quickly he dropped the pretense of letter writing. Working from rudimentary drawings which I believe he had created himself, I struggled on an electric typewriter to master these *Universal Action sequences*, as he called them. The same thing you have just demonstrated so perfectly. For some time, I believe, I was the most proficient student he had, although I never made satisfactory progress. It did something to my mind, something most distressing. He was disappointed. Eventually he excused all of us from his program, after he found someone more adept."

Dr. Toss opened the bag at her side and reached in. She pulled out and set on the stage beside her two objects: a silver, rectangular box the size of a large dictionary, and a small wooden container, vaguely the size of an iPhone shipping box.

"I assumed I had heard the last of Professor Nowak when I left his program. But then, four years later, came the endowment. After that another fourteen years went by, and then one day he appeared in my office. He looked... well, at that point he had begun a decline, and he may have been mad. But he begged me to do one last thing for him." She nodded to Preston, and patted the objects at her side. "He told me that these were for you. That is, he said that if you were ever born, boy or girl, and if you came to me, and if you were able to reproduce the *Universal Action sequences*, that I should pass these to you."

"Why not keep them and give them to me himself?" Preston protested.

"He seemed very certain that if a grandchild of his were ever to appear under these circumstances, he would be dead."

Dr. Toss drew her feet up beside her then, and stood, looking down at them. "I'll leave you. I have work to do, and you surely have dinners to get back to. Here is an email address where you may contact me if you have questions later. It has been a tremendous pleasure to meet you. All of you."

She laid her card on the stage floor and turned to walk back the way she had come, but Preston stopped her. One of the last things she had said had stuck in his mind. "You said he, my grandfather, excused you from his program. Because he found someone more adept. Do you know who that was?"

Dr. Toss shook her head. "No. None of us had ever seen her on campus before. She was an older woman, perhaps as old as I am now."

"You don't remember her name?"

"No. I remember very little about her. But that was long ago, you understand." She thought for a moment. "There *is* something I remember. Something odd. She had a condition."

"What condition?"

"She did not like being touched. She told us that she bruised very easily. I remember now, she always wore gloves. Black, tight fitting gloves. Is that helpful?"

Preston could hardly move. But after a moment he did manage to nod. And with a final smile, Dr. Toss bid them goodbye.

TWELVE

Holding the bag propped on the handlebars in front of him, Preston led the others back to his house. It was uphill from Caltech to his home, but he was glad. He pushed himself. He wanted to wear himself out. He wanted to be so tired that he would stop having to think. Because all the thinking he could do right now just led him in circles. Or into dark corners.

When they got back to the house it was getting late, and typically his friends would have been leaving at this point, but none of them was ready for that. Getting on their bikes to come back from Caltech they had said very little to each other, but the ride home seemed to have loosened their tongues, or given them a chance to sort their thoughts. Not that there were that many thoughts. There really was just the one.

They closed Preston's door, and Jacey's voice was carefully neutral as she said, "So, I don't know, did Dr. Toss's description of Professor Nowak's intern sound familiar to anyone else?"

"Yes," Regan said. "But it can't be Sally. Toss told us the woman was old. And that was sixty years ago. She would be dead by now. That is a simple fact."

Everyone nodded. They had all worked the facts out already. The problem was that over the last several weeks, the *fact* category had become a lot dicier. It used to be a fact that circles of light did *not* appear above your head when you held hands with your friends. And it had been held as a truism that telepathic voices would never interrupt you while you were in the middle of a hackathon. Their concept of the facts, it seemed, needed an update.

"It was an exact description of Ms. Fredrick," Jacey insisted.

"It's a coincidence," Matias stated. "It must be a coincidence."

"I'm not so sure," Regan said.

"You just said it couldn't be Sally!" Matias protested. "She would be dead by now."

"I am reconsidering. The fear of contact, the gloves — "

"I can't take this anymore!" Preston burst out.

"We are simply debating the merits — "

"Nothing makes any sense!" Preston had had enough. The ride back had not helped. He was not tired enough, or smart enough, or strong enough to force this picture into focus. He had tried. For weeks, he had tried, and failed, and the pressure had built, and built, until now he felt the dam bursting and all his fear and fatigue came tumbling out.

"I'm some kind of *Object*," he scoffed, though he knew it to be true. "Ms. Fredrick is 150 years old. My grandfather was a crazy physicist who killed Albert Einstein and taught magic at Caltech. I feel like I'm losing my mind. I need to figure out what's going on — someone tell me what is going *on!*"

He sank down onto the floor, on the edge of tears but holding them back because he knew that if he went that direction it would be hard to stop. His knees were drawn up to his chest, while his friends glanced at each other, wondering how to help. Finally Jacey sat beside him.

"Preston, we'll figure this out."

"I feel like I'm trapped in quicksand! I can't make any progress, and I'm sinking!"

Regan came to sit by him too, and he put his hand on Preston's. "Between the four of us, we will solve this mystery. We have brilliance on our side. Even you, surprisingly, are revealing yourself to be insightful. Quite possibly a genius."

"He's a Spynncaster," Matias boomed. The others looked up at him, standing like a statue, unblinking. Solid as stone. "We must confront certain facts. We must do it now. Though they contradict all previous concepts of our reality, to deny them would be unscientific. And dangerous." His voice was expressionless. He ticked points off on his fingers. "One: unidentified actors are guiding or participating in our actions, communicating telepathically, and possibly influencing us in ways we are not aware of. Two: there is, in the universe we currently inhabit, an energy that most accurately can be described, as Preston has done, by calling it *magic*. Three: Preston has demonstrated an ability to wield this magical energy in the form of Embodied Phenomena, and to affect the physical world in dramatic ways. These are facts. We must confront these facts if we're to resolve these mysteries. Preston is a Spynncaster. This is real."

"But I can't even *do* Spynncasting," Preston protested. "I almost died when I tried it last time. It's useless."

"That is a problem we must solve," Matias said. "We must investigate every identifiable data point."

"That's what we've been trying to do," Preston snapped.

"Yes," Matias answered. "Let us continue now. Why are we waiting?"

Jacey snarled at Matias, "Leave him alone, Matias! Sometimes you're just *too much Spook* — give him a break!"

"But new data — "

"Matias!" Regan stopped him. "Drop it!"

"But what about the data — "

"WHAT *DATA*?" the three of them demanded together.

Silently, Matias raised his arm and pointed to the bag in the corner. The bag from Dr. Toss. He raised his eyebrows questioningly.

"Oh right," Regan nodded. "That data."

Preston had completely forgotten about the satchel Dr. Toss had given him. He had been that overwhelmed. But Matias was right. The only way out of this was to keep moving forward, keep turning over every rock they came across. So he pulled the bag closer to him and carefully took the wooden box and the metal case out. Rising, he set them on the bed. The fabric of the satchel had a faintly floral smell, as though steeped in perfume from a bygone time, and this aroma clung to the boxes.

The first thing they saw was that, if the metal case was a box, it was a very strangely designed one, because it had neither hinge, clasp, nor lid. It did have a faint groove connected around the top on all four sides, where a lid might have been expected to close, but it did not shift or lift or bend. There was no obvious way to access whatever lay inside the metal container.

The wooden box was more conventional. It was beautifully built. Black and brown woods laced together in complex geometric shapes on the sides and lid. This box had hinges and a clasp. And a keyhole.

"No key," Jacey growled, turning it in her hands and giving it several frustrated blows.

"Jace," said Regan, putting a calming finger on her arm, "perhaps vandalism can be our *backup* plan."

Preston held out his hand, and Jacey gave him the box. There could be only one key which would fit this lock, he knew. He drew it up on the cord from around his neck.

"From Grandpa Nowak's shoe box," Preston said, before they asked. There was not a breath in the room as he brought the key to the lock. Pressed it in. Twisted it. And started as the lid popped up a half inch.

Inside was an insert of stitched black silk, seamlessly drawn around a delicate, raised stage. Within a perfectly formed hollow on this stage lay a crystal. A rhombus, diamond shaped, with a tiny hole bored through one tip. It was milky white, polished, with simple facets. Preston reached for it tentatively.

The moment his index finger touched the polished finish, the crystal glimmered with blue light. It was a color all of them had seen before, twining above their heads when they were Synched. Preston snatched his finger back and dropped the box on the bed.

"You saw that, right?" he asked, not taking his eyes from the crystal.

"Yeah," Jacey said. "It's purdy."

"Should I touch it again?" he asked. "It didn't hurt or — "

"Do it," Jacey told him.

Regan looked less certain but said nothing.

"The wisest course would have been not touching it at all," Matias said with a shrug. "Now that you know it won't kill you, what's the harm?"

Preston studied the box for several more seconds. Then, as he reached the tip of his index finger toward the smooth facade, Matias spoke again.

"Although maybe it only kills you the *second* time you touch it."

But it did not kill him. This time he left his finger against the crystal's slick side. The surface was cool and smooth. Light sprang forth. It grew to a gentle glow, throwing a soft aqua splash on his hand, the covers, the metal case beside it. And Preston felt Spynn.

This sensation was similar to what he sensed when he was charging the battery in his phone with a trickle of energy from his own body. But this was a more powerful flow, not a trickle but a surge. And it was flowing *into* him, not out of him, filling him up like water fills a pot. He drew his hand away and the Spynn that had pooled inside him instantly drained back into the rhombus in the box, which then stopped glowing. He touched it again, less hesitantly, and understanding grew.

"Guys, I know what this is," he breathed, his voice soft in awed comprehension. "This is a storage container. Like a battery. It's a battery full of Spynn."

He touched the stone, and the energy coursed into him again, palpable and warm. He was an empty receptacle that the crystal pumped full, until Spynn saturated his every muscle, every bone, every cell. It shifted him, subtly but powerfully, elsewhere. Into a slightly different world. When he took his finger away again and the Spynn left him, it was as if he himself were dropping back into his normal world.

"What are you experiencing?" Matias asked.

"Nothing. I mean, I feel good. Normal." He could not put it into words, but he knew that Matias was mostly asking whether anything bad was going on.

"Now, what could the good Professor have been doing with a Spynn battery?" Regan mused.

"He was a Spynncaster," Jacey said. "Obviously."

"But his hands," Regan said, "were in no condition to do what Preston does."

Matias turned to look at Preston's timeline, still laid out on the bed.

"Somewhere earlier in his life, Professor Nowak must have been like Preston. But something happened to him. Perhaps," he said, turning back to Preston, "it was Spynncasting itself that maimed him."

Preston frowned. "I don't think he would have passed this battery down to me just to maim me."

Carefully he threaded the cord holding the key through the small hole drilled in the crystal's tip, then hung them both around his neck. Spynn suffused him. He saw that it also spread around him into the room, coating everything, painted everywhere. He stood in a field of Spynn, and everything there — himself included — was an Object in that field. It was like a rubber sheet had been stretched out very, very thin, and all the objects in the world had been pressed up into it from below, so that they emerged within that unifying field as molded blue *Objects*. The bed, the posters on the walls, tiny motes of dust floating in the air, they were all separate, real world items *and* Objects in this Spynn field, enmeshed and connected. Spynn connected him to everything. Spynn connected *everything* to everything.

"Jacey, I see it," he breathed. "What you saw — it's all Objects. Everything is an Object. Spynnlang is a way to program them — Object Oriented Programming! The *Embodied Phenomena*, that's a way to make new Objects in this field, and it's a way to make Setters and Getters to control... " the scope of the idea rocked him. What he was seeing. It was beyond belief.

"To control what?" Matias asked.

"Everything," Preston whispered. "Anything. All of it." He moved to the bed. An idea was occurring to him. It might be a bad idea. But the only course of action left to him now was to move forward. There was no going back. "I think Grandpa Nowak wanted me to use this battery. That's why he gave it to Dr. Toss. There's something important we have to do."

He lifted the metal box from the bed and turned it in his hands, inspecting the metal, feeling the corners and the cool, smooth sides, and at the same time inspecting the Spynn shape of it, featureless and perfect, moving in perfect unison. He traced the thin line around the top edge with the tip of his finger.

"Couldn't this be a lid?" he asked.

"Welded shut?" Matias ventured.

"I don't think welding did it," said Preston. "I think it's been *Embodied*. I've seen it in the coursework. A Phenomena called *Seal*." Another moment of examination and he was sure.

"I know how to get it open," he said.

He set the box on the floor in the middle of the room. Without being instructed, the other three stepped back. The room was full of anticipation and sheer nervousness. Jacey was staring at the box on the floor and tearing at her nails. Regan kept running his hand through his bushy hair. Preston sat at the computer and placed his hands over the keyboard. Then he twisted, inverted, pressed and bent through a quick set of Spynnlang fingerings. The screen blossomed with icons as he went.

He began to understand the power of the Object Orientation in the Spynnlang code. He pictured circles on a white board, the ones

Ms. Fredrick had drawn, with Parent Objects linked to Child Objects, and below that a chain or hierarchy. He realized he could create an *Embodiment* that would affect just this individual box, or he could take a step up to the Parent Object of this box and create an *Embodiment* to affect *all* boxes. He could keep climbing higher and higher up the tree, creating more and more powerful *Phenomena* that would affect a broader and broader set of Objects. At each step up the chain, the Casting would require greater and greater amounts of Spynn. Planets, stars, *universes* worth of Spynn.

Keep it simple, he told himself. Just this box. A single purpose Embodiment.

At then, after many minutes of careful double checking, he was done. He deployed the updated app containing his new Embodiment. All four of their phones chimed.

"Keep away from the box," he said. "I'm not sure exactly how this is going to work. Either I'm not good enough yet, or there's part of the process that's just random chance."

Regan looked dubious. "I feel odd being the person urging caution at this juncture. But you yourself pointed out that the last time you attempted to use one of these Phenomena you almost died. And also, I thought you could only cast *Embodiments* onto another person who had a phone. And I also think we should research this idea more thoroughly before — "

But Preston had raised his arm and pointed his phone toward the box. All or nothing, he thought. If I want understanding, I have to act.

"*Unseal,*" he said, casting the orange ball out of the phone and toward the container.

Several things happened at once. He felt the Spynn suffusing his body rush into his phone and leave him. The stream was so powerful it sucked him a few inches forward by the wrist, and it rippled his shirt sleeve as it passed down his arm. Then the crystal hanging around his neck gave a powerful throb, and a new allowance of Spynn rushed into him.

While this was happening, a starburst of intense blue light was growing on the metal container, about an inch from the top — right on the line that might have been a lid — while a hiss like an endless sheet of tearing paper rose in the room.

The blue starburst flared and they had to squint. A searing white prick of heat appeared in the center of the blue. Then it darted forward. It shot swiftly down one side of the container, following the lid line with great precision, turned the corner and sped down the next side, hissing and flaring its way until it had circumnavigated all four sides. It was done in a matter of seconds.

And then it flashed and was gone. They rubbed their eyes to clear the glowing afterimages. A tangy, bitter smell hung in the air of a shocked and silent room. Four pairs of eyes studied the box on the floor without moving. Anything might happen now. A bomb could go off. Poison gas could sweep out. A dragon could emerge, breathe fire on them, steal their phones, and fly away, a possibility which only a month before would have caused them to roll their eyes in derision, but which they now would have been willing to consider as a real danger.

Another moment of silent waiting. Matias asked Preston softly, "Weakness? Voices?"

Preston shook his head. He held his hands up and looked at them. His phone was very hot. But other than that he felt no different. "I did it," he whispered in wonder. "I just did that."

The box on the floor gave a loud bang, the way cookie sheets do when they are cooling in the sink, and the lid — it was a lid, they saw — popped up. They had been leaning closer despite themselves, but now they leaped back. It was nerve wracking, to want so badly to lift the lid off a box, and at the same time fear that you might be eaten by monsters if you did. It was the classic battle between curiosity and caution. But curiosity triumphed.

Jacey was the first to the floor, though Matias and Regan were only a second behind her. Preston was slower, still stunned that the Casting had gone off just as he had imagined. This is real, he kept saying to himself. It is real, and I know how to do it. What else is possible now?

While Preston was standing with a dopey, wide eyed expression, Jacey was lifting the lid with careful fingers. There were only two items inside. A very worn, brown leather journal, and a rolled paper scroll. Matias lifted out the scroll and unrolled it.

The Entanglement Matrix, read the title at the top of the long, curling sheet. The paper was brown at the edges, and covered with hand written characters. The title was the only element they could read instantly. The rest of it, four scrolling feet of tiny, precise writing, was a mathematical formula.

Regan pulled out the journal and opened the leather binding to the first page. It was written in the same hand as the scroll, but in English.

"It's a journal," Regan said. "Look. *Preston Oliver Nowak*. It's your grandfather's. The first entry is August 21, 1933. That makes him 16, right?" Preston nodded. Regan read from the book. "*First day at Caltech. Met Albert Einstein in the quad. Pointed out a mistake in his molecular theory of heat. He did not dispute it. He asked me to join his seminar. I think we will be great friends.*"

Regan thumbed ahead a few pages. "Okay, he is certainly a cocky little bastard." He turned a few more leaves, read randomly from the entries he saw, then flipped back to the beginning. "Huh. Something changes pretty quickly in his style. I cannot quite put my finger on it... "

And just then Mrs. Nowak came into the room. She sniffed.

"What's that smell?" she asked.

Preston hated lying to his parents. "We were doing some magic," he said.

His mom snorted. "I see. For your Vegas stage show."

She surveyed the mess on the floor and the collection of photos and papers on the bed. "It looks like you've been having a party. Very nice!" Mrs. Nowak loved parties. But she also loved a well-followed routine. So now she glanced at her watch and looked at the dark-ening sky outside Preston's window.

"Isn't it time for everyone to be getting home? Tomorrow's a school day, you know."

"Yes, Mrs. Nowak," they said, almost in unison. It never ceased to amaze Preston how quickly and effectively she could organize a room or a group of people into coordinated action. It was just easier, in the end, to do what she wanted, the way she wanted it done.

She left, and they heard pots and dishes being maneuvered around the kitchen. Time to go.

"Preston, I want to take this journal tonight," Regan said. "There is something about

it... " The typically precise and focused Regan had a faraway look in his eyes. Preston shrugged and nodded. There was too much material to review, too many things to think about. He had no problem delegating some of it to the geniuses in the room.

"And I would like to study this scroll," Matias said, holding out the rolled *Entanglement Matrix*. "The math here is unlike anything I've ever seen."

He walked them out. The streetlights came on as he stood on the porch and watched them hurry away. The air was cool, and the sunset muted, but Preston felt electrified.

Now that he was outside the confining walls of his room he saw that the field of Spynn expanding outward from the crystal did not stretch everywhere. It draped down from him, and spread out around his feet in all directions like an enormous robe in a circle, perhaps a hundred yards in diameter. It moved with him when he walked, and stopped when he stopped, but the boundary of the field was sharp and constant. It raised a small blue glow over everything it touched, though he was confident only he could see it.

What did it mean? He understood now that Spynn was a force connecting all things, and that things — all things? — existed in this field in the form of Objects. But it looked as if he stood in the middle of the only Spynn on the planet. Beyond the perimeter of his field the night was dark. The blue luminance ended very abruptly. If his battery powered a Spynn field that was limited to the area immediately around it, where was all the other Spynn? Was it there, but he just couldn't see it? Or was it somehow missing?

He stepped off the porch and walked out toward the road, his field moving around him. He stepped outside the gate onto the sidewalk, and now the Spynn flowed across the road and slipped up over the parked cars on the other side, and into the neighbors' yards to his right and left, flowing over everything. It was as if a helicopter were flying above him, following him with a huge, dim spotlight.

Three blocks down the street he saw Jacey, Matias, and Regan turn the corner beneath a faltering streetlight and vanish from sight. The night had grown dark quickly, or else he had been standing outside longer than he thought. Deep thoughts played funny tricks with time, he had noticed. He was beginning to feel a little chilly, too. Time to go in.

As he swiveled toward his door, trying to see if the Spynn field rotated when he turned his body, he caught a flicker of light from the corner of his eye, far up the street. It could have been a headlight. It could have been the flash of a camera, or a street light coming on. Something ordinary. But it was not any of those things, and a part of his brain knew it.

Now it was rushing toward him. For a second he thought he had made a mistake, that it must be a motorcycle, it was coming so fast. But this light was not electric headlights — this was a dense blue glow, and it was streaking down the sidewalk straight at him, swinging and moving like a running body. A running body covered with a field of glowing Spynn.

He stumbled back, away from his gate and away from the shape speeding toward him. So fast! He did not know why, but without a doubt he labeled it a threat. His mind told him *not* to look away, not to lose track of it, but he caught his foot as he shuffled backward and he crashed to the ground, blinked, scrambled back up, and then the thing was there.

It stopped, just beyond the periphery of his Spynn field.

Preston's breathing was loud, but otherwise the night was completely quiet. The shape, flush with blue fluorescence, seemed to be the height and width of a person, and shifted quickly from side with bouncing steps the way a person would, agitated, but it was without arms or legs or head. Preston sensed, though, that there was a living body beneath the glow.

The Spynn of the other did not spill out around it on the ground. It was a soft-sided shaft, brighter than Preston's field, but confined to whatever body was generating it. Before Preston could move, it had flashed up over the hedge separating the neighbor's property from his, and it skirted the edge of Preston's field and dashed up to the side of Preston's house. And then it seemed to walk *up the side of the house*, until it stood on the roof. It flashed across the eaves to the other side of the roof, and walked down the wall on that side, standing straight out. When it came to the ground it stood again, normally, and seemed to be turning. Searching.

He had seen that before, that wall walking. When the door in his mind had opened, when the memories or the visions had spilled out — in the background there had been walls, and the creatures had run up one side, and down the other, with no effort at all. The Dark Folk. Was he looking at one now? Or was this, too, just a hallucination? A broken memory, roaming free?

It arranged itself between him and the house. It stood a moment as if watching him, though he could neither see a face nor be sure what direction it was facing.

And then it moved to the front door, threw it open, and disappeared inside. He heard the screen slam. No hallucination. Something was in the house.

"No!" yelled Preston. All he could think about was his mom and dad. He crashed through the gate and raced up onto the porch. It took him only seconds but he felt like he would never get to the door, which was now hanging open. Light from the living room poured out onto the warm concrete of the porch. He could not see the thing inside.

And then he was in the house. His father slumbered in his reading chair, his book slipping from his hand onto the floor. Preston ran toward the back of the house, past the kitchen — and there he saw his mother, collapsed on the floor, a frying pan of chopped vegetables scattered on the tile beside her.

"Mom!" He dropped to the floor beside her. He lifted her head. "Mom, can you hear me?" He saw that she was breathing. Not dead. Not dead!

Then from the back of the house, in the direction of his room, he heard a scream, of rage it seemed, and a crash. And without even stopping to think about what he was doing or what he would find, he ran toward it.

The door to his room was open, which was probably the way he had left it, and the lights were off. Everything was dark at this end of the house. He slowed his headlong rampage down the hall to a crawl. Then he stopped. And listened.

He heard nothing but his own breath. He pressed himself against the wall, and slid, step by step, toward his bedroom door, until his head was inches from the doorjamb, pressed against the drywall. His ears seemed to pick up every tiny sound, a car horn nine blocks away, the chirp of a baby bird three houses down the street, but nothing from his room. Nothing at all. He could not wait, but he could not move. Until at last he jumped into the open doorway. And shivered.

The room was empty. But the window was open. The screen was hanging loose, pushed out from the inside.

He rushed to slam it shut, and lock it. Then he ran back down to the kitchen to check on his mother. She was blinking and groaning. He ran to the living room. His father was opening his eyes. He saw Preston, and noticed that his book was on the floor, and shook his head as if he had water in his ears.

"Wow. How about that? Must have taken a little nap."

"Dad," Preston yelled, "Mom fell in the kitchen. I think she might have hit her head." He ran back to help his mother, who was now trying to stand but slipping in the oil from the spilled frying pan, and a second later his father was beside him, still a little groggy himself. Between the two of them, they got his mom into a seat at the kitchen table, and brought her glasses of water, and an ice pack for her head, which she had bumped on the floor.

Preston cleaned up the food in the kitchen, and then eventually they ordered pizza for dinner and his mom and dad seemed to forget that any of it had ever happened, although his mom did go to bed a little early complaining about a headache. Preston, however, could not forget a single second of the entire sickening chain of events.

Alone in his room, he double checked that the window was locked, and then sat with his head in his hands, trying to get it all straight in his mind.

Something had come into the house. And he had to assume that whatever had happened to his mom — and probably his father too, who had just been lucky enough to be sitting down — had been caused by the intruder. Then it had come into his room. And screamed. And left through the window.

Why? What had it been? Some creature or person who had their own battery? Or who had a field of Spynn that came from their body, like Preston's trickle charge but far stronger? He stared around the room. It had come straight here. What had it wanted? Nothing seemed missing. The two boxes, now empty, lay where he had left them.

As he sat looking around the room, and at his locked and darkened window, he began wondering not about why it had come, but whether or not it was going to come again. The muscles on the back of his neck went stiff. He had already checked all the locks on all the doors and windows before retreating to his room. What else could he do? This thing, whatever it was, had unearthly speed. It had leaped the hedge and jumped to the porch like a superhuman gymnast. What could he do if it came back? What defense did he have against a Spynn infused monster?

A distant memory came to him then, from a scene he did not remember having lived. He remembered voices shouting at him. And something tumbling thought the air. A... piano? The voices. They kept shouting the same thing.

Shield.

He flipped on his computer and pounded at the keys. He kept looking at the window. Any second he expected to see a glowing face there, or eyes, or a hand begin pounding from the outside. He kept getting the URL wrong in his haste, but finally he had the Embody Phenomena coursework page open. He scrolled down the list he had worked through the week before: Fog, Gravity, Insight, Stickiness, Orbit, Elasticity, Eating, Friendship, Dog Walking, Digestion, Shield. *Shield!* How do you defend against a Spynn-infused monster?

He hoped, he desperately hoped, that you used a Shield.

With trembling hands he fingered the Phenomena, and then he deployed the update to his phone. He took the phone and left his room, and went to stand in the hallway beside the linen closet, which was his best guess for the center of the house. He took a deep breath and let it hiss out between his lips. Again, he was not sure exactly how this *Embodiment* was going to work. Was he going to cover the property with a huge, glowing ball of energy that would instantly betray him to the neighbors? Was he about to chop his roof off? Was this the right thing to do?

Did he have a choice?

No. No choice. So he pointed his phone up into the air above him, Cast the orb out of the device and into the ceiling, and called out *"Shield!"*

Spynn rushed up along his arm, and his arm actually recoiled with the force of the departing *Phenomena*. His crystal throbbed, and new Spynn rushed in to replace what he had spent.

And nothing else happened.

He waited. Listened. But could detect no change.

He looked out the living room window. Nothing. He opened the front door, but the night was perfectly silent, perfectly dark, and perfectly normal. So he stepped cautiously outside, scanning the street and the yard, and then went to stand on the sidewalk just outside the gate and look back at the house.

And from that vantage point, he could see his *Shield*, a shimmering blue half dome encompassing the entire house, shot with veins of sparkling white fire. When he saw it he knew it would be invisible to anyone but him. Then he caught himself. It was likely that there was at least one other living thing in the neighborhood who would be able to see this *Embodiment*. The thought made his look behind him.

That is when he realized that the Spynn field that flowed from the crystal and down around his feet no longer reached across the road to the parked cars. Now it extended no more than halfway to the other side of the street. The field had shrunk, very dramatically.

Apparently, he thought, this battery had a limited charge.

THIRTEEN

The sky above the schoolyard was cloudy the next day. Rain was expected. The novelty of rain in Southern California was enough that when lunch came, the entire student body was filled with a certain wild, anticipatory zest. Regan was late to the Reading Garden, and Jacey said he had been missing from their classes that morning. So Preston took the opportunity to fill them in on the events of the night before. And then all of them began to get very worried about Regan. Had he had a visitor? Was he unconscious on a floor somewhere?

But soon they saw him striding in the main gate of the school. Today, despite the overcast sky, he wore gold plastic sunglasses with small pink flamingos at the corners. He stopped before the bench and drew the lenses down his nose slowly, for maximum drama.

"It is fortunate you are already sitting down," he said. "I have something to show you." From his backpack he took a folder.

"Wait, first," said Preston, "did you see anything strange last night? Or, did you, like, pass out, or... anything?"

"That is a delightfully bizarre question. Why do you ask?"

Preston ran through the story again. Regan shook his head.

"Nothing like that. I pulled an all-nighter to parse out this journal's secrets." He took the leather journal from his pack. He looked disappointed. "I had thought my news would be the high drama of the day. I am very glad you are all right, Preston."

"What's your news?" Preston asked. He badly wanted something to take his mind off of last night's intruder, because his mind seemed determined to think about that and very little else. It was exhausting.

"Well," said Regan. "I read the journal." He gave each of them a stapled pack of laser printed paper from his folder, then held out Grandpa Nowak's leather bound book. "And it was actually two journals. One, the daily entries you see written in plain sight. And two, an encrypted second layer of information contained within the first. I will not bore you with the cryptographic details, but suffice it to say that your grandfather, Preston, was an extraordinary genius. I just happen to be his equal. Though barely. And I had at my disposal gigaflops of supercomputer resources which he could never have imagined."

The wind was pushing through the schoolyard in cool, sharp gusts now, and the clouds were darkening and scudding lower. The papers they held were flapping in their hands and attempting to fly off in many different directions. Regan suggested a move to the library, and they all agreed willingly. Once inside, they sat at their usual stations, but Regan faced them instead of Ms. Fredrick.

"There is a lot of information to cover," he began. "The dossier I have given you is word by word transcription of the coded entries, but I can add context if I simply tell most of it to you, and reference passages. Acceptable?"

He did not wait for them to agree. He looked at Preston.

"Very well. In 1934, your grandfather, Preston Oliver Nowak the First — I will call him PON1 — in conjunction with Albert Einstein, Robert A. Millikan, and other Nobel winners of the day, formed a secret society to save the world. It was called The Entanglement Matrix Project. Mostly they just called it the Project."

"Save the world from *what?*" Jacey asked.

"PON1 never explicitly states. But even in 1934 they had a date: July, 1957. At that time a portal of some kind was to be opened. Each member of this secret group had separate responsibilities. Resources were pooled. This was to be a marathon, not a sprint, with milestones achieved over the course of the next two decades. PON1 was given an assignment along with the others. Can you guess what it was?"

Regan looked at them in anticipation. None of them cared to guess. Steepling his fingers to heighten the drama, he said, "He was tasked with building and operating a shoe store empire. This, obviously, was the genesis of Nowak Shoes."

"Wait," Preston said. He had wanted something to take his mind off the events at his house last night, but he was not sure that this was what he had been thinking of. "You're saying that Albert Einstein *told my grandfather* to open a line of shoe stores? As part of a project to save the world?"

"Yes," Regan said. "In fact, Einstein put up most of the money." "Why?"

"The journal does not tell us," Regan said. "Remember, the coded layer of this journal mainly contains notes to himself, and information he wanted to keep secret from the rest of the group. Which, as it turns out, was quite a lot. But I am getting ahead of myself."

Jacey threw her hands on the desk. "No big mystery. They started the shoe stores because they needed money for their Project. Just like I want us to open a web development company so we can live in Arkansas."

Regan rolled his eyes. "A nationwide shoe store chain would not be the most obvious choice as a funding vehicle. Less even than making horrible little websites for neighborhood thrift stores. But again, we can come back to this."

Regan took his glasses off and looked at the papers he had printed. There were pen marks in various colors scrawled all over the face of the printed text. He looked tired, Preston thought. He had not been exaggerating when he told them he had pulled an all-nighter.

Outside, a light rain had begun. They could hear it on the roof, and the row of tinted skylights high in the peaked ceiling had grown darker. The entire library was darkening, in fact, but none of them felt like getting up to turn on a light. Regan flipped on the flashlight in his phone and continued.

"Now, in the next set of coded entries we learn of his difficulty mastering the Universal Actions. You recall, he later attempted to teach these to Dr. Toss. But neither he nor any of the other scientists on the Project could do it. PON1 speaks of mental issues very similar to what you experienced, Jacey. So at this time, it does not appear that Grandpa Nowak was a Spynncaster. But someone was trying to teach them. Who do you think that was?"

Jacey pounded her fist on the table. "Regan I swear, if you're going to do this Socratic Method crap the whole way through, you're not going to leave this library alive. Get on with it!"

Regan sighed. "You have a remarkably limited appreciation for the theatrical, Jacey. Very well. In a nutshell — it appears that Albert Einstein was the Spynncaster, and it was *he* who was attempting to teach the others the Universal Actions. *Casting,* as Preston refers to it."

A thunder crack sounded, hollow and distant. The rain began pounding harder on the windows in the ceiling, and outside, the wind had begun to moan and pull, whipping past the eaves and blowing debris against the door. This really was an unusual storm. But it paled, Preston thought, in comparison to the story he was hearing now.

Matias rose from his seat and came to stand beside Regan, looking at his paper in the shine of Regan's flashlight.

"Could there be a mistake?" he asked.

"The text is very clear," Regan said. "Almost ten years pass then, with very little journaling, perhaps twice a year. The Project proceeds apace. And then, in 1949, PON1 begins to speak of a disagreement which has surfaced between him and Einstein over the date their Project is pointed toward. Einstein believes in the original date, July 1957. But PON1 has done additional calculations, which lead him to believe that they should be pointed toward April 1955 instead. And, I'm sorry Jacey, but I simply must ask — do you know what *does* happen, six years later, in April 1955? No? Einstein dies of a brain aneurysm. And the universe, according to PON1, begins to fill with Dark energy."

"What's the connection?" Matias asked.

"I will tell you now," Regan said, with a profound satisfaction on his face. "You see, though? When I offer you a small piece of fore-shadowing like that, it increases the drama, and engages you in the story so that — "

"JUST TELL US!" Jacey yelled, standing. "Regan, you're driving me freaking crazy!"

Thunder crashed then, directly above the library, and the rain pounding on the roof became so loud that Regan had to raise his voice to be heard. Again the thunder crashed, and again. The inside of the library was dark as night now, and the others turned their own flashlights on. Preston saw his friends, all lit from below by the reflected light off their phones, casting eerie shadows. The combination of the story he was hearing and the ferocity of the storm gave him the sensation that he was experiencing something supernatural. Something from another world.

All four of them were standing by now, and instinctively they crowded closer. They bent over Regan's paper where he had set it on the table.

"It appears," he said, pointing, "that PON1 usurped control of the Entanglement Matrix Project from Einstein. He was afraid they would miss what he considered to be the essential deadline to open a *Portal*. He appropriated the Entanglement Matrix on April 18th, 1955. And we know Einstein died that *same day*, April 18th, 1955. And then there are four months where no journal entries are made. And do you know why? *Jacey, wait.* I will simply tell you."

He lifted his flashlight and shone it on his own face. They could not help but stare, captivated.

"No journal entries were made for four months," he intoned, "because PON1 fell into a coma, which he did not awake from until August, in a hospital. With his hands destroyed."

"I was in a coma," Preston said dully.

"Yes," Regan said, "I am aware of that. That is why I shone the flashlight on my face, because of the supremely dramatic — "

"Be silent Regan," Matias interrupted. "Preston, think. Had you ever heard of the Entanglement Matrix before your coma? Could there be a link?"

Preston, shocked, could only shake his head. Had his grandfather *really* somehow killed Albert Einstein? Had he had the same kind of coma that Preston experienced? There had to be a connection, didn't there? But his own hands had not been destroyed. And as far as he knew he had not killed anyone.

"After this the journal entries become extremely labored," Regan continued. "PON1 can barely write. But he does continue. He seemed to have an indomitable will. He speaks of having Inherited an Object from Einstein, and he is devastated to learn that Einstein has died. At this point, honestly, he begins to go crazy. He marries a woman he barely knows, as quickly as possible it seems. She becomes pregnant. This baby is your father, Preston. PON1 has a plan to kill himself at the moment of the child's birth. But instead, the pregnancy goes tragically awry, and his wife dies. So he does not kill himself, but continues on to raise the child. He is tortured by failure, now believing he erred in his calculations and caused Einstein's death, and that he failed when he was unable to kill himself at his child's birth. And here we enter the last chapter of the tale."

A first flash of lightning streaked over the school, and the fork threw electric shadows down through the skylights and against the book stacks, strobing them in unearthly hues, causing the four wide-eyed sixth graders huddled together before their papers to jump.

"What is up with this *storm?*" Jacey yelled. "They said rain, not apocalypse!"

Preston was holding his grandfather's journal open, transfixed by the cramped, childish writing. It must have taken the author painful hours to produce such work. What had driven this man? What was he feeling? What was he hiding?

They jumped when Regan began speaking again. It was as if they were being told a ghost story that they *knew* was true. The tension in the library was viscous, it squeezed their lungs and bowed their necks, and every time the lightning struck or thunder broke like trucks crashing overhead they leaped and shuddered. Regan's voice trembled as he spoke.

"After his wife dies PON1 looks for other people to teach the Universal Actions to. Dr. Toss is mentioned. He is disappointed with them all. And then he meets a woman he names Dorothy C. Older, averse to touch, and wearing gloves. Dorothy surpasses all the others in her lessons. PON1 seems excited that he might have found the pupil he was seeking. He tells her about the Entanglement Matrix. He calls her a polymath, a genius. Over the course of four years she grows proficient in the Universal Actions, though not entirely to PON1's satisfaction. And then — she betrays him. She uses the Entanglement Matrix, though for what I cannot determine. But afterward, she *also* falls into a coma, apparently unaware that this was a possibility."

Regan took a breath and looked at them all. Then he shrugged, and continued. "So, this last bit of the story? It is, how should I say... insane. And gruesome. Just to set the scene. PON1 finds Dorothy beside the *Primary Node*. This was apparently a feature of the Entanglement Matrix that the journal does not explain. She is comatose. And when he strips her gloves off to take her pulse, she transforms."

BOOM! Thunder rocked the building. Rain beat the windows above them like rocks in an endless avalanche. The main door to the library reverberated as wind hit it, a living wind that wanted to come in, come inside! The strokes of laser-white lightning flashed continually, throwing shadows everywhere. It was a storm like Preston had never seen. But he blocked it out, he blocked out everything except Regan's story. Reagan acted out these last few sentences, his face a mask of horror.

"She transforms into what he describes as a grotesque, gangling monstrosity. Long fingers. Very ancient. A decrepit gown. He searches her; she has nothing but a few odds and ends in her pockets, some pathetic jewelry. And then he stabs her through the chest with a shoehorn."

"A shoehorn?" Jacey demanded. "What is *that*?"

"Long piece of metal that gets thin on one end," said Preston. "You use them to get shoes on, if they're tight."

"Yes," Regan said. "And then he leaves. Distraught and virtually out of his mind. But he returns later that evening. And he finds that she is alive again, though still comatose."

"Alive again? You mean he failed to kill her?" Matias said.

"No. He is very clear. He kills this creature. But he returns to find her alive again. And so he kills her a second time. And soon he sees her return to life. And he repeats this gruesome routine, he does not say how many times, with the same result. So at last he carries the body into the Angeles Crest Mountains in the back of his car, and he rolls it off a cliff."

"This is horrible!" Preston cries.

"Yes, I warned you. At this time, 1966, he sells all the Nowak Shoes and at the same time he disassembles the Entanglement Machine, although he leaves the Primary Node standing, whatever that means. He funds the Caltech department for Dr. Toss. His only hope is to wait for a grandchild, he writes. Many years pass. The last entry is 1981. He has clearly passed the bounds of rational objective thought; his writing wanders and his thoughts are disjointed. He has seen *her* again, he writes in a moment of clarity. He proposes to take some items to an old colleague for safe keeping, presumably Dr. Toss. His final instructions are to his grandchild, if that person should ever find and decode the journal."

"What does he say?" Jacey cried.

"He says, *Recharge the battery in the Primary Node. Answers are there. Beware the creature. She is the most dangerous thing the world has ever seen. Please forgive me. Please forgive me.*"

For two seconds there was silence.

Then the door of the library crashed open. Lightning flashed and threw into shadow a figure in the doorway. It lurched into the room.

Regan screamed. Matias spun and snarled. Jacey swept up a chair and held it out, shouting incoherently. Preston stood fixated. There was something familiar about the black silhouette. Horribly familiar. Rain blew the fringes of a dress around the legs of the figure, and stringy shoulder length hair hung dank and wet.

"What are you *doing?*" screamed a voice. A hand rose, pointing. "You will be. *Late. To. SOCIAL STUDIES!*" The hand flicked on the overhead lights, and there stood Mrs. Vargas, soaked to the skin and glaring at them.

"You students should not be in this facility without express permission from a teacher or unless you are raising money for the school. Somehow." This struck her as a hopeful thought, and her glare softened for a moment. "Are you?"

When they shook their heads, they were all herded out of the library, through the rain, and back to their classes, soaked and shivering. And deeply disturbed by what they had learned.

CHAPTER
FOURTEEN

T he storm passed swiftly, as they usually do in Southern
California, so that by the time Preston and his friends had
left school and arrived at the sidewalk in front of his house,
there was nothing but sunshine, wet lawns, and the occasional
shocked squirrel to suggest that anything as untoward as a rain-
storm had troubled the city. The kids, however, were still suffering
the effects of Regan's dramatic reading. In fact, Jacey was not talking
to Regan at all at the moment. Somehow, irrationally, she seemed to
blame him for the thunder and for Mrs. Vargas's startling entrance.
Regan did not seem bothered by this.

"Fabulous art is always disturbing," Regan said to no one in
particular.

Preston stopped at his gate. He could see the outlines of his
Shield, still enveloping his house, harder to view in the daylight but
still visible.

Matias saw him looking at something that the rest of them could
not see, and guessed what it was.

"What exactly does the Shield do?" he asked Preston, who
shrugged.

"I don't exactly know. Ward the house from Spynn. Keeps out moths? All I know is it cost a lot of Spynn to put it up, so it had better be worth it."

They passed quickly through the house and shut the door of Preston's room. This was their first opportunity to talk through the things they had learned from the journal. They went back and forth about it for an hour, adding pieces to the timeline that Preston now kept pinned to the back wall of his closet so his parents were less likely to see it. The last lines of the journal kept coming back to Preston.

"What's the Primary Node?" he asked. Matias had been very silent through their discussions. Preston poked him. "Hey, you with us? You're the one working on the Entanglement Matrix."

"I've made no progress," Matias admitted. "There are variables here that are difficult to fathom." He pulled the scroll from his backpack where he had it wedged between a biology textbook and his lunch. He unrolled it on the floor and pointed to elements in the calculations.

"You see, in essence it's a blueprint of some kind. I believe it's a way to entangle an elemental particle. But there are issues, perhaps issues of scale, and I'm not able to bring the formula into focus... " Matias drifted off as he stared at the roll. His eyes were motionless below his black brows. The other three bent to the floor and lost themselves in consideration of the lines of numbers and calculations.

Preston quickly felt the now-familiar sense of disassociation as he contemplated the math, and soon he was following complex elements of it. But of course, *he* was not doing it. *He* had gotten a C- in Beginning Algebra a few weeks before his coma. His comprehension of the algorithms and mathematical expressions written here came from somewhere else. If it had not been so beautiful, such a joy to have such insight into the indisputable numerical mysteries of the world, he might have been terrified.

After fifteen minutes he pointed to a series of individual expressions within the larger formula. "Look," he said, "here, here, and here. These are dependencies, they define the positional relationships of many of the other elements described. Could these be the Nodes? There are more of them," he observed, "all through the equation." Regan and Jacey looked surprised and impressed. Preston had trouble feeling good about that, since these observations really had nothing to do with anything he had earned, or even been born with. He might be talking like a genius, but he did not think he was one.

Matias nodded. "I had seen those. But that is where the issue of scale arises. There is a variable missing. Or a variable I can't see."

After a moment he rumbled, "You must Cast an *Insight* Embodiment on me, Preston. We need these answers, as quickly as possible."

"I can't do that," Preston said.

"I accept the risks. You have the Spynn available in the crystal. But we need to understand this equation."

"We need something else more," Preston said.

He had a plan to propose to his friends, but he did not think they were going to like it.

"If I Cast an *Insight* Embodiment on you," he said, "that's going to use up a lot of Spynn. And we're going to need all the Spynn there is for what we have to do next."

"And what is that?" asked Regan.

Preston stood up and gazed at his timeline. "This woman. Dorothy. She wore gloves, she was afraid of being touched. My grandpa called her a genius." He turned back to make his point to his friends. "And then she turned into a creature when my grandfather touched her. The most dangerous thing in the world, he said."

"Yes," said Matias. "Although your grandfather was insane."

"No he wasn't!" Preston shouted. They all drew back in surprise. Even Preston was not sure where that had come from. He held his hands up in apology. "Look, I'm sorry. But everyone's calling him crazy, and I don't think... what if he wasn't crazy at all? What if he was just desperate? And he kept trying to do things and it all kept going wrong, and getting worse and worse, and he was the only one who knew the truth?"

After a moment, Regan spoke. "What, then, do you propose, Preston?"

"We have to find out if Ms. Fredrick is — if she's the same person. If she is involved. If she is Dorothy, or the thing my grandfather... killed."

"Several dozen times," Regan observed.

"Yes," Preston agreed.

Jacey snorted. "How are we supposed to do that? Ask her?"

Preston nodded. "Yes. That's how we should start. She needs to take off her gloves and let us touch her."

"She won't do it," Jacey said.

"Then we'll make her," Preston said.

"*How?*" Jacey wanted to know.

"*Embodiments*," Preston said. "First we ask her, then we make her."

His friends looked shocked. It even shocked Preston, to hear himself say it out loud. But he was moving forward on an intuition. He felt as if he had read the instructions.

"But what if she says no," Jacey persisted, "and you use an *Embodiment* to force her to let us touch her, and it turns out she was saying no because, I don't know, she has a *well-reasoned fear of being touched* because she's had a *terrible condition all her life?* What happens if she's just got a really sad problem? She's going to hate us. She's never going to forgive us. She'll report us to the police."

Preston shook his head. "I think she's the same person."

"But if nothing happens when you touch her?"

They were all watching him. "I have a plan for that too. We can just make her forget. Forget it ever happened. Another *Embodiment.*"

They were quiet, considering his plan. And him.

"Can you really do these things, Preston?" Matias wondered after a moment. "Because if you can it's... staggering."

Preston took a breath, and he nodded. "I can."

. . .

THE REST of that afternoon was taken up with planning, and more work on the Entanglement Matrix, not that anything fruitful came of any of their calculations. And then Preston walked his friends out to the road as the evening came down like a cool cloak over the city. He stood on the sidewalk a moment watching the flicker of light from the *Shield* covering the house. It seemed a very insubstantial defense against the growing list of threats they appeared to be facing. All he could do was hope it would help, if the time ever came.

That evening he stayed in his room, on the pretense of a looming English paper due date, and he began the next section of Spynnlang coursework.

After bringing up the main URL and navigating to the course-work page, he saw that another link in the list had become un-blurred. It read, *Synch.* There was only one link left after *Synch,* and it was still blurred. He thought about all the work he had done to this point. This, at least, he could claim as something he had earned. *He* had done this. *He* had felt the pain, and struggled, and persevered. Spynncasting was his.

He clicked the link.

"Congratulations, Preston Oliver Nowak!"

"Computer Programmers are Royalty, and you can be one of that pantheon! In fact, you almost are! Rules do not apply to Computer Programmers! Everyone will work for YOU! Laws will be changed to accommodate YOU! Visit other planets, control time and space, invent astonishing machinery by snapping your fingers and looking bored — the world will bow to your power!"

Then came the fine print.

"If you are not Preston Oliver Nowak you are legally obliged to eat a poisonous Wanta Lizard and then use your resulting Highly Acidic Saliva to destroy this computer before the Wanta horn growing downward through your brain kills you. Failure to eat a Wanta Lizard constitutes legal agreement to these Terms and Conditions."

Blah blah blah, he thought. Always with the legal mumbo jumbo. He read the last of the introductory copy.

"You have reached a rare stage in the career trajectory of any Computer Programmer — and by ANY we mean only you, since Computer Programming is basically impossible for anyone not named Preston Oliver Nowak! Preston Oliver Nowak is the Object of everyone's affection, you could say!

In this section you will be learning the intricacies of Synch, the Spynncaster's best friend! Synch connects a Spynncaster to the Spynn fields of others, and grants insight, and allows the Casting of certain Embodiments not possible alone! Isn't that exciting? Yes! It is! Very exciting!

"Remember, there is no hurry, so take all the time you need to peruse this collection of the greatest knowledge ever assembled on your planet! Even if taking lots of time is lazy and self-centered! Remember, The Dark Folk will be here very, very soon — the clock is ticking and if you are unable to complete this course quickly enough, your universe will be reduced to straw and lint and carbon atoms! So work as fast as you possibly can without even stopping to eat or to go to the bathroom!"

Within him he heard a pounding at his memory door, as a host of green horrors tried to reveal themselves, but he was adept by now at denying them. He pushed that door back and locked it shut. And then he began to work. He stayed up for hours, swiftly moving through the *Synch* positions and fleshing out the concepts, the whole time thinking about all the things he was about to do with this knowledge. And keeping one eye on his darkened window.

THE NEXT DAY WAS TUESDAY, and without even talking about it the four of them exited the main gate after school and headed to Preston's house. They talked together in hushed tones, tones that seemed to form a bubble around them. Preston followed the conversation as the other three volleyed theories and questions back and forth. How dangerous was the thing that had invaded Preston's house, since it had not hurt anyone? What was the best way to approach Ms.

Fredrick about taking off her gloves? How could they get to the real meaning of the Entanglement Matrix?

Listening to them, brilliant and weird and funny and, amazingly, fond of him, he could not help comparing them to friends he had had in the past. Not long ago his best friendships had revolved around playing video games, and once those games had faded from the picture, the friends had too. He had known Regan and Matias and Jacey a very short time, but he already understood them better and cared for them more than any other friends he had ever known.

"Let's look at Spynncaster," Preston said when they got back to his room. "I added a bunch of stuff last night. I want to see what you think."

So they took out their phones and launched. Through all the craziness of the last few weeks, the one thing they seemed not to have talked much about was the game they were building. Which was ironic, since it was the software around which all their adventures seemed to be pivoting. One reason, of course, was that none of them could do any of the construction except Preston, and Preston himself only had a loose grasp of how he was building it. And there had been so little time. They seemed to have so many other problems.

But after updating it last night with material from the *Synch* coursework, Preston had really taken a look, and gone through the flow and the game mechanics and the rules that had seemed organically to fall into place to shape the game play, and he had realized that he was proud of it. It was, he thought, a pretty awesome game. It *deserved* to be in the final round of the hackathon. It was not just a boring orange ball anymore, it was a complicated, real-time, multiplayer game, and if you did not know that it had been built with a weird, semi-magical programming language, it would have fit right in with some of mobile gaming's most accomplished titles.

"So, I've been doing a lot of work on it," he told them. "Log in with your accounts." They did.

"Ok, this is extremely impressive," Regan said. The sections following the log-in contained all the art Regan had produced at the last Code Portal, explanations of game play, and examples. It had grown to be a fully fleshed experience. Jacey and Matias were equally impressed.

"The next thing you have to do," Preston said, "Is choose your character type. There are four types of Spynncaster. Orb Mage, which is like an illusionist, casts things like invisibility. Field Mage, which is a battle class, casts broad effects like Fog and Earthquake. Sling Mage does quick, highly targeted individual damage, like a knife fighter. And Spynn Mage, which manipulates the Spynn of his own team and the opponent's."

Each of the classes had pictures, and, whether he had tried to do it or not, Regan had created portraits that resembled himself, Matias, Preston and Jacey. As if it were the most natural thing in the world, they each chose the character class with the picture that resembled them: Jacey as Orb Mage, Matias as Field Mage, Regan as Sling Mage, and, of course, Preston as Spynn Mage.

"Next thing is, we create teams. I'll invite Matias to join a team I created. Jacey can invite Regan." It took them a few minutes, but he was happy to see that they were quite easily able to move through the setup.

"Ok," Preston said, "now one of us creates a match. I'll do it." He tapped a few buttons. "My team is hosting, Jacey's team can join." Again, a few taps and it was done.

"Now, when the game starts, an orange ball drops onto each player's screen with a name of a person on your team. You pass the ball to that person off the *side* of your phone. Then that player Casts the ball back over to the other team off the *top* of the phone. See? Pass to the side. Cast off the top. And if a ball comes over to you and you *catch* it, you can place an *Embodiment* on it before you Cast it back. And then the other team has to deal with Fog hiding the ball, or an Invisible orb that's super hard to grab and Cast back. And the more time the orb is on your side as you try to find an Invisible orb, or a Decoy orb, or an Orb buried in Fog, the more points you lose. First team to lose all their points loses the game."

They played for much of the afternoon. At first they were squealing and complaining when they could not get the balls to do what they wanted, but quickly they got the hang of it, and then the competition got deadly. At the end of an hour Preston and Matias were slightly higher on the leader board, but only by a few points. Jacey and Regan caught them soon after that. Then Preston and Matias pulled back ahead. They played round after round. It was, they all agreed, one of the best games any of them had ever played.

"There is something I am still trying to figure out," Regan said to Preston when they had finally stopped. "These Embodiments we are Casting here, this is not real Spynn. Right?"

"No, it's just a game," Preston said.

"But you use the same app to Cast real *Embodiments*. Why is this happening?"

Preston had been thinking about this himself. "I have this feeling that when the app is done, it has a job. It will be like a machine. And in the meantime it's like training wheels for Spynn or something. There is going to be a time when Spynn is everywhere. Maybe a million years in the future or something. I don't know. And then you won't need an app to cast Embodiments. You'll just... "

An image flashed into his mind. Figures on a hill. Orbs of Spynn passing from one to the other, and being hurled out into the void.

"Just what?" asked Jacey.

"You'll just do it," he shrugged. "Right now phones are like end points. I use them to identify a person as an Object so I can Cast to them. I guess phones are like Getters. They're a way to get information about an Object, if we're thinking Object Oriented Programming. But when Spynn is everywhere, when *everyone* has an Object in the Spynn field, you'll just... connect." It was clear in his mind. But he could tell his explanation was not satisfactory to any of his friends.

"You Cast *Unseal* onto the box," Matias observed. "But the box had no phone."

"Inanimate Objects are different from human Objects," Preston said. "I can't explain it. Humans are much more complex."

"Are the phones Objects too?"

"Yes. But phones that have the app on them, those are a special kind of Object. Like a Spynn channel. They have special properties. Look." He had them lay their phones on the bed. Then he closed his eyes and held out his hands. The phones were like beacons in his mind. He was connected to them. Even if he had not been wearing the crystal battery, once they had the Spynncaster app installed, they seemed to become like an extension of himself, although he knew that once he was more than fifteen or twenty feet away, the connection faded. Softly, to himself, he whispered, "Levitate." He heard Regan gasp. He opened his eyes.

The phones were hanging in the air above the soft green covers on his bed. He gestured, and the phones descended, slowly settling back where they started. "I can do that without using any Spynn from the crystal, as long as I'm close enough." Matias was fascinated. The other two were a little speechless.

"So proximity is required?" Matias asked. "How close do you need to be?"

"I don't know. But it's like I'm converting the electricity from the phone batteries into Spynn. There are all these ways that the Spynncaster universe and ours overlap. It's almost like we were meant to be connected to them."

Matias picked his phone up. "Yes. The battery is drained. Surprising."

Soon Matias insisted that he needed to go back to his own house, where he had taped together a long roll of paper to try to make more sense of the Entanglement Matrix by doing a side-by-side deconstruction of the formulas. Regan and Jacey followed soon after. And Preston retreated to his room, pushing further into the *Synch* coursework.

Wednesday passed in the same way, with little progress on the Matrix, but exciting additions to the game. Jacey, Regan and Matias fed Preston suggestions and ideas, and Preston implemented them. Whatever the theme of the final Code Portal Hackathon, they were going to go in with an app that was as polished as it could possibly be. For the first time, Preston actually started to think that maybe they were going to win. It was possible. The game was that good.

The one subject they did not discuss much was Ms. Fredrick. When it came up, all they had been able to agree on was that none of them particularly liked the plan. But the creature was out there, according to Preston's grandfather. Preston knew it was important. He tried to tell himself that he was being rational, that he was doing the obvious, logical thing. His grandfather had warned them, *beware the creature.* He had called her *the most dangerous thing the world has ever seen.* And he had understood everything so much more clearly than they. What choice did they have?

And then Thursday was upon them. The school day flew past, bringing the Programming Club meeting closer and closer. This is a behavior exhibited by school days that Albert Einstein, in all his wisdom and brilliance, never managed to explain. Or maybe he had never noticed. But it was indisputable — the slower you wanted a school day to pass you by, the quicker it went, and no known math accounts for it.

Finally the hour was upon them. As they walked into the library, Regan spoke softly to Preston. "So, are we sure about this?"

Preston nodded. But only because he felt it was his job to be encouraging, not because of any great confidence. He had begun to think of this as one of those things his dad talked about, that build character through being unpleasant or horrendously difficult.

Assuming that Ms. Fredrick *did* transform into a creature — and thinking those thoughts in that explicit way made the possibility seem unlikely — he hoped he would be able to do whatever was needed next. His grandfather had not been able to kill her. Preston was not sure he could even bring himself to try. He would have to attempt something different.

Ms. Fredrick had her back to them at the whiteboard when they came in, but she turned when she heard them.

"There you are!" She clapped softly, her gloves meeting as gently as cat's paws, and she smiled. "I must tell you, I am so very proud of your progress. It is both exciting and nerve wracking, is it not?"

She looked at them expectantly. Jacey looked away. Matias continued toward their table with his usual impassive expression. Regan gave a nervous chirp of agreement. Only Preston met her look.

He tried to see deep into the gray depths of Ms. Fredrick's eyes. What was she hiding? Was there some kind of creature lurking just below the surface? This was turning out to be more difficult than he had expected. None of them spoke as they moved up to stop at the edge of the desk. Slowly, Ms. Fredrick's look turned questioning.

"Cat got your several tongues?" she asked. And then, after another moment of silence, "Is there something wrong?"

Preston was at one of the terminals, pulling up the Spynnlang page so he could deploy the app to Ms. Fredrick's phone. When he did, there was a soft chime from her pocket. She did not seem to notice. He faced her again, waiting as she became noticeably more puzzled, and finally he could wait no longer. His voice was remarkably steady, he thought, when he spoke.

"Ms. Fredrick, we would... " It had all been planned out in his mind. But now, as always seemed to happen when he prepared things to say before he was ready to say them, the words were gone.

"Yes?"

"What — why do you wear gloves all the time?" he heard himself ask. It had not been part of the script. It was not a strong start.

"Ah," she said. She looked at her hands, then sighed. "I suppose it might be a little disconcerting. Perhaps you have noticed that I go to great lengths to avoid touching or bumping other people? Yes. I go about hoping no one will... you see, I have a condition, which results in rather terrible bruises if I am bumped, or pushed even a little. If I strike my hand against a door. So I wear these gloves to protect my hands. And to hide, I suppose. I'm afraid it tends to create something of a barrier. Interpersonally, I mean. But I feel as though we in this room have been able to rise above that. Would you not agree?"

"Yes," said Regan. "I think that explains it. Do you agree, Preston?"

But Preston had been watching Ms. Fredrick very, very closely. And he had seen — he was sure he had seen — something flicker in her eyes. Something hidden. Something watching. And suddenly he was absolutely sure of himself.

"No," he told Regan. Then, to Ms. Fredrick, "We would like you to show us your hands."

The silence in the room was like the dead quiet that lives in the darkest bowl of the deepest cave in the world. Not a clock ticked. Not a drop dripped. And no one moved. Until Ms. Fredrick stirred. On her face there was something complex. Something shifting. Surprise. Anxiety. Indignation. And something else. It shifted again, and was gone, leaving nothing but the features of a woman stoic in her discomfort, and wishing she were somewhere else.

"I'm afraid I cannot do that, Preston. Please do not ask me, do not ask me ever again." Her tone was level, and seemed strangely divorced from the emotions floating over her face.

Preston's friends were not looking at her now. They were watching him. From the corner of his eyes he could see that Regan and Jacey were ready to drop it. They were sorry they had started this. Matias did not seem to be following the emotional nuances of the conversation, but watched curiously. And all Preston could think of was his grandfather. And the warning. And his certainty grew.

"I'm afraid I have to ask, Ms. Fredrick." He stepped out from behind the table, and approached her. She backed away. The indignation on her face had now been replaced by uncertainty. She moved away from Preston, then tried to go around the other side of the table to place it between them, but Matias stepped into her way. So she moved backward, toward the wall.

"Children," she said. Her voice had begun to tremble. "This is very... please stay back. I have a condition. I... " She held up her hands, showing them. She looked like a cornered rabbit. Her eyes were wide with panic. And then suddenly she turned to run for the librarian's office and the rear exit.

Preston shouted to Jacey, who was closest, "Stop her!"

But Jacey seemed frozen. And Ms. Fredrick was very fast. She was going to make it to the door, and their chance would be lost; Preston could see the whole plan falling to pieces. There was nothing else to do — he pulled his phone from his pocket and pointed it at Ms. Fredrick's fleeing back and cried, *"Weakness!"*

Spynn shot down his outstretched arm like water through a fire-hose, tugging him firmly forward along with it. The crystal on his neck pulsed and pumped new Spynn into him to replace the discharge.

And Ms. Fredrick, running toward the stacks in the farthest section of the library, staggered. Her knees buckled. She went down like a rag doll, collapsing to the floor without putting out her hands to stop herself. Then she lay still, crumpled on the carpet as if made of rubber, her arms and legs splayed at unnatural angles, motionless. For a moment they all stood mesmerized. And then Matias was moving toward her prone body, and Preston and the rest were following.

When they got to her side they could hear her sharp, uncomprehending breaths. Her head could not turn, but she followed them with her eyes as they approached. "Children," came her enfeebled sob, "What is happening to me? Please... why don't you answer?"

Preston's certainty was fading. She looked so helpless. But that shifting look in her eyes — it had not been fear. It had been more like triumph. Or even glee. But why would that be true? He was about to unmask the creature. Why would that make her happy?

He dropped to his knees. Ms. Fredrick's barely audible sobs faltered; she could not escape or protect herself, but her eyes moved, and they were blank with terror.

"No," she shivered as he reached for her arm. He rolled her sleeve up and gripped the tag at the top of her glove.

"Preston," Jacey said in a whimper. "This is too cruel. Stop."

"Please, no," Ms. Fredrick's fading voice pleaded. "That is private, it is — ahh, no... "

Then he pulled the glove down her arm. Jacey and Regan let out murmurs of horror. The arm and the hand were a mass of bruises. And as they watched, a bruise formed on her cheek where she had fallen on the carpeted library floor. She watched Preston's other hand as it drew close to her wrist. A moment of hesitation. And then he touched her flesh.

Nothing happened. He tried again, pressing harder, and a bruise formed where he pressed. What was he doing wrong? He knew that there should be a transformation. He knew it with a certainly that he could not explain even to himself, knew it as surely as he knew his own name, knew how to ride a bike, knew how to *talk*.

But he could not deny the evidence in front of eyes. Somehow... somehow he had made a mistake.

He stood up. "I don't understand," he stammered.

"Why?" Ms. Fredrick whispered. "Why are you hurting me?"

Jacey let out a deep moan of her own, and held her hand up over her mouth as if she would be sick, and staggered back. Regan was aghast, motionless, gripped by the sight of Ms. Fredrick, stretched on the floor and helpless before them, like the victim of an unspeakable crime. An ongoing crime.

"Preston," said Matias calmly. "Preston." And Preston realized that Matias had been saying his name for several seconds. He turned to look.

"If you are planning another *Embodiment*, I don't see any reason to wait. Clearly we will not see the kind of transformation which your grandfather witnessed. And if Ms. Fredrick is able to recall this incident, I fear we may be expelled. Or worse."

Preston nodded. He was numb. How could he have been wrong? Was this a mistake? If that were true, it was horrible. If he had been wrong, then Ms. Fredrick was nothing but an innocent, a helpful woman with a sad condition, and *he* was... Preston was not sure what *he* was in such a scenario. But it wasn't good.

He was still holding the glove. So he knelt and threaded it back upon her limp fingers and stretched it up her arm, as careful as he could be not to apply any pressure. And then he stood.

Preston held his phone out and pointed it at Ms. Fredrick.

"No!" She pleaded, her forced voice a husk, a pathetic wail. Though she was not able to move, she was aware of everything. Tears slipped from her eyes. "Please, *PLEASE*, don't hurt me! I — "

"*Forget,*" Preston said, casting the one Embodiment and cancelling the other. Spynn surged down his arm and flew away from his phone. And then something faltered. The crystal around his neck gave a throb, but nothing came out. The battery was dead. The Spynn was gone.

Ms. Fredrick stirred. She blinked, and looked all around, surprised to find herself on the floor. Her hand went to her cheek, where the bruise spread.

"Whatever... has happened?" She stood slowly. She faced the four of them. Then she looked back to the carpet. "Was I — was I on the floor?"

"You fell," Preston said. His voice cracked. Jacey and Regan backed slowly to the whiteboard. Matias stayed beside Preston.

"I fell? That is so very odd. I do not remember, I feel — I think I will need to cancel the rest of our meeting this afternoon. If I have fallen then I must check for... I will need to go home. Please excuse me. Please... " Her voice trailed off, confused. She moved back to the table, lifted her small bag, and then holding her cheek, with her face twisted in dismay, she stumbled from the library.

"This is *horrible,*" Jacey breathed after a moment. "That was basically just *torture.* That was a crime!"

"She will not remember the experience," Matias offered.

"I don't care! What kind of people are we?" she asked, indicating all of them but looking at Preston. "How could you do that to a person? Just because you had the power?"

"I was so sure," Preston said, his own voice stunned.

"Did you see her face?" Jacey cried. "The way she looked at us. She was powerless. I'll never be able to... " Jacey turned and bolted toward the door.

Preston called out to her. "Jacey wait! Don't go!"

She whirled. "Why even bother to ask me? Why not just *Embody* me if you want me here? Isn't that what we do now? Whatever we *want?* What are we even doing any of this for? Who *are* you, Preston?" She glared into the room at the other three, and then spun again and was gone. Regan followed her quickly, stunned and ashen.

CHAPTER

FIFTEEN

The next day, Friday, was a dark day for Preston. The clouds were back, though no one expected rain this time. Neither Jacey nor Regan had come to school. Matias did not know where they were. Preston hunched miserably on the Reading Garden bench and felt the mosaic of Albert Einstein gaze accusingly at his back. Matias sat with him, eating his cubes of tuna fish sandwich and seeming unconcerned. Preston wished he possessed Matias's capacity for blissful detachment.

Instead, what Preston had was a sick feeling and a gnawing self-doubt. Part of him was mad at Jacey and Regan. They had known what might happen. They had discussed it together, all of them. But the other part of him, the larger part, the sickened part, was admitting that the entire incident had been driven by him, and him alone. And it had been a gigantic mistake.

And now, not only had he lost his friends — Matias counted, but sometimes being friends with Matias was like being friends with Siri — he had also lost the crystal. He was surprised at how much he missed the pool of Spynn flowing around him at all times; it had quickly become a natural extension of his other senses. His knowledge of the world was deeper when he saw both the Objects pressing up through the Spynn field and the physical world superimposed over it. Now he felt like he was missing crucial information, as if the color had been bleached out of the world.

After school Matias went back to his own house to continue his research on the Entanglement Matrix, and Preston went home alone. He did not have the heart to work on Spynnlang. He confirmed to his parents that he would be leaving for the final stage of the Hackathon the next morning, and then he went to bed early.

And that night his single dream was of being suspended in space, once again, where he hung before an orange circle. It loomed over him, as big as a continent. Irresistible. Insistent. And growing larger.

Remember, it insisted to him, pulling at a door in his mind, pulling to break it open.

"Remember *what?*" he yelled, his dream throat clenched with frustration, wondering what could possibly be hiding behind this door.

Remember, it repeated. And pulled.

And all night long, there was only the message, and the unopened door.

Saturday morning Preston walked to school and found Matias already waiting. Ten minutes later Ms. Fredrick's black Suburban whooshed up to the curb.

"Where are Jacey and Regan?" Ms. Fredrick asked.

"I don't know," Preston told her. He was not prepared to say that they were not coming, although that was what he suspected.

"Well, we'll wait for them." She smiled and settled down in the driver's seat, reading something on her phone. Preston studied her profile, and the back of her head, and the set of her shoulders, for any sign that she remembered the Programming Club fiasco. But what would that look like, anyway, he wondered? She would probably not have shown up at all if she remembered what they had done to her. She would *probably* have called the school and reported them.

But she was her usual cheerful, optimistic self. She gave them a few thoughts about how prestigious Code Portal was, and how wonderful it would look on their college resumes. Even getting to the Third Stage was wonderful, and how outstanding it would be if they were finalists or, by some chance, were one of the three winners. Every supportive observation she offered made Preston feel worse about what he had done to her.

When thirty minutes had passed, Ms. Fredrick said they would have to go without the others or they would be late.

"Will the two of you be able to carry the torch for the team?" she asked.

"Preston does the bulk of the work," Matias told her.

"Oh?" she said, raising her eyebrows. She watched him, puzzled. "Well, Preston, it is quite extraordinary to hear that. You must have made some *very* dramatic progress since you joined the Club." He shrugged and looked out the window. The last thing he wanted to do was talk to Ms. Fredrick about Programming Club.

The trip to Anaheim passed in complete silence. Walking into the hotel, he began to feel like an accused boy being marched to trial. The restaurants and cell phone stores seemed to watch him go by, and pass judgment. What was he even doing here? If Jacey and Regan had not been so determined to enter an app in the Primary Category, he would never have come to begin with. And now he had driven them off.

Stage Three was back in the space with the attached break room, but now there were only about seventy-five people, and the room looked much larger by comparison. Approximately twenty teams at tables were arranged around the center of the conference space. He and Matias took their seats, logged into their accounts, and waited. And as he sat there, and watched the other teams talking, excited, ready to build and create together, he made a decision. It had been a mistake to come without the rest of the team. Jacey and Regan might want to remove themselves, but that was not possible. There was no team if all four of them were not together.

"I'm not going to do anything more on Spynncaster," Preston

said, leaning close to Matias. "Without Jacey and Regan it doesn't feel right."

"I do not understand that decision." Matias considered him, looking closely at Preston's chin, his usual stare. "Are you feeling well? Perhaps you should go throw up. Then you can return and program your application."

"No, Matias, without all of us together it's — "

"HELLO FELLOW HACKERS!" Boomed their familiar host, followed by his usual uncertain tapping on the microphone. "WEL-COME TO THE THIRD AND FINAL ROUND OF CODE PORTAL!"

"We might as well leave," Preston told Matias.

"But I do not want to leave without submitting a build."

Preston rose. "Well, I don't know how that's going to work. I'm not doing any more Spynnlang. I'm not doing any more work on the game." Matias regarded him without expression. It was one of the things that made Matias a difficult friend; you could never really fight with him.

"I'm getting some water," Preston muttered. "Wait out here all day if you want." While the announcements droned on he walked to the break room. It was empty, just as before. He was grateful. He had no desire to mingle right now.

He poured himself a drink from one of the pitchers and stood by the wall holding it. He had not wanted water. He had only wanted to escape. But what was he supposed to do now? Spend the entire day here with the vending machines? Go stand around in the lobby? If Matias wanted to remain, then Preston would have to find some-where to wait. He was still standing, water glass full, indecision complete, when Matias found him fifteen minutes later.

"We can go now," Matias announced.

Preston was surprised. "That's — yes. Good."

Together they left the break room and moved toward the confer-ence room exit, where they saw Ms. Fredrick. She stood, concern on her face.

"What made you change your mind?" Preston asked Matias.

"About what?"

"Staying until we submitted a build."

"I did not change my mind," Matias said. They went a few more steps.

"Then why are we leaving?" Preston asked.

"I submitted a build."

Preston stopped Matias by grabbing his arm. It was like trying to stop a steamroller, but he hung on and after a few steps Matias noticed.

"What are you talking about?" Preston asked.

"You deployed the app to my phone at your house, you recall. I simply upload that binary to the admin server."

"But what's the point?" he demanded. "We'll just get cut. I didn't hear the theme, but I know I didn't add anything to the app based on it."

"That is the curious thing," Matias said. "The Stage Three theme they just announced was *Team Multiplayer*. And you had already programmed team multiplayer functionality from the *Synch* course-work. Remember when we played in your room, you had us create teams and play team versus team? So now we can go home early, and I can continue my study of the Entanglement Matrix."

It was an outlandishly unlikely coincidence. But Preston had to agree. If the Stage Three theme was really *Team Multiplayer,* then somehow he had already done the work. Which meant he did not even get to abandon the project and make a dramatic point about friendship and team unity. Instead, he seemed to be careening help-lessly forward, caught in an avalanche of events too big for him to control. He had no idea where he was being taken, but he had a growing feeling that the bottom was coming up fast.

WHEN HE AWOKE the next morning, Sunday, the first thing he did was check to see if Jacey or Regan had emailed him back. He had been writing once a day since Thursday. All he wanted to do was explain.

Even if they never spoke to him again, he wanted the chance to tell them how badly he felt, and assure them that he was not a power-mad monster. But their silence continued.

He did, however, find an email from Ms. Fredrick with the subject *Congratulations, Hackathon FINALISTS!*

We are one of only five teams selected for the award ceremony! Two runners up, and three medalists. This is an amazing honor. I am very proud of all of you. The ceremony will be this Tuesday in Anaheim. We will arrange for the Team to take a field trip from school that day. I'm sure you are all as excited as I am! Please have your parents sign the attached permission slip. Yours, Sally Fredrick

Preston was not surprised. The avalanche he was caught in seemed to be picking up speed. Avalanches crush people, he thought. It doesn't matter how smart you are. Regan and Jacey probably saw that early enough to jump off. But not him. He was caught.

He wandered into the kitchen a few minutes later to find his dad making pancakes, and no sign of his mom.

"She said the sweeping could wait today until everything had already been broken," his father said, shrugging. "Do you want to help me hang a new mirror in the hall?" Preston asked to be excused from what was likely to turn into a disaster. But he did push the permission slip and a pen beside his father's coffee.

"What's this?" his dad asked.

"There's an award ceremony. We're not going to win," Preston assured his dad. "But we might go anyway. Could you sign it?" This was perfect. If his mom had found out about an award ceremony, she would have insisted on going. His dad never wrote anything on the calendar though, so he was likely to forget. Preston's impulse was to try to hide the entire experience from anybody who did not need know about it. Partly it was shame. Partly it was fear. A huge part of it was simple confusion.

"You've seemed a bit down, lately," his dad said as he whipped through his signature. "You ok?"

"Just some stuff at school, I guess," Preston said.

"You know you can talk to me about anything," Mr. Nowak told him. "I might not have any answers. But then again, I might. Don't try to carry the weight of the world by yourself, Pres."

Preston gathered the form after his dad finished signing. He tried to imagine talking to his parents about the events of the last few weeks. Where would he start? He had no idea. How would it sound? Absolutely insane, that's how. Maybe after the Hackathon. Maybe things would be clearer. He badly wanted to unburden himself. But now was not the time. Before he returned to his room, a question occurred to him.

"Did Grandpa Nowak have any friends?" he asked. "Do you know if he had anyone to talk to?"

"No he didn't, Pres," his father said softly. "Not a single friend, not at all. Your grandfather was the loneliest man I ever knew. And the saddest."

Preston nodded. That was the answer he had been afraid of.

He spent the day reading. He even tried to play some video games. But he was just avoiding his real job, he knew. So that night after dinner, he went back to his room and flipped on his computer.

The last link on the Spynnlang coursework URL was visible now. It said *The Spynn Portal.* He clicked it.

Congratulations, Preston Oliver Nowak! It's the final step! Once you open the Spynn Portal, your career as a Computer Programmer begins! Then, when the Dark Folk arise, you can look at them and know that you have done your job — and that's all anyone could ever ask! Practice this sequence in your mind. But do not enter it until you are ready for the Portal to open!

And that was all. No fine print. No extra instructions. He scrolled down the page. There was only a single sequence displayed. It was not very complicated. Within twenty minutes of practicing — in his mind — he was confident that he could perform it flawlessly.

What he was not at all confident about was being ready to open a Portal. Whatever that was.

· · ·

MONDAY MORNING before school he stood in the main gate, waiting for Jacey and Regan to pass. He was going to demand a chance to talk. But he had hardly been there two minutes before he was scooped up by Mrs. Vargas.

"Well here he is!" she said, bending down to deliver her widest, most lipsticked smile. "Our conquering hero! Our own six-million-dollar man! Come with me." And she grabbed him and pulled him into her office like a hunting animal dragging home its prey.

Once there, she pinned him to a chair with an intense recitation of her plan to change the school into a technology magnet, and she promised him a seat on the Student Technology Council she was forming, and even suggested that he might also be interested in special lunchroom privileges.

"That's great," he said, head spinning.

"I'll be making a proposal to the school board next month. Would you like to speak?"

He shook his head. She nodded in understanding. "Yes, you geniuses are terribly shy." She lifted some papers scattered on one side of her desk and scattered them carefully onto the other side. And then she looked up in surprise, as if a thought had just at that moment occurred to her.

"I've heard there's a substantial cash prize at stake in your contest," she observed.

"If we win," Preston said.

"Of course, of course. Which I'm sure you will." She got a faraway look. "And all because of the money and resources the school has poured into its hallowed programming club, at great expense to the rest of the student body. You must feel very lucky." She gave him an encouraging look. "Do you feel lucky that we have expended all these resources on you?"

He squinted, trying to think of a way he could possibly agree with her and bring the conversation to a close. But he could not do it.

"We have bathrooms that aren't going to fix themselves, Preston. I don't need to tell you that. Now, we're planning to dedicate a commemorative urinal. It's a once-in-a-lifetime chance for a suddenly wealthy student to go down in school history. The urinal will be known as the Blank Blank Commemorative Urinal. Blank Blank is where the student's name will go. There's going to be a plaque. I see we understand each other. I don't need to say any more, do I?" Preston shook his head. He wished she had stopped saying anything a long time ago. He really wanted to confront his friends before school started. But then the bell rang, and Mrs. Vargas drove him from the office as if it had been his idea to come there in the first place.

At lunch he went back to sitting alone in the lunch area, keeping an eye on the Reading Garden so he could march over if the opportunity was presented. Earlier he had caught a glimpse of Regan ahead of him in the hall, but he had disappeared; he and Jacey were obviously avoiding him. So he sat and ate without hunger and watched Matias alone on the Garden bench. Matias did not seem to notice. His routine never changed, tuna sandwich in cubes, juice box. Chocolate cookie dipped in milk. Then lunch was over.

He tried the same lying-in-wait tactic after school, hiding behind the corner of the gate. He knew they had to come out. There was no way they could avoid him. Nothing was going to stop him this time. He jumped when Matias appeared behind him.

"Preston, we must go immediately to your home," he said.

"I can't, Matias, I'm waiting for Regan and Jacey."

"They have already left," Matias said, pointing behind him at the exit doors on the cafeteria. Preston hung his head. Of course. This was going to be impossible if he had to be in two places at one time.

"Preston, we must go immediately to your home," Matias repeated.

"Why, Matias? Can't it wait?"

"I have made a breakthrough on the Entanglement Matrix. Would you rather discuss it here?" He slipped off his backpack and began digging in the zippered depths. Preston stopped him and sighed.

"No, it's fine. Come on."

"THESE NODES YOU IDENTIFIED?" Matias said, once they were situated in Preston's room. He was pointing to sections of the Matrix scrolled open on Preston's bedroom floor. "These Nodes are the keys."

Preston glanced at the math, but had to fight to keep his mind from spinning off into calculations the moment he laid eyes on them. He struggled to concentrate on Matias, and finally had to tear his gaze away from the scroll entirely in order to listen to what Matias was telling him. His problem with math was getting worse.

"I'm now convinced," Matias said, "that this Matrix is a mathematical description of the dimensions and power settings for a device to entangle a quantum particle. A particle of Spynn." Matias's voice was soft. He seemed to be amazed by what he was saying.

"Spynn is made of particles?" Preston asked, feeling thick. It was an all-or-nothing thing, his higher thinking. He either relinquished himself to the numbers and found himself wandering beautiful fields of equations and neglecting what was being said around him, or he was just regular old Preston but could keep track of a conversation. There was no in between.

"It's both a particle and a wave," Matias said. "It's a quantum phenomenon, like light. I believe your grandfather entangled a particle of Spynn, and that is what provided the power for your battery."

"So the Matrix is a... what?"

"It's a blueprint. To build a machine to entangle a particle, as Dr. Toss explained, using quantum entanglement. Contemporary technology exists for this, at Caltech in particular. Perhaps relying on your grandfather's designs. But that technology requires that the Nodes be subatomic in size." Matias turned to him, his face blank with unanswered questions. "Such miniaturization was not possible in your grandfather's time. So how was he able to build this machine?"

"Maybe he didn't."

"From the journal, we know he did. And you have your battery."

"How small do the nodes have to be?"

"I'm not certain. The scale is the one piece of the math where there is some ambiguity. The machine is either the size of several atoms, or the size of...", Matias struggled to imagine the scale, "the whole country. It would depend on how you interpreted certain equations. Here," he pointed, "and here."

Preston mused aloud, "In his journal, he says he broke apart the machine except for the Primary Node. We're supposed to go there. Where is it?"

"There is no way to tell," Matias shrugged. "If everything is nano scaled, how would you even be able to access just a single Node? It would be like choosing between individual atoms on the head of a pin." Matias did not like this kind of mystery. He was grunting and he had begun to pace. "Then again, if this machine was completed in 1942, it could not have *been* nano scaled. You see my problem, Preston? It is a paradox."

Preston watched Matias. It really was a problem for him. He might lose all his friends, and he might be confronted by magical energies that turned the world upside down and gave sixth graders the power to take control of other people's bodies. But what really bothered Matias was the paradox.

Preston started an email. "I'm going to write to Dr. Toss. I'll give her the main points and see what she thinks." He typed up a paragraph outlining what he and Matias had covered. "So, the Nodes," he said as he was typing. "I'm saying the scale seems wonky. Anything else? How many of them are there, do we know?"

"There are exactly eighty-eight nodes, each precisely placed in relationship to the square of — "

Preston's head snapped up. He threw his hand over his shoulder to stop Matias, then spun slowly in his chair to stare. Matias waited. "Have I said something interesting?" he asked.

"Eighty-eight Nodes in the machine?"

"Yes. When it was functional. Now there is only the Primary."

"Nowak Shoes," Preston whispered. His eyes went to the old map pinned to the wall, showing all eighty-eight Nowak Shoe Stores, marked with stars, scattered from one side of the country to the other. "Eighty eight shoe stores. A machine the size of the Unites States."

Matias thought for a moment. But then shook his head. "The machine requires a way to charge and manipulate subatomic particles. There would have to be something at each store to capture and transmit radiation." Matias's voice trailed off as Preston rose, went to the poster, and placed his finger beside the smiling woman with her foot bones exposed on the x-ray screen of the Ped Meter. *Every Store a High-Tech Marvel,* read the caption.

"This is it," Preston said. "It has to be. In the journal he says he tore the machine apart after Dorothy betrayed him. We know he sold all the stores at exactly the same time. The stores *are* the machine." The whole picture becoming clear to him. "You know what that makes the one store he left open? My dad's store?"

Matias was matter of fact when he said, "The Primary Node."

"Yes," Preston nodded, amazed. "And he said there would be answers there. Let's go get some answers, Matias."

IF THE CITY of Pasadena was a river, then the Nowak Shoes Building was a boulder this river had detoured around for decades. Since 1942 the city had been rushing past its granite flanks, and over the years had worn away many less substantial structures, or carried them off and rolled new edifices in to replace them, but Nowak Shoes had remained. With its deep roots and thick bones it had hunkered down and refused to budge, and in the end had become something of a local celebrity on Historical Society tours and for film crews shooting period exteriors.

For Preston it had been like a second home growing up. His father was always either at home or at the store. His babysitters had often been Nowak Shoe employees. His earliest playground had been the aisles in Men's Dress Shoes. It had been the least mysterious place in his life. But now, belatedly, he saw that it had harbored secrets, right beneath his nose.

It was a twenty-minute bike ride to the store from his house, but Preston and Matias did it in ten. When they arrived Preston pushed in, out of breath, and the bell above the door echoed in the cavernous space. There were only a couple of salespeople on the floor. Preston knew his father would be in the office in back. The question now was, where should they start looking? And for what, exactly?

They stood before a sea of organized footwear. The interior of the store was an open, vaulted expanse, two stories high. Boxed shoes lined the lacquered wooden shelves on the ground floor while a wrought-iron balcony, running along the second-story walls, gave access to specialty shoes and extra stock. Arching high above it all was a mural of the heavens, where footwear from all the ages of man floated, suspended among clouds in a timeless blue sky. And along the base of the dome were the words *"Before you judge a man, walk a mile in his shoes."*

"The Ped Meter should be our target," Matias said when he had his breath back.

"That's the problem. There is no Ped Meter. I don't know where to look."

"Could it have been thrown away?" Matias asked.

"My grandfather wouldn't have done that. Not if the Ped Meters are the key we think they are."

"Is there a storage area?"

"A basement. But there's no way you could have gotten that thing down the stairs. It was five feet across, and it looked like solid steel."

As they peered up at the balcony and down the shoe stacks, Mr. Harwood, who had been at the store since long before Preston was born, tottered into view among the canvas slip-ons, performing his patient, endless rounds restocking. He had never moved any faster than a turtle, as far as Preston could remember, but he was constantly in motion.

"Mr. Harwood," Preston called, dodging down the aisle. Matias followed him.

"Hello Preston," he blinked. Preston's father claimed that Mr. Harwood had forgotten more about shoes than most people ever learned in their entire life, so from a young age Preston had thought he had a very bad memory. But now he hoped that was not what his father had actually meant.

"Mr. Harwood, do you remember the Ped Meter they used to have at the store?" he asked. No time for casual lead ups.

"Hmm. The Ped Meter, is it?" said Mr. Harwood. He was moving forward a few feet per minute, which made talking to him an awkward undertaking. It was a real challenge to move that slowly, that relentlessly. The best approach, Preston had discovered long ago, was to take a position several feet in front of Mr. Harwood and talk while you waited for him to catch up.

"To x-ray people's feet," Preston said, facing him. "To fit their shoes."

"Oh yes. Oh yes. That's gone." Mr. Harwood nodded.

"Do you know what happened to it?"

Mr. Harwood pointed straight up to the ceiling. "They put it in the basement," he said. Preston and Matias followed Mr. Hardwood's finger skyward, trying to understand what the ceiling had to do with the basement. "They had to winch it up, you see, and then Old Man Nowak cut a hole in the floor. They lowered it through." He dropped his arm and pointed to the floor. "We had to move all the orthopedic pumps and the slipper boots three sections over. Terrific mess, that was."

"Thanks, Mr. Harwood," Preston called, and sped to the other side of the store, stopping before the door to the basement. It bore a sign that read *Employees Only*. Preston pushed it open and stepped in. Matias followed.

The electrical switches in the basement had never been updated from the 1940s, and were all brass buttons, one for *on,* one for *off.* Preston pushed the lights on. He peered down, Matias behind him. It had been many years since he had ventured down these stairs. He had never really liked it as a boy. Too dark. Too musty.

But now there was no choice. The stairs creaked as they descended.

"I'm not sure what all is down here," Preston said. "I was never supposed to go down when I was a kid. I snuck around a few times. I remember there were boxes of shoes from Grandpa Nowak's time."

At the bottom of the stairs was another switch. Preston pushed it on. A set of hanging lightbulbs glowed to life to reveal a deep and murky room. Thousands of shoeboxes in neglected stacks stood along the walls. Dust was everywhere. Rows of old wooden shoe racks stretched from near them back to the shadowy, distant walls, and many of these racks were cocked at odd angles, no longer aligned, like the cars of a train that had crashed or derailed.

Matias was looking at the ceiling. He pointed to a span toward the middle of the room.

"There. That is where the hole was cut in the floor above." Preston could see where boards had been severed and replaced with lighter wood, and the whole area braced with new supports. Below it were more shoe racks. No sign of several tons worth of metallic x-ray machinery. They slipped through the space between misaligned racks and crept down the aisle. The light was bad here. They both pulled out their phone flashlights. When they stood directly below the repaired ceiling they shone the lights up.

"So where's the Ped Meter?" Preston asked himself quietly. "It should have come down right here... " He turned his flashlight to the floor, and when he brushed aside the dust with his foot he saw a deep mark scored into the concrete, as if something heavy had been dragged away and had cut into the surface as it went. He shot his light toward a distant wall.

"He lowered it," Preston said, picturing his grandfather in his black suit and his bandaged hands, directing the operation, "and then he dragged it. Then he put all these racks back in a hurry. Come on!"

Coughing and blinking, they threaded their way to the wall, over, through and around the cases, until at last, covered in dust and feeling as if they had breathed in the decomposed remains of a thousand leather loafers, they came to a set of shelves running from the floor to the ceiling, standing against the wall. Faint scrapes disappeared beneath it.

"There's something back there," Preston said to Matias. The dust here was the thickest they had seen. They had left the hanging bulbs far behind them, and the darkness was only held back by the meager light from their phones. Shoeboxes were piled on every shelf before them, all the way to the ceiling. Preston reached a tentative hand out and pulled the nearest shelf toward him. It did not budge. The shelves were fastened to the wall.

Matias had been playing his light closely along the edges of the shelves. Now he followed one of the central vertical braces to the floor and motioned Preston over.

As Preston stepped closer, Matias's phone slipped from his hand.

"Oh!" he called, and grabbed for it. But he only bounced it higher into the air, and then it was falling, out of his reach, the light sweeping circles though the room in a disorientating whirlwind.

Without thinking, Preston threw his hand toward the falling device, and said *Float!* in his mind. The phone froze in midair, light pointed back into the darkness from which they had come.

Matias reached out, but stopped before he touched the phone, examining it hanging in midair.

"Astonishing," he said. "You say proximity is required. How close do you need to be?"

"I don't know. Farther and farther these days. Grab it, the longer it hangs there the more the battery drains, and we need the light," Preston told him. What surprised him was not what he had done, but how casually he had done it. And how unsurprised he felt now. Matias gripped the phone as if it might squirm in his hand and bite him, but finally turned it back to the bookcase to show Preston what he had found.

"Look," he said, pointing the light. "The unit is split, from the top to the bottom. I think it's a massive door. It must hinge outward."

"How do we open it?" Preston turned, looking for some clue. If the doors were going to open outward then a dozen of the racks would have to be heaved out of the way first. The doors were obviously intended to be hidden. There was no reason to disguise them as shelves otherwise. But it seemed an odd design to have to drag a bunch of heavy wooden shoe racks out of the way every time you wanted to open your secret doors.

Then he had a thought. What if they didn't hinge outward at all?

"Matias, stand over there." Preston pointed to the right-hand side of the shelves. He positioned himself on the left, then he grabbed the end of the shelves and had Matias do the same, so they were facing each other.

"Now *pull*," he said. And as he and Matias pulled in opposite directions, the two halves of the high, dusty shelves creaked slowly apart and an opening appeared. They had to push the doors together after a few inches because the mechanism stuck, then pull again, over and over. Each time they did, the space between the doors got wider and wider. Finally there was a high, dark opening just wide enough for a person to step through.

Preston peered through, then shone his flashlight in as he squeezed into the space. He saw a confusion of shapes: shelves, books, tables, jumbled papers, beakers, pipes... It looked like a laboratory, but one in shambles, with everything pushed up against the walls. The reason for this was obvious. The center of the lab had been cleared to make room for what now sat in it. A hulking, gray machine: the Ped Meter.

"Can you see a light switch?" Preston asked. Matias came in behind him and started hunting for a switch. After a moment he found one and pushed it on.

In the light, the lab looked even more chaotic. A huge collection of equipment, much of it quite delicate and intricate-looking — scales and burners and metallic funnels in long glass cases, antennas and wires and sockets — had haphazardly been pushed backward, as if a high tide had washed in and cleared the center of the lab, then deposited the Ped Meter and retreated.

The Ped Meter was built upon a solid circular base five feet in diameter and about eight inches tall. It was made of a rough gray metal, like lead, inlaid around the outside surface with long strips of chrome and silver rivets. In the middle of this raised base was a seat made of the same dull metal and cushioned in red velvet, and in front of the seat rose a cylinder of metal, cut at an angle and studded with knobs and buttons. On that surface was what looked like a TV screen from the 1940s — rounded glass resting in a polished wooden frame. The entire machine looked like something from a black-and-white science fiction movie, like a set piece.

Preston walked around the machine. On the side opposite from the doors he found a single cord leading from the Ped Meter to an electrical socket in the wall. Grandpa had left his machine plugged in.

He climbed up on the base and sat in the chair. At floor level, in the bottom of the cylinder with the controls, was a hole into which you were obviously intended to put your foot. Very carefully, Matias stepped up beside him.

Below the TV was a large red button.

"Should I push that, do you think?" Preston asked Matias.

"That seems very unwise," Matias said.

Preston nodded. Then he pushed the button.

The lights dimmed all through the basement. A hum began at their feet, an electric pulse that juddered unevenly for a few seconds, then stabilized into a throb. The TV screen came to life with a popping sound, as white light spread from the center and shimmered slowly brighter.

"I'm surprised the wiring can still sustain this current, after all these years," Matias observed. "Your grandfather must have created a very robust and redundant system." Preston was feeling a little wild eyed at what he had just done, and he gazed around the room at the sounds and the dimming lights. But despite his advice against pushing the button, Matias did not seem alarmed. Preston wondered if Matias would seem alarmed even if he were being eaten alive by ravenous panthers.

The pitch of the humming rose higher, and several of the other buttons on the console in front of Preston began winking on and off. He felt like he was sitting on top of a riding mower that had just been fired up, shaking and sputtering. He was beginning to think it might be time to stand back up from the seat when, from a spot in the side of the cylinder somewhere near his knees, a small drawer slid open.

Exposed wiring ran up from deep inside the guts of the machine and threaded out onto the little drawer. The wires fed current to thin, tapered electrodes posted into the insulated surface. Each of the electrodes had a glass top like a clear lollipop where streamers of yellow-orange electricity danced, arching and twisting within their transparent vessels as if trying to escape confinement.

And nestled between the electrodes was a familiar form. An empty rhombus. A diamond-shaped cutout, silver and perfect, exactly the dimensions of his grandfather's crystal.

Preston pulled the crystal up out of his shirt and slid it off the cord. The size seemed a perfect match, when he held it a little above the drawer.

"This seems pretty obvious," Preston said to Matias after a few seconds. "Right? What do you think I should do?"

"You appear to put very little stock in any advice I might offer."

"But *this* time — what do you think I should do?"

"I think you should turn the machine off and review your options."

Preston considered. Then he dropped the crystal into the tray.

Instantly the lights dimmed further, and the humming dropped several octaves and grew much louder. The crystal sat in the silver form like a glittering piece of jewelry, and the current streams within the tiny globes now arched down and began crawling along its surface. They left a blue glow where they twitched and danced, which faded when they jumped to another point. But slowly, over the course of less than two minutes, the crystal began to radiate a steady blue light. And just when Preston was beginning to worry that it might not stop, that it might glow so brightly that it blew up, the dancing fingers of current ceased.

The humming rose back up several octaves and the volume went down, and the lights brightened to their previous dim but sufficient level.

"What do you think I — " Preston began.

"Please do not ask," Matias sighed. "It's a waste of time. Just do whatever it is you are planning." Preston thought he almost sounded snippy.

So he reached to lift the crystal from its socket. And when his fingers touched it, Matias, the machine, the lab — everything— vanished. He was standing upright, staring into an all-encompassing field of static. Then he was thrown forward, as if the ground had been pulled out from under him. And when the static cleared, he found himself on a hilltop.

CHAPTER

SIXTEEN

He was on his hands and knees, and the dirt beneath his fingers was soft. A few crushed blades of grass splayed out beneath his palms. A cold wind blew against his cheek.

He raised his head. Around the hilltop spread a vast and empty plain. Above him lofted a cloudless, twilit sky. Distant stars were even now appearing. It was silent, except for the gusts of wind pushing up the long slope of the hill. He stood. He had been to this place before, when Jacey and Regan and Matias and he had Synched in the library the first time. And there were other memories, specters floating on the outskirts of his mind, wisps of fog too insubstantial to grasp. There was more to this hilltop. If only he could remember. *Remember* he thought he heard a voice whispering. *Remember.*

But before any recollections came to him there was a sizzling sound on his left, and a figure vaporated into place beside him. Twelve feet tall, dressed in formal black robes, with a head of wild white hair and a beard and eyebrows to match. Preston looked up in stunned surprise.

"Albert Einstein?" he said.

The figure regarded him for a moment.

"It takes one to know one," said Albert Einstein.

"What?"

"That's a saying on your world, right? Meaning, you have to *be* something in order to recognize another manifestation of that thing?" Einstein watched him carefully. Preston nodded just as carefully.

"Well," Einstein continued, "that is only a local translation in any case. You are an Einstein Object. I am an Einstein Object. But only here, in this space-time, does the label Einstein Object have relevance. You understand?"

"Totally. I mean, not *at all*," Preston breathed. "Where am I?"

"This world is called Ceaseless. The mother world. Cursed by strife. You have come here because it is the world of first transition." Einstein bent his extremely large face down to look into Preston's uncomprehending eyes. "You have no context to understand anything I am saying, do you?"

Preston shook his head. "You look like Albert Einstein, just super huge. But he's dead. Am I dead?" Preston did not feel dead. He actually felt a little bit cold.

Einstein took a breath. The huge funnel of his mouth drew an enormous stream of air deep into his lungs and it sounded like wind whistling through a hollow drainage pipe. He let the breath out. His snowy mustache flapped like a palm frond in a hurricane.

"I see. We require a quick explanation," he said. Preston could tell he was trying to be patient. "There is much to say, and you cannot remain here long. Soon you must return to your world and open your Portal." Einstein crouched to his haunches beside Preston. It took ten seconds, partly because he was old and partly because he was enormous. It brought his head even with Preston's head. Einstein launched in, without explanation, and Preston followed as best he could.

"There are many Universes in the Omniverse," he intoned. "They are pressed together in bubbles of reality that collapse and expand where their edges touch. All are unique. But they share one fundamental commonality — all are made of just two forms of matter-energy. The local translation for those forms are *Spynn* matter-energy and *Dark* matter-energy. When a Universe comes into existence it is sealed shut, and its Dark and Spynn matter-energies do not mix, and other Universes are locked out."

"But as a Universe matures, the time arrives where it must open its borders or perish. And so it naturally exposes two portals, a Dark Portal first, and soon afterwards, a Spynn Portal. Then Dark matter-energy and Spynn matter-energy flow in from other Universes, and the next stage of that Universe's existence begins."

"What next stage?" Preston asked. Hadn't Grandpa Nowak been trying to open a Portal in the journal? Hadn't he had a disagreement about when to do it? And wait, of course. The final stage of the coursework was *The Spynn Portal.*

"Your Universe comes alive in new ways once the Portals are both open. Spynncasters arise to walk your lands. And the Dark Folk spring into being. This is a natural result a Universe maturing."

Preston nodded. It all sounded so reasonable when Albert Einstein said it. Although it was not just Einstein's brilliance and unbelievable charisma. Preston also somehow *knew* it was true; there was some experience twisting like mist past the edges of his memory that told him it was all true.

Remember, he heard again.

"You have very little time," Einstein told him. "So listen. In your Universe there is a problem. The Dark Portal was opened, but the Spynn Portal failed. Dark matter-energy began pouring unchecked into your Universe. A terrible imbalance now exists."

"Yes!" said Preston. "Too much Dark energy. I know about that. Most *everything* in my universe is dark energy and no one knows why." His eyes flicked to the horizon, then up into the air above him. Something falling? He was starting to feel jumpy and exposed up on this hill.

Remember.

But he needed more information.

"Can we go back to the part about the Dark Folk for a second?" he asked. "What are they? Who are they?"

Einstein sighed. "You Objects are all the same. Obsessed with the Dark Folk. All right. The Dark Folk. Sometimes called Fairies. Think of them as a coexistent life form, dramatically different from yours, sourcing different energy and heeding different rules, but appearing concurrently in your world. They lie dormant within every Universe, alive but asleep, until the Dark Portal and the Spynn Portal are opened, and the two matter-energies mix. And then they materialize. They are like exotic quantum particles, which spring into being only under very specific conditions. Just because you cannot see them does not mean that they are not there."

"Are they evil?"

"Some are. And some are not. But their powers *are* chaotic and unpredictable. The Spynncasters are simply the counterbalance to that chaotic force. Or that was so until Ceaseless was cursed. Now we are more diametrically opposed."

And then the world faded to static for just the tiniest moment, then flickered back, and Preston jumped.

"You are being drawn home," said Einstein. "But you have your answers now."

"No!" Preston cried. "I don't know anything. Why am I even here?"

"You are the Einstein Object. You are the Object which will open the Spynn Portal in your Universe, so the dark matter-energy can be rebalanced."

"How am I supposed to do that?"

"After the ceremony. There must always be a ceremony."

"But why me?"

"Just lucky, I guess."

"But I didn't ask for this, I — "

"Listen, quit complaining. You are Albert Einstein, and that's just the way the cookie crumbles."

The world flashed to static again, this time for several seconds, then steadied once more.

"What?" Preston shouted. "I'm not Albert Einstein! My name is Preston Oliver Nowak."

"Hmm," said Albert Einstein. "You are not Albert Einstein?"

"*You're* Albert Einstein!"

"I just appear this way for your benefit. You and I are both Child Objects of the same Parent Object. I opened the Spynn Portal in my Universe, just as you will do in yours."

"But I'm not Albert Einstein!"

Albert Einstein picked Preston up with the greatest of ease, and held him straight out, ten feet off the ground. He chewed on his prodigious mustache. He squinted his eyes and tilted Preston from side to side like a prize piglet he was judging.

"How was your Setter addressed?" Einstein finally asked. "Did it say, local translation, *Computer Programming is impossible for anyone other than Albert Einstein?*"

"No, it said for anyone other than Preston Oliver Nowak."

"I see. It is a calibration issue. You are most certainly the Einstein Object. But you are clearly Preston Oliver Nowak as well." Einstein almost dropped Preston then. "Could it be? Dual Inheritance? But that — "

The world flashed to static once more, and this time it did not cycle back, but faded in and out, until it became nothing but dancing snow, and all Preston heard were a few more words, "... dual Inheritance... danger... Portal opens... "

And then he was back in the basement of Nowak Shoes, standing on the platform of the Ped Meter, watching the bulbs in the room fade completely to black. It only took a second. The humming of the machine ramped down and disappeared. Stray electric snaps and pops came from the metal panel in front of him, and the only real illumination in the lab now was the soft blue glow from the crystal. Preston found that he was reaching down to touch it in its socket, the same position he had been in just before being transported to Ceaseless.

"Matias," he said, into the dark.

"I'm here."

"I'm back," Preston said, and he raised the crystal up out of the Ped Meter and held it aloft for light. "What happened?" There was a burning, sour smell in the air, and fumes that seemed to be making his eyes water.

"You touched the crystal and then the Ped Meter shorted out." Matias's phone light flashed on. "And now you're asking me what happened."

"I've been gone for — I went back to the hilltop. Where we were when we synched," Preston told him, stepping down from the Ped Meter. "I was there for an hour." His crystal was full of Spynn again, and he could sense the Objects within or on top of the things around him, impressing themselves into the Spynn field. While he strung the cord back through the crystal and hung it around his neck, he explored the sensation. He felt as if the world was in color again, as if he had gotten back a sense that had been stripped away. He felt complete.

"I am afraid the Ped Meter is now beyond repair," Matias said, after it had given one last, explosive bang.

They closed the sliding shelves in front of the lab, and then, through the darkness the short-circuited Ped Meter had thrown across the basement, they picked their way back to the stairs. As they went, Preston told Matias what he had learned. And he tried to make sense of it himself.

"When is this Portal to be opened?" Matias asked. "And how?"

"After the ceremony," Preston said. "Whatever that is supposed to be."

"There is one ceremony coming up," Matias observed as they left the stairway and emerged into the light of the sales floor.

"The hackathon awards ceremony," Preston breathed.

"Has it struck you as odd, at all?" Matias asked, as they crossed through Men's Hiking Boots. "The name of the Hackathon is Code Portal? And you are now called upon to open a Portal?"

"Yeah, Matias, it's odd. So what else is new?" Once they left the store they saw how late it had become, and Matias immediately walked off toward his own house. So Preston walked home alone, thinking how very, very odd *everything* was, and how little of it he understood. And how much easier it would be if he could only have his friends beside him. That night, he got very little sleep.

Instead he stayed up, staring at the last page of the Spynnlang coursework, *The Spynn Portal,* and wishing he were someone else, in some other life, on some other less complicated world. All he knew was that he was getting very tired of everything depending upon choices that he had to make. And he wanted that to be over. He needed to open this Portal, and give responsibility for the universe over to whoever or whatever else came next.

TUESDAY DAWNED, and he tiptoed through the morning getting ready for school and calling as little attention to himself as he could. His plan had worked so far — his father had forgotten the awards ceremony, and if he was just a little bit lucky he would be able to get to school without either of his parents realizing that they were missing a chance to see him receive a certificate.

And then he was walking up the front steps of the school, his eyes bleary from staring at his dark window all night. But not so bleary that he did not see Matias, Regan and Jacey standing by the railing, waiting for him. Watching him. He stopped when he saw them. Was it an ambush? Were they going to confront him? He did not know what his next steps should be.

"For the love of Zeus!" Jacey yelled. "Hurry up, Preston, you colossal dork!" The three of them turned and ducked through the gates, and Preston ran up the stairs after them.

He saw Regan standing in the open library door, and he hurried to follow, his heart in his throat, and then he was through, and the three of them were facing him.

A moment of silence, and then Preston, Jacey and Regan all spoke at one time.

"I'm sorry — "

"We shouldn't have — "

"It was all — "

They stalled. Then Jacey spoke.

"I'm sorry I ran off. Ever since I got caught in that loop trying to get inside Spynnlang, I've been — "

Preston interrupted her. "You don't have to apologize."

"But we do," said Regan. "The weight of this has fallen onto you, and because we could not face the consequences of our actions, we abandoned you."

"Matias told us about the Ped Meter," Jacey said. She gestured to Regan. "We've been working on something. Can we show you?"

Regan had a laptop in a case, and as he slipped it out Preston turned to Matias.

"When did you tell them about the Ped Meter?" Preston asked.

"Immediately after I left you last night," Matias told him.

Jacey nodded. "Matias has been helping us all weekend."

Preston looked at Matias. "You could've told me you were working with them. You could've told me what they were doing!"

"I didn't know it would interest you," Matias shrugged. "You didn't ask."

Regan had his computer open. He spun it so Preston could see the screen. It was a version of the timeline Preston had created on the back wall of his closet, but very tastefully illustrated and organized. Definitely Regan's work.

"The information about the Ped Meter brought it all together," Regan said. "Let me walk you through the material we have assembled. I think you will be amazed."

"I'll do it," Jacey said quickly, but Regan held up a regal hand.

"No. You will fail to emphasize the suspense and mystery. Seldom in our lives will we have an opportunity to — "

"There's no time for flash and drama, Regan!" Jacey snapped.

"Jacey, darling, you actually cannot physically tell this tale," Regan shrugged. "It is too long. You will become bored. You will skip important elements just to get the story over. Many of the less pleasant facets of your personality will come out as you grow weary of talking, while I *never* grow weary of talking, and my personality does not have — "

"Ok, fine, just *do it!*" Jacey snarled, but then was silent. Regan nodded. He squinted and looked into the distance, a master assembling his materials. Then he began speaking to Preston, indicating points on the timeline as he went.

"In 1934 Albert Einstein, the physicists Niels Bohr and Erwin Schrodinger, and your grandfather begin building an enormous Machine for a purpose we have yet to determine. This Machine spans the American continent from one side to the other, and is comprised of the linked and precisely aligned energies of all eighty-eight Ped Meters in the Nowak shoe chain."

"Einstein, who is a Spynncaster, leads this project. He has determined that the Machine must be turned on October 12, 1957. But your grandfather comes to believe that his calculations are wrong, and that the Machine should be turned on two years *earlier* than that, on April 18th, 1955. He cannot convince Einstein to change the date, however. And Einstein is the only person who has the power to activate the Machine. So when that date arrives, April 18, 1955, your grandfather uses — or more likely *misuses* — the power of the Machine to create an Inheritance event, whereby he Inherits an Object from Einstein. Probably to become a Spynncaster himself. The Object is stripped from Einstein, causing Einstein's death."

Preston pointed to timeline on the screen. "The Einstein Object! That's the same

thing I — "

"Yes, Preston. We will get to you," Regan nodded.

Jacey scoffed. "It's going to take twice as long if you interrupt him."

Regain continued as though he had not heard her.

"Your grandfather planned to turn the Machine on as soon as he Inherited the Einstein Object on that day in 1955, but instead he falls into a coma and misses the date. He awakens months later, and only then does he realize that Einstein's 1957 date was correct all along. At this point he is a Spynncaster, but he cannot use his hands, so when the 1957 date arrives he is unable to activate the Machine. He has now killed his friend, confused his calculations, missed his dates and achieved nothing. But apparently he feels that the Machine can still be activated. Years later if needed."

"As quickly as he can, he marries. His intention is to have a child and pass the Einstein Object to them— let the child *Inherit* the Einstein Object, you see — by killing himself at the exact same moment that the child is born. He hopes this child, who will presumably Inherit Spynncasting in this process, can learn to activate the Machine. But, tragically, his wife dies giving birth, and your grandfather cannot bring himself to abandon his son by committing suicide and leaving him an orphan, so this plan fails as well."

"He then tries to teach Spynncasting to others. Dr. Toss, for one. He is still looking for a way to turn the Machine on. And then he meets Dorothy, who has just enough ability with Spynn to give your grandfather hope, but instead she betrays him. He teaches her everything he knows, but she does not turn the Machine on — she probably is not able to do that since she is not a Spynncaster — but she uses the Machine and she falls into a coma. We think that she herself forces an Inheritance event and steals an Object from *someone* else. We do not know who."

"Once your grandfather realizes that he cannot kill her, he tears the Machine apart because he is afraid of what she will do. Years pass. He declines in mental ability. We think it is because of his use of Spynn. Dorothy then reappears. Your grandfather hides his items with Dr. Toss. Soon after that he is placed into an elder care facility. He is there almost twenty years. And then you are born, Preston."

On the screen there was a blinking red dot sitting right on Preston's birthday. Regan could not seem to help himself. He lowered his voice. His eyes grew wider. He stepped closer to Preston and held his hands in front of him as if he wanted to bring the scene to life right there in the library.

"And at the moment of your birth," Regan whispers, "your grandfather dies. He must have killed himself for the timing to be so perfect, though he was deep in dementia by then. It is a mystery how he was able to achieve such precision. But, one way or the other, he did it. And you, Preston, inherited the Einstein Object. From your grandfather."

They drew closer together, all four of them. It was somehow impossible to resist Regan's dramatic delivery, even when they knew what he was up to. Preston felt chills as he listened to the end of Regan's story.

"And now, at last, we come to the Spynncaster Application," Regan said. "Your grandfather built the Entanglement Machine, but he was forced to destroy it. And you, Preston, have built this Application." His eyes got misty, and he held his arms out to his sides, tense and fervent like a preacher. His voice grew in volume.

"The Machine and the App, both created for the same purpose! One, destroyed by betrayal, brought down by pain and failure, never to shine its light upon the world. While the other, delayed down three long generations only to rise, like a plant seeking light in the darkest cave, like truth flowering in the inhospitable soil of — "

"And," Jacey interrupted, "we're *done!*"

"Regan," insisted Matias at the same time, "you must stop talking now. The story is over."

"So you're saying the Spynncaster App and the Entanglement Machine are two versions of the same thing?" Preston asked.

"Bingo," nodded Jacey. She turned to Regan. "See how easy? One sentence."

"We don't know what either is intended to accomplish, however," said Matias.

"And there's more, Preston," Jacey said. "We don't have anything definitive. But look."

She spun Regan's laptop toward her and opened a succession of documents.

"Here," she pointed. "The week you fell into your coma. That *same week* the school district hired Ms. Fredrick. Strange coincidence. And then the same day she got hired, she got assigned to replace Mr. Heart, the Programming Counselor we used to have. That's more than strange. It's like she skipped a dozen steps, and just appeared here."

"Her credit and other digital records are thin," Regan said, pointing to other documents. "We think they may have been manufactured. There is no record of her having a loan for a Suburban, or any car. There are just a host of things that fail to add up. We cannot find a record of her at the schools she has listed for her Teaching and Computer Science degrees. She is a ghost."

Preston sat suddenly, and they watched him. "So, what — you're saying you *do* think she's Dorothy, the lady from my grandfather's journal? The creature?"

"We don't know, Pres!" Jacey said. "But I know a hacked digital record when I see one. When you combine that with all the other things we know, or think we know: avoiding contact, the gloves, the journal... " she held out her hands, asking him for understanding. "The sight of her paralyzed on the floor, begging us not to hurt her... that's always going to make me feel sick. But I don't think I believe her anymore."

"Well, I don't know what else to try," Preston told them at last. "Even if we wanted to try again with an Embodiment, she already — "

"And that is another thing," Regan broke in. "We do not think you should cast any more Embodiments. Matias has told us the crystal is charged. But the records are clear, and we have performed content analysis on the journal. Your grandfather grew increasingly disturbed — his insanity grew, until at the end he had dementia and was placed in a home — and there is good evidence suggesting that this was due to manipulating Spynn from the crystal. We are afraid for you."

"But Spynncasting is... " Preston could not think of the word. He only knew that it was natural. It was as natural as breathing.

Jacey sat beside him. "Promise us, Pres. You can't use the crystal. It's dangerous."

"I concur," said Matias. "The crystal was made by your grandfather. For ends we don't fully understand. We *do not know* what mistakes he may have made. There are too many variables. It's too dangerous."

Slowly Preston nodded. "Ok. If that's what you guys think, then I guess I won't use the crystal." He stood. He wanted to give them a hug, but he was still a little uncertain of his status. Was all forgiven? Or was there nothing left to forgive? Were they friends again, or was he presuming too much too soon?

Then Regan stepped forward and hugged him, and Jacey joined them. She even dragged Matias, looking surprised and a little confused, into the embrace. And then all his questions were answered.

Well, maybe not *all*.

"Ok. Hey guys," he said, breaking away at last, "I have to go wait out front."

"For what?" Jacey asked.

"Pickup. Awards ceremony today."

"You're joking," Jacey said slowly. He shook his head.

"After what we have just told you? About Ms. Fredrick?" Regan said. "Surely — "

"I want this to be over." Preston said it quietly, and they saw that he was not arguing. But there was no way to change his mind. "I've been through a coma, I've been flung out onto other planets, my family's been attacked. I almost lost my best friends. I have to finish it. After the award ceremony, I have to open the Portal."

"But how?" Matias asked.

"The last stage of the coursework," Preston told them. "It shows how to deploy the application to the app stores. That's it. I don't even need to cast an Embodiment, it's just a few lines of Spynnlang, and push the Enter key."

"And then what?" asked Regan.

Preston could not answer that question, but he did not care. Once the Portal was opened, presuming it actually did open, events would take whatever course the Universe, or Albert Einstein, or quantum physics demanded, but it would no longer be in his hands. And that was exactly what he wanted — for things to be taken out of his hands — his inadequate hands. They were not big enough to carry this adventure forward any farther. He wanted out.

"We're coming with you then," said Jacey. Preston felt a surge of relief. It was selfish, he thought. None of them could pretend any longer that there was no danger. And he suspected that the closer anyone stood to him, the greater the danger got. But his friends wanted to help, and the truth was that he wasn't sure he would be able to take these final steps without them.

So together they left the library, and went to stand on the curb in the cool morning air, waiting for whatever the universe sent them next.

Which was, of course, a black Suburban. It rolled up to the curb just as the tardy bell rang. Over the previous few weeks this arrival had been a signal of exciting things to come, but now all Preston felt was dread. He could see it on the faces of his friends as well. None of them knew what they were getting into. But it didn't even matter, this was the only way forward. And so, as completely as he could, he pushed the issue from his mind.

"Why the long faces, my champions?" Ms. Fredrick called as the passenger window eased down. She seemed in very high spirits. "Jump in, the last thing we want to be is late for our laurels!"

"We're not even sure we won anything," Preston pointed out as they climbed in and fastened down. "There are five team finalists, right? And only three awards."

He watched her very carefully as he spoke. Was she hiding secrets from them? Was she something other than what she appeared to be? But there was nothing to be seen other than her buoyant smile, and her lively eyes in the rearview mirror revealed only affection and excitement.

"Very true! Let us not count our chickens before they are free of their eggs!" she said. And off she swooshed, the big car cutting an effortless path through the local traffic, and then out onto the freeway, while the four children in the car held on to their seat belts and wondered what lay waiting for them at the end of the road.

THE CODE PORTAL Awards Ceremony was being held in the same hotel they had been visiting for the last month, but this time they were led by Ms. Fredrick to a new section of the hotel.

"They are pulling out all the stops, children," she said. "They have rented the theater. Just like the Oscars!" They took a different route through the hotel lobby this time, and then ahead of them they could see stanchions holding red velvet ropes, and lines of people waiting to get through a set of double doors. Ms. Fredrick led them down a side hallway until they came to a door that said *Greenroom.*

"Are all those people coming to see the awards?" Preston asked, puzzled.

"Yes, it looks like it," Ms. Fredrick said, eyeing the crowd. "It's not a proper ceremony unless there is a full house, don't you think? Many of the previous teams have been invited back to watch. And there are industry professionals here. Winning Code Portal would be a very important step in the career of any computer programmer." She opened the door and then stepped aside. Within the room they could see comfortable chairs and couches, and a number of other people arranged among them.

"I'm afraid I will have to leave you here," she said, looking at her watch. "The ceremony will begin in half an hour. Only team members are permitted beyond this point. And it *is* a bit crowded for me in there. But I will find a place in the audience and cheer when you win!"

Preston and the others found seats together in the greenroom, conscious of their age for the first time. Everyone else in the room was an adult, and they were all watching the Einsteins with emotions ranging from amusement to disdain. There was a heavy feeling of nervous energy in the room, and it was effecting everyone differently. Some paced. Some talked with anyone who would listen. Many surfed on phones or computers, but did so either standing in place or drawn up into chairs in tense, uncomfortable positions.

Preston felt affected as well — he found himself getting sleepy. The long night worrying and staring at *The Spynn Portal* page was catching up to him. He was sitting next to Regan at the end of a deep, comfortable leather couch, and after fighting to keep his head up and his eyes focused for a few minutes, he finally lost the battle and plunged into a fraught, powerful dream.

He was floating in space, hanging before his enormous orange circle. But now the difference in size was more pronounced than ever before. The disk was the size of the sun, and he was nothing but a grain of sand suspended, insignificance itself, like a supplicant before a god. And, as had been the case in each of the previous dreams, the disk wanted something from him. He could feel a radiating force pushing his mind to some open — no, forcing a door within his mind to open. Pulling, like reverse gravity off a super massive star. This force was compelling him. Demanding action.

Remember, demanded the circle, with a final, unstoppable surge against his locked and hidden door. *REMEMBER.*

And then, finally, he remembered. And the door swung open for good.

Light and sound came flooding in, and he saw the night he fell into a coma. He saw himself in bed, bestowing gravity onto the circle on his phone, and then being expelled from his body and hurled backward through space.

He remembered the sight of a planet beneath him, the planet called Ceaseless, and the feeling of plunging toward it, and the surprise of assuming the body of one of the figures on the hilltop. And then standing with them as they Synched and began casting Embodiments.

As he watched this, he had an insight into the way that Spynncasting worked. Spynnlang was not dependent on machines like phones or computers or Entanglement Matrixes. It was universally flexible, and took whatever form was most appropriate, wherever it was being used, to affect and manipulate Objects. He saw that its purest form was actually just hand gestures, the motions these Spynncasters used without a keyboard. And he saw that, after the Portal was opened, this was the way Spynn would be Cast on Earth.

Next he saw the hordes of Dark Folk coursing in a dark tide toward the hilltop, pouring in from all sides, and he saw the fear on the faces of the other Spynncasters when he failed to Embody a Shield. And then he was watching them fall, one after the other, crushed, or frozen, or burned. Until he was alone on the hilltop.

And the Faerie was there, the one they had called the Dark Crone. She had the appearance of a sixty-year-old woman, dressed in classic business clothes, her hands encased in dull, heavy metal gauntlets. She bent down beside him. He saw himself reach for her, and he saw her raise her gauntleted fist to deflect his hand. He saw his fingers strike her face, and the transformation began — the green skin and the black tongue, the pointed teeth like pencil tips. But he saw it now in slow motion, and from very close, as if he were watching a magnified instant replay on TV.

And he saw her blink. She blinked just before his hand struck her face. Her eyes were closed, for just that single instant when his hand connected.

And then his own eyes flew open and he was in the greenroom, and a man with a clipboard was making an announcement.

239

"... and all of you have positions marked onstage. So have fun, and good luck!"

The other teams in the room were standing, but Jacey and Regan and Matias were looking at Preston.

"Finally," Regan said. "I could not get you awake —"

"I need a computer," Preston said. He remembered everything he had just seen. He knew what he needed to do.

"They want us onstage in five minutes," Jacey said.

Preston clawed Regan's laptop bag open and ripped his computer out. "Then we have to *move*," Preston said. "Log me in, go!"

Regan's fingers flew over the keys and he handed the unit back to Preston without a word, and then watched as Preston loaded the Spynnlang page. He began the deployment figures, the sequence used to place the Spynncaster application on a mobile device. But then he stopped. He was trying to deploy to one specific device, one single, particular unit, but he did not know exactly where it was or how to identify it. How could he deploy the application to it if he could not identify it?

For a moment he was stuck, and then he thought of his Object Oriented Programming lessons. He thought of the power of OOP. Each Object a Child of a Parent, Inheriting everything the Parent had. He visualized the branching tree in his mind. An individual phone would be a Child of the Parent PHONE, and PHONE would be a Child of the Parent MOBILE DEVICES, and — yes, it was clear to him. If he changed a Parent high enough up the chain, the change should propagate back down through all the Children. And the device he was seeking would be included by default. It seemed like it should work. But what if it created some kind of ripple effect? Some unintended complication? All he knew for sure was that he was running out of time. So he began a complicated series of high level Spynnlang fingerings.

The line of other contestants was beginning to file out of the room when Preston finished. Then he took a deep breath, and initiated the code.

Suddenly every device in the room chimed. The phones in the pockets of all the people in line, Preston's phone and Jacey's, an Android tablet one of the other team members was reading, the iPad that the stage manager was using to organize the event.

"What the — what was that?" Jacey demanded.

"I'm not totally sure," said Preston, "but I think I just deployed the Spynncaster app to every mobile device on the planet. I hope so, anyway."

Then he stood up and followed the end of the line out the green-room door, through the darkened backstage area, and onto the stage. His friends followed him, and though they did not say anything, either to him or to each other, he could tell that they were wondering if he had finally lost it. Honestly, he thought, it might be true. But if he was going to accomplish what he wanted without resorting to the Spynn stored in the battery around his neck, this was the only plan he could think of.

The contestants all took their marked seats, and a host came on to tremendous applause. The audience was full, the lights were bright in Preston's eyes and hot on his clothes. He felt exposed — exposed as a fake, exposed as a bad friend, exposed as a failure. But there was only one direction to go now. There was only ever one direction.

Five teams, and the first two honorary mentions were called. The Einsteins were still in the running. The third-place finishers were declared, and received the award and gave a small speech. Now it was down to the last two teams. Strangely, Preston felt very little nervousness about winning. It was actually at the very bottom of the list of *Important Things He Had to Worry About.*

So when the second place finisher was called, and it was not the Einsteins, he barely noticed. He was running over his plan. His *crazy* plan, he had just about decided. It had very little chance of success, he should just abandon the idea, there would be other opportunities —

"And the first-place award of one hundred thousand dollars and an iPad Pro goes to the Albert Einstein Programming Club! Let's give them a big hand!" The audience erupted in applause. The host gestured for the team to stand, and they did, and then pushed Preston forward, smiling. They were happy, even now. They did not understand the stakes. They did not understand, as he had come to, that the Code Portal Hackathon was nothing but a giant setup.

The host handed him a check in an envelope, and an iPad Pro in its box. Preston handed the envelope back to Jacey, and then stepped up to the microphone to deliver the required acceptance speech. The audience grew silent, and Preston stood, without talking, facing them. It seemed like he stood for ten minutes, but it was probably only a few seconds. He was looking for a specific face. And then he saw her. Preston held up the iPad box.

"We came a long way to get to this place. I mean, not just from Pasadena," he said, to laughs, though he had not been attempting to be funny, "I mean, in our lives." He began to unwrap the iPad box as he talked. "The power to program is the power to change the world," he said. The iPad packaging was tight; it was hard to open. He needed to keep talking until he got it free. "None of us are islands. We learn this power, programming, and we carry it forward in our lives. But if we forget the people who taught us, then we commit a terrible injustice."

Finally, it was free of the box. He held up the black-and-silver tablet.

"This machine is a source of world-changing power. And we Einsteins, we remember the person who brought us here. Who taught us so many valuable lessons. And we know that this device belongs to her. Ms. Fredrick," he said, pointing to where she stood, off by herself in the aisle. "Come up here."

He pointed more urgently. "She's right there. She's shy. No! Don't let her leave!" People in the aisle moved good-naturedly to block her when she tried to escape. People sitting in the chairs reached out to encourage her, and she ducked and shifted so that they did not touch her. "Come up here, Ms. Fredrick. Help her up, she's shy!" Preston said, trying to keep the banter light, but feeling a horrible tension in his stomach. Because there was nowhere else to go, Ms. Fredrick dodged down the aisle and came up onto the stage.

"Preston!" Regan whisper-shouted, though no one could hear him, since the theater was full of laughter and talking as Ms. Fredrick was herded up. "What are you doing?"

But Preston was focused on Ms. Fredrick. Now she was stepping up onto the stage, and she was looking at him in the most peculiar way. Not fearfully. Her face was set in a very neutral, watchful expression. He gestured for her to come closer, and the audience members who had shepherded her onstage moved in, and she glided forward until she was standing next to him.

"Ms. Fredrick is so shy, she would never ask for this, but we know the truth. All of this is due to her." He turned to look her straight in the eye, and smiled. He had to maintain the fiction just a few more seconds. "Ms. Fredrick, please accept this iPad Pro as a thank you for everything you have done for us."

He held the device out to her. The audience began to clap, and the clapping rose in volume, and they waited for Ms. Fredrick to reach out and accept the gift. Preston held his breath. At last she reached out two delicate, careful hands, and never taking her eyes off his face, she took the iPad from him.

He turned back to the microphone, and as he did so his hand went to his pocket. Now was the real test. Had Spynncaster actually been deployed to every device on Earth? He put his finger on his screen. *Adhesion,* he said in his mind, and pictured the orange circle flying from his phone to the iPad.

He swung back to watch her.

Ms. Fredrick studied him quizzically for a moment, as if to say, is that all? She then smiled, and went to lift her hand to wave. And both Preston and she saw, at the same moment, that her gloves were affixed to the device. She pulled briefly, and then she turned slowly and faced him. He saw in her eyes that she knew she was trapped.

Gravity, he said, and her arms were pulled straight down as the iPad she was holding suddenly grew to weigh fifty pounds.

The audience was beginning to understand that something was going on, and the laughter was dying down. They watched the two motionless figures on the stage. Preston did not spare a single second of his attention for them. He stepped closer to Ms. Fredrick.

"I know who you are now," he said to her softly.

"I am only a chaperone," she said, "for a group of increasingly selfish children." There was a tiny smile on her face. He increased the gravity of the iPad, so that it pulled her down more forcefully. But she bowed very little. He ratcheted up the weight on the device until it weighed a hundred pounds, and Ms. Fredrick bent just the smallest amount again, but seemed barely to notice.

"My goodness Preston, this iPad has grown so *heavy*," she told him in silky, innocent tones, "as if someone is trying to break my arms." There was dead silence in the audience as people strained to hear what was being said.

"Not your arms. It's your fingers," he told her, soft but intent. "I know how strong they are, because I've had them around my neck. I want your fingers straightened out in your gloves." He held his right hand up as if he was going to touch her face, and positioned his left hand at his side, hidden. "So that I can do this."

And with that he powered the gravity of the iPad up from a hundred pounds to a thousand. It only took a millisecond, and burned through the battery instantly, but under the sudden weight the device plunged straight to the floor — and it tore her gloves, still affixed to the device, straight off her hands.

Exposing her flesh.

In that second, before she understood what had happened and turned her eyes down, he reached out with his left hand and touched her bare wrist.

And just as she had on the hilltop on Ceaseless, she changed. One second Preston was looking at a young woman in a dark turtleneck, with brown hair and amused eyes, and the next he was recoiling from an ancient abomination. Its eyes were saucers of ink. White hair sprouted in patches on its scalp and fell past its hunched and bony shoulders. Its green skin was torn with scars and growths, and covered in shreds that once had been clothes — a gown. Its black lips pulled open to bare terrible, infant-sharp teeth, in a grin so wide and broken it seemed a grotesque puppet mouth.

She assessed the new dynamic in an instant. She reached out to take him by the neck now that her hands were free, in a deadly, familiar gesture, her strength irresistible, her fingers extended like tongs: jointed and murderous and hard.

The audience surged to its feet, and the screaming began. The creature turned to look at them and hissed, and the sound was a jet engine hurling hate, and the screaming grew louder.

She turned back to Preston. "So," she said, her voice thick liquid, pulpy and fetid, pouring from her mouth, "you think you know *me*? You know *nothing*. I made you. I made you the night I killed your grandfather, the murderous, incompetent cripple. I have watched, have waited, for this moment. Now, I seize it." She closed her hand tighter and her fingers embraced his throat like vines of steel. She squeezed, with a luxurious squint of her eyes, watching him realize that he was powerless to stop her.

And then she released him.

"Do your job, Einstein Object."

She stepped back, and Preston closed his eyes and fell to his knees. When he looked up, she was gone.

CHAPTER
SEVENTEEN

The theater erupted in chaos, filled with screams, and the audience rushed to escape. Participants from the other teams were leaping off the stage to run toward the exits, then finding themselves caught, some falling to be trampled. Before Preston's throat was open enough for him to even breathe, he was surrounded by Matias, Jacey, and Regan. Matias lifted him in a fireman's carry.

"Where?" Matias roared.

"Back," Regan pointed offstage. "The greenroom!"

They ran. Once offstage where the curtains and flats separated them from the seats, the noise dimmed enough for Preston to wheeze, "Put... me... down!"

Matias spun him like a doll and propped him on his feet, steadying him until he could stand. Preston's eyes were watering, and his throat burned, but as soon as he got his bearings he pushed Matias forward. "Go. Go!"

The backstage was a terrifying obstacle course of ropes and unexpected walls and shadows. Around every dark corner they expected to find a looming monstrosity, reaching, with hands like

246

pitchforks, for their throats. But they found the door, and once they were inside the greenroom and had closed and blocked the entrance with a chair, they paused.

"Preston. What just happened?" Reagan asked. The greenroom was empty. By this time Preston had his breath back.

"Ms. Fredrick is a Faerie," Preston said. "Some super powerful... I don't know. They can disguise themselves. But if you touch them it destroys the disguise, unless they *see you do it*. Remember, my grandfather touched her when she was unconscious. And I touched her when she was blinking, on Ceaseless, when I... " He ground to a stop. It was too much to explain at one time. He scanned the room. "We have to get out of here. Hotel security will round up anybody they find. We need time."

"For what?" Jace asked.

"For opening a Portal," Preston said, "and ending this." But where could they go? Where would they be least conspicuous? In plain sight, he decided.

"This way," he called. "Regan, grab your computer!" Then without waiting to see if they were following him, he ran out into the corridor and turned down toward the lobby. Ahead he heard screaming, and when they rounded another corner he saw people pouring out of the theatre doors and spilling outward past the convention rooms and into the hotel reception area.

He mixed in with the crowd for a moment, and let the press of people carry him into the glittering, cavernous space, and then he stepped away and headed for the shops. The tables there were all empty, their occupants having run either toward or away from the chaos. He headed for a table with four chairs situated in front of a yogurt shop, and only then did he think to look for his friends. They were close behind, scouring the crowd. Looking for a quick flash of green, he felt sure.

"Here," he said, "sit down, look casual." They sat. But they were the absolute opposite of casual, Preston thought, perched on the edges of their seats like rabbits. They needed to blend in. They needed to look like normal kids. He pulled out his phone and sent off a group text, and all three of them heard it and looked.

Keep looking at your phones. Be normal :) I'm going to set up the code to open the Spynn Portal. Regan, unlock your computer.

Regan keyed his password quickly and pushed the laptop over to Preston, and then Preston began inputing the Spynnlang sequence for *The Spynn Portal*. It was very simple. He had practiced it in his mind many times over the last two days. The icons danced into place on the page like strange living creatures as he bent and flexed his hands through the positions.

He had come so far. What had once seemed difficult — almost impossible — was now as simple as breathing. He did it without even thinking, and he realized that everything he had been through since that night on his birthday almost five months before had been leading him to this moment. Opening the Portal. Like the final word in the final sentence of a long and disturbing book. After this he would be free.

"There," he said when he had finished, and all he had left to do was push the Enter key. "Are you ready?"

Jacey reached out and pulled his hand back.

"Wait." She looked at the others, then back at Preston. "Explain this again. What are you doing?"

Preston was ready to go. He felt a powerful force inside him now, which — almost against his will — was driving him to execute the final step. But his friends deserved an explanation. He owed them far more than an explanation, in fact. It was the least he could do.

"Remember how Dr. Toss said 95 percent of our universe is made of dark matter and energy? And there's no explanation for the imbalance?" He waited for his friends to nod, which they did, impatiently. They were geniuses, they did not need a primer on physics.

"Well, there *is* an explanation," Preston said.

He marshaled his thoughts, trying to find the words to explain what he had so far only thought about as ideas and images. "There are two kinds of energies. There's Spynn, and there's Dark. And they are supposed to be present in equal amounts. The universe is supposed to have two Portals opened. But our Dark Portal got opened, and the Spynn Portal *failed*, somehow. And Dark energy has been pouring in ever since, filling up the universe. So I have to open the Spynn Portal. So I can bring balance."

His friends all looked blank.

"*Bring balance,*" said Regan with a touch of distaste. "That is just a wee bit... trite. A fantasy novel trope. Would you not say?"

"You can't deny the science," Preston shot back. "It doesn't matter whether you think it's trite or not. The universe is filled with Dark matter and energy, and no one knows why. So *bring balance* — it sounds crazy, but is it any crazier than anything else that's happened?"

"Absolutely," said Jacey. "Much crazier."

"Precisely what is supposed to happen when this Spynn Portal opens?" asked Regan carefully.

"The two energies mix. Dark Folk appear. Spynncasters walk the land." Even to Preston that sounded off the deep end — and he had stood atop a hill on Ceaseless and had *seen* the evidence rushing across the plain to kill him.

"I mean, Dark Folk exist already, but they are dormant," he continued, sounding less and less certain, "they're like exotic quantum particles, they can only exist when certain conditions are met... " He realized he was not making his case at all. He stopped talking.

"Oh... kay," said Jacey, separating the sounds slowly. "Well I, for one, think we have enough Dark Folk around already. Does anyone disagree?"

Not one of his friends disagreed. Jacey turned back to Preston.

"Let's wait. Let's do some more investigation." She was looking at him earnestly, imploringly. "It can't hurt to just wait a little longer, can it?"

"I don't know," Preston said. He glanced at the screen. His fingers itched to press the final key.

"We can consult Dr. Toss," Regan said. "We can involve some prestigious scientific experts. Think how *that* will look on our resumes." His weak attempt at humor died when Preston looked at him.

"This is real," Preston told him. "Don't you believe me?"

Irritation — and more than irritation, some irrational kind of anger — was flaring inside Preston. Jacey put her hand on his arm again.

"Yeah, Pres, we *do*," she said quietly. "That's the whole point. We *do* believe you. We are considering this very seriously. We've seen the things you do. We believe that Spynn is real. So shouldn't we be methodical? There is too much we just don't understand."

"What's there to understand?" Preston snapped.

"Many things," Matias said. "For instance, you say that when the Spynn Portal is opened, Dark Folk are no longer dormant — they appear. But one of them is apparently already among us, and she seems far from dormant. How do you account for that?"

It was true. Preston hadn't really thought that through. The Dark Folk were supposed to be dormant until the Spynn and the Dark Portals were opened and the energies mixed. So what was Ms. Fredrick doing here?

"The decision is yours, Preston," Regan said. "But can it hurt to do just a little more digging, when the consequences of making the wrong decision could affect... well, all of reality? And I say that fully acknowledging how ridiculous it sounds."

Try as he might, Preston couldn't think of any reason not to wait. *Because I want to do it now* was not a good enough answer. Slowly, and unhappily, he nodded.

"I will summon an Uber," said Regan. And then, from the yogurt shop, they heard a familiar voice.

"Oh, children," said Ms. Fredrick. "I am so very disappointed." As though she had been standing there the entire time — and maybe she had, Preston could only assume — she now stood between Jacey's seat and Matias's. They jumped back. She put her hands on their shoulders as they started to rise, and both of them fell forward, asleep. Regan pushed his chair back and made as if to run; Ms. Fredrick gestured softly in his direction, and he slumped down, unconscious.

"You will not run from me, will you, Preston?" she asked. Moving calmly and with an almost motherly affection, she stood behind Regan's chair and pushed it in to the table. Then she leaned him forward, so his arms pillowed his head on the tabletop while he slept. She arranged both Jacey and Matias in the same pose. Then she pulled a fifth chair up to the table and sat.

"Look at the darlings," she murmured. "This long day has worn them out. Or so any passing observers will assume." She put her gloved hand on Jacey's shoulder and stroked it as she spoke.

"It was you that night," Preston's choked. "You broke into my house. You put my parents to sleep."

"Guilty," said Ms. Fredrick. "You see, your grandfather stole something from me. Such a funny story. I was lying unconscious, defenseless, and he was attempting to murder me, viciously, again and again."

She laughed. She really did make it sound like she thought it was funny, but from her eyes Preston could tell she felt only cold, deep hatred.

"That sort of behavior seems to run in your family, Preston. Assaulting helpless victims."

"Are you a Spynncaster?" he asked. He was desperate to keep her talking, while he tried to think of what he could do.

"Oh, no." She shook her head. There was prim revulsion in the gesture. "Not that."

"But you were coated in Spynn that night," he said. "I saw you when you ran up."

Ms. Fredrick reached down into her turtleneck shirt, and pulled up a cord that held a crystal, an exact replica of the one he had himself.

"You should not be surprised," she admonished. "There were

eighty-eight of them, you know. But I am a Faerie. I can manage only the most rudimentary Spynncasting, and it disgusts me. A glamour, for instance, to mask myself within the Spynn field of another adept, as you saw that night. I *was* able to use your grandfather's machine to keep the Dark Portal from collapsing. Dual inheritance, just like you, Preston. But if I had true Spynncasting ability I would have opened the Spynn Portal myself, and we would not even be here having this conversation. Speaking of which... "

Ms. Fredrick indicated the computer, the page of Spynnlang awaiting execution.

"You have a task to complete. Open the Portal."

Preston was by now absolutely convinced that his friends had been correct. They needed to understand this thoroughly, and they needed to work together to make the decision. If the Faerie wanted the Portal open, that alone was enough to make him wait.

"I'm not going to do it," he said.

"Oh dear," said Ms. Fredrick, her bored voice still somehow thick with threat. "What will I do?" Her eyes lit theatrically. "Here's an idea. I will brutally flay these three small children until you come to your senses."

Before he even realized that she was standing, she was up, and she reached across the table and snatched Regan's laptop. Then she whirled to pull Jacey, Matias, and Regan into her arms, heads loose and rolling like flop dolls, holding them with no more effort that it would take to carry a paperback book. It was all done in three seconds. She was horribly fast, and monstrously strong.

"Let's not forget your devious little toys," she said. And quick as blender blades, her hand flashed out to the table, cupped the four phones lying there, and crushed them to splintered pieces in her hand, the snapping and popping more reminiscent of celery stalks than glass and aluminum. She cast the pieces back on the table like a handful of dirt.

"Now to move our party where blood and snapping bones will attract less attention," she said. "Find us in room 1028." And carrying the bodies like bags of dog food, she ran. At first Preston thought she was heading for the inside of the yogurt shop, but then he saw that she was aiming for the wall. And when she reached it, she leaped — out, up — and her feet struck and held, and she was running *up*. He watched her, leaping higher, story after story, toward the top of the glassed-in atrium, passing the balconies of the rooms that overlooked the lobby.

It did not appear as if anyone else saw her. The clamor and rushing of people from the theater had not diminished, and no one was paying any attention to the group of kids sitting quietly at the table.

Just at that moment a squad of security officers rushed through, and Preston ducked his head. When they were gone he looked back up, trying to see where Ms. Fredrick — or the Faerie, or whatever in the world he was supposed to call her — had vanished. The atrium extended far above him, at least ten stories. He could not climb after her. So he dashed to the elevator, and punched the button for the tenth floor.

All other considerations had fallen away, and as the small box rose swiftly upward, the only thing he could see in his mind were the bodies of his friends, hanging in the arms of Ms. Fredrick the creature, cross stacked and bundled skyward toward a lair of some horrible variety, and to who knew what fate. Preston had no doubt at all that the Faerie would follow through on her threats of bone snapping and blood. He did not know what he was going to do. But he had to stop her.

The elevator doors opened on the tenth floor. He stepped into quiet, air-conditioned luxury. The red patterned carpet and the tasteful, opulent wallpaper seemed drawn from a different world than the one on the ground floor, full of strife and terror. This world was silent, smooth, catered.

He rushed silently down the hallway, ticking off room numbers as he passed them, until he came to room 1028. And there he faltered. The door was slightly ajar. He knew he needed a plan. But he could not think what options he might have. He was long past his promise to his friends not to use the Crystal. But unless he could find an extra phone in the room, he had no way to cast Embodiments. He needed the Spynncaster app. He needed his orange ball.

Or did he? Hadn't he told his friends that the phone was nothing but a transitional stage? That Embodiments would ultimately be Cast through the Spynnlang gestures alone, once the Spynn Portal was open? He had witnessed other Spynncasters performing this feat, on the hilltops. What was stopping him from doing it now, with the Spynn hanging around his neck?

He knew that there might be many answers to that question, and that most of those answers would probably involve pain and regret on his part. But it was the only plan he had. If the opportunity presented itself, he would use it.

Without knocking — because really, the time for politeness was long past — he pushed the door open and stepped into the room beyond.

It was a suite, with large sliding glass doors looking out onto a balcony, and beyond the balcony the very top of the glass atrium. A huge bed and headboard rose against one wall, and a sitting room and well-appointed work area stood opposite. He noticed Regan's computer on the table, opened to *The Spynn Portal* page.

And then he saw his friends. Suspended from the wall, beside a painting of yellow flowers, was a thick black net, hung from a metal post driven deep into the cracking plaster. The mesh bag swayed, stretched tight like a fishing net drawn up on a winch. In it were his friends, pressed against the ropes, upside down and sideways and crushed against each other. And they were awake.

"Preston, look out!" yelled Jacey, as Ms. Fredrick stepped into view around the corner from the sitting room.

"Oh, my dear," she laughed. "He has nothing to worry about. It is you who are in peril." And she walked languidly past and strummed the cords of the net like piano strings, and set the bag to swinging.

"Let them go," Preston growled.

"I don't think I am going to do that," said Ms. Fredrick. "My three little piggies. All set for slaughter. Open the Portal and I may reconsider."

Preston scanned the room. He could see no phones or devices. He was left with nothing except his dubious plan. In his mind, he pictured the Embodiment he would attempt. A binding. An impenetrable box to ward her away from the world for the rest of time. He braced his feet and waited for the right moment, while Ms. Fredrick continued to pluck at the cords of her net.

"It will only take you a moment," she said to Preston. "And then all *this* will be yours." She turned to face out toward the balcony, holding her arms wide to indicate *everything*.

And when her back was turned, he began. He held his arms in front of him. He knew what he wanted. He could picture the fingerings. It was exactly the same sequence as if he were at the keyboard, preparing a new build to deploy to his phone. But since he had no phone, he needed a different place to focus the charged Spynn Object he was creating. There was only one other place. He concentrated on his hands.

Ms. Fredrick was across the room from him, looking out the open sliding doors. Preston funneled Spynn down his arms, and out into his fingers, and he saw a tiny orange globe form between his palms. From his fingertips to his forearms a thin nimbus of light shimmered into being, as if he had dipped his arms in blue wax that flexed and glowed as he moved. The crystal at his throat grew hot and throbbed, and Spynn poured from it across his chest, over his shoulders, and down past his elbows. And as the blue halo around his hands expanded, the orange sphere between his palms became larger.

He worked quickly, silently, hooking and arching and pressing his fingers through their tortuous positions, racing to finish before the creature turned, but his friends could see him, and there was terror on their faces. Not terror for themselves. For him. He was doing the exact thing he had promised them he would not do, he knew that, but what choice did he have? They glanced in desperation back and forth between him and Ms. Fredrick at the window.

She turned back to her captives. Something in the way Regan was staring made her glance at Preston.

She saw the glow; orange and blue reflected up onto his face, and onto the walls. With a shriek of anger she closed the gap between them, all pretense of disguise dropping away as her green, horrible face came clear. Preston stepped backward. It was finished. His arms were dense with Spynn, the ball in his hands was thick with power. He knew that now it *must* be Cast.

He pulled from the crystal to unlatch the Embodiment from his own Object and Cast it away. He stumbled farther back. The Faerie, a slavering and furious animal, bounded at his chest and reached for his throat. But not his throat, he saw. Her long, cruel fingers curled around the rhombus on its cord at his neck. She gripped it. And *squeezed.*

Steel presses the size of mountains would have shattered against that stone. But her ancient bones were hard beyond imagining, her strength as unstoppable as the orbit of planets. Preston heard bones in her hand fracture despite all this.

But she broke it. She broke the crystal. It splintered to dust.

She fell back. Her breath heaved. She looked up at him. A twisted expression came over her face. It was curiosity.

The Spynn amassed in his hands began to smolder. He could not Cast it now. He lacked the last dram of Spynn needed to unhook the Embodiment from his own Object so it might be hurled away. And, un-cast but fully primed, it turned back against him.

He fell to his knees. The creature backed away, watching with great interest. Preston felt fire now, which began at his fingertips and ran up his forearms. He badly wanted to scream, but his breath was locked in his throat. Bubbling agony grew. He watched in horror as his hands blackened and began to smoke. His fingers twisted. Then they burst into flame.

The orange ball exploded. Concentric ripples pressed outward over the surface of everything visible, as if the room and the furniture and the people were nothing but a reflection on the surface of a pond. Preston was thrown backwards against the wall, and the creature was thrown the other direction. And then there was silence.

The room swayed for Preston, coming in and out of focus. Something terrible had just happened, but for a second or two he could not clear his head and think what it was. Then he looked at his hands, and was confused. He did not have hands. He had incinerated, blackened lumps. Charred skin fused, his knuckles twisted and his fingers folded back, blasted apart as if tossed in a salad bowl. I can't use my hands, he thought. A strange thought, but a clear one. Maybe his last one for a long time? Because the pain was starting, and he could tell that very soon it would overwhelm his ability to do or think anything at all.

The creature rose slowly. She pointed at Preston. And a voice thrust itself into Preston's mind. A very familiar voice.

I tire of these games, Einstein Object.

It was the Faerie's voice, thick and distant. She strode to the wall where his friends hung in the net and lifted them off the hook with one hand, while with her other hand she retrieved Regan's laptop. Then she leaped outside, onto the balcony, and held the bag with the children over the edge with a single, steel-hard finger. She offered him the computer.

Open the Portal. Or watch your playmates die.

Preston staggered to his feet, his hands held before him.

"It was you," he gasped, his voice a broken husk. "You saved me when I cast the *Insight* Embodiment on Jacey at the Hackathon." He struggled out onto the balcony, every faint caress of air against his hands like the agonizing lash of a whip. But he understood something. Something new.

"You are as incompetent as your grandfather," the Faerie scoffed. "So yes, I was forced to save you."

The balcony overlooked the pond and the lobby, ten stories

below. Preston had never liked heights. His fears were not eased by the small plaque fixed to the balcony: *Caution, do not lean over railing.*

"You were *forced* to do it — " Preston doubled in pain, and for a moment he could not speak. But he saw his friends, suspended, ten stories above the ground. He had to save them. There was only one way left. A terrible gamble. He could only hope he was guessing right.

The net creaked as it swung from the Faerie's finger. She held the computer toward him, open on her other palm like a serving tray.

"You were *forced* to save me," Preston continued. "You told me yourself, you made me. You killed my grandfather at the moment I was being born, so that I would Inherit the Einstein Object. You can't let me die. Because if I die, if the *Einstein Object* dies, then the Spynn Portal can never be opened. Isn't that right?"

"There is only a single key left to push," she said, ignoring his question and pushing the computer closer. "And then I can heal your hands, and I can free your friends. You have done everything else. It is time for you to rest. You can fight me no longer. Deploy your code."

"That must have been hard for you," Preston told her, his voice breaking. He knew what he had to do. He needed tools. He needed weapons. He stepped closer to her, talking to keep her distracted. "My grandfather tried to destroy you. Did you hate saving his grandson?"

"The Portal," she said, giving the net a vicious shake.

He held up the smoking, butchered wrecks that were his hands. He reached for the Enter key.

"Preston, *no!*" shouted Jacey.

"You shouldn't be leaning on that railing," Preston told the Faerie. "Don't you ever read the instructions?"

And then he sprang forward with the last of his strength, throwing himself over the top of the railing and off the balcony.

At first the sensation was like not falling at all. Time slowed down, as if he were being given the opportunity to regret his choice, but not the power to change it. He seemed to hang in space with his feet on one side of the balcony and his body on the other, like a high jumper coming down over the tallest leap he would ever make. And then time went to double speed, and he plummeted.

He could have reached out to touch the windows of the suites as he fell past them, backward, facing the sky. He could see his reflection beside him in the glass, his bloody, mutilated hands held away from his body at an angle, like a doctor prepping for surgery. The balcony on the ninth floor whooshed by. He felt the wind begin to pull at his clothes, and he heard a cry of rage from the platform he had just abandoned. By the time he reached the fifth floor the wind was a seventy-mile-an-hour-torrent. He saw a woman in a housekeeping uniform sweeping the balcony and for an instant their eyes met, and he saw how tired she looked, and careworn, and then he fell past, head back, legs and arms reaching for the ceiling.

And he thought, looking back toward the tenth floor, *was I wrong?* The ground was almost upon him. He had failed. He had guessed wrong.

But then — at last — he saw, high above him, a shape dropping over the balcony. He held his breath, and his eyes watered in the wind from his dive as he tried to see which of two shapes it was. A net bag? Was it a net... no! The shape was traveling faster than a falling body, running down the side of the glass and steel hotel. Running.

He was only thirty feet from the floor, and his speed was close to terminal velocity, a hundred miles an hour, when he looked to his right and saw a figure pacing him. It was the Faerie, leaping downwards on the face of the hotel wall, racing him as he plunged. She bared her teeth and reached out, grabbing him by the leg. She set her feet against the metal column beneath her and began to skid, holding Preston by the ankle. Lower and lower they fell, closer and closer to the floor, shedding momentum, the building material under the Faerie's feet cracking, buckling in waves, melting from the friction.

And then Preston's head was a mere eight inches from the floor, and he had come to a stop. He swung in the Faerie's grip. His leg felt broken where she had sutured her fingers around it. But he was alive. And he had what he needed.

Proximity. Was he close enough?

She dropped him, and he fell on the side of his face and slammed his broken and useless hands against the tile floor. The pain swamped him, forcing him into a mental retreat, and when he came back to his body he saw the Faerie bending over him. She tossed the net bag with Jacey, Matias, and Regan behind her and it skidded across the floor, bowling through chairs and tables and coming to rest against the wall near the yogurt shop. He turned to look at the stores beyond them. Was he close enough? Would it work?

"*Enough!*" she spat in fury. There was screaming behind and around them. She seemed to have that effect wherever she went. She bent even closer, as if she would lick him, or kiss him, or shred his face with her teeth.

"You are not dead. I will not allow it. Oh no, not yet. You achieved *nothing* with this. Nothing but to *infuriate me!*"

Preston's arms were extended out to his sides, and he was lying on his back, but he could see the line of shops. He closed his eyes and reached out with his mind. Slowly, painfully, he curled what there was of his hand into a claw, and pulled it toward him.

"*Flight,*" he whispered. Then he opened his eyes. Would it be enough?

The Faerie watched, blank faced.

"What?" she demanded. And then she heard the sound. They both heard it. A hollow rumble that rose in volume behind her. She turned, and spun her head one way and then the other while the sound grew, and grew, until it was like a hundred empty barrels tumbling down a hill.

That is when the window of the store beside the yogurt shop — the Verizon Wireless store — exploded outward, showering glass and metal across the lobby and releasing a dark cloud of chrome and plastic up into the air of the atrium. It rose, this throng, and boxes and packaging fell from the shapes in the mass. It rose, blotting out the light from the sun, and turned in one motion, like a flock of metallic birds. And then the shapes dove down.

"What is this?" screamed the Faerie, stumbling backwards.

But she saw. The shapes were phones, slicing through the air — Preston was calling them from deep within the buildings in flocks, connecting to the Spynncaster app that each of them now hosted, burning through their own batteries to fling them high, and bring them diving down.

The Faerie ducked and rolled away, and Preston levered himself up.

"There is nowhere for you to go!" she screamed. He gestured again, and from behind her a shining swarm plunged and drove her to the floor.

"*Adhesion!*" he cried, and they formed an interlocking panel on her back. But she stumbled to her feet, confused now, and enraged beyond belief.

"*Gravity!*" he yelled, and the weight of each was multiplied a thousand times so the Faerie was driven to her hands, then to her knees. But she was strong, so strong, and she staggered, and rose, and turned to face him. Now some of the devices were falling away in drops of melted slag, their batteries consumed too fast, too hot.

"*Flight!*" he called, and another storefront, the Sprint store, blew outward and expelled a deluge of black and pink and white forms into the air, and these too dove forward and bore her down.

But three Embodiments, *Flight* and *Adhesion* and most of all *Gravity*, were too much at one time, and the phone batteries were consumed like matches dipped in gasoline. She was too strong; it took too much weight to pin her down. Even now she lumbered toward him, phones clinging to her back and shoulders, the tiles beneath her feet snapping under her weight, huge chunks of the floor breaking beneath the force of her heels.

She reached to grab him; he stumbled back. Her great weight levered a piece of the subfloor up and one of the tables was sent flying high into the air. Of course, he thought suddenly. So simple. Not down, *up.*

He dismissed *Gravity,* thrust both his ruined hands out in front of him, and raised them toward the top of the atrium.

The Faerie shot skyward, shrieking in rage.

Clouds of multicolored devices coursed in great circles around her, five stories off the ground, and dove when an opening appeared on an arm or shoulder to fasten to her body, while a cascade of consumed and ruptured devices poured off her like a rain of broken birds, cracking and splintering upon striking the floor. She screamed, but her strength was useless in the air.

Around him in the lobby he saw devastation. Terror-stricken guests ducked or sprawled behind kiosks around the pool, or dashed down hallways, crying in fear. Broken tables and tile and storefront material were strewn across the perfect and welcoming foyer, mixed with the smoke of burning phones and the smell of combusted electronics. Above him the Faerie screamed and thrashed helplessly, her fury at being held against her will overwhelming her reason. Her inchoate shrieks echoed through the vast atrium, monstrous and primordial, while the flock of phones orbiting and diving around her body drove her to strike and swing and screech. Soon, he could see, he would run out of phones with charged batteries, and he would no longer be able to hold her safely aloft. She would descend again, free to enact her vengeance.

He ran to the wall where the Faerie had flung his friends, and went weak-kneed with relief when he saw all three of them standing, pulling themselves free of the net.

"Preston!" Jacey cried, and almost embraced him, but stopped. "Oh — your *hands!*"

"No time," Preston croaked. He was barely able to stand, but he swept his mind back and up, and four phones dropped down to hang, one by one, in front of each of them.

"Take them," he cried. "We have to leave."

"We cannot escape," said Matias calmly. "The Faerie is invulnerable. To flee under these circumstances is not logical."

Preston shook his head. "No," he said. But he could explain no more. There was no time. Even now the cloud of phones was growing thin. The Faerie was drifting lower.

"Hold the phones," he told them, and each reached to grab a floating device. He dropped the phone hanging in the air before his chest slowly into what was left of his palm, and the excruciating pain of contact almost took him out of his body. But he battled to focus. He had only one last job. He had brought them all to this, and he had to pay the price.

With the stub of his other hand, he clawed open the Spynncaster game and drew up an Embodiment.

"An Embodiment? But you have no Spynn!" Regan shouted. "If you do that — "

"If I don't, the Faerie catches us. We all die."

"Preston, no!" Jacey cried. But there was nothing she could do to stop him.

He flung the orange ball from his phone, Casting it out onto all four of them. He felt the Embodiment bite deep and begin to draw Spynn from his body, the Object surging into existence. He felt himself drawn down, down into darkness. And he knew. He knew he could not survive this.

But he had done it at last.

"*Ceaseless!*" he called. And fell.

CHAPTER

EIGHTEEN

Three are certain steps you take in your life from which there is no going back, and falling into an inter-dimensional Portal is one of them. It should only be done with the greatest care and foresight. It should not at all be done the way Preston did it.

As anyone who has ever fallen into a Portal will tell you, it's no walk in the park. These passages have pockets of anti matter which you cannot touch under any circumstances, and there is no internet, and unless you fall in wearing a jacket it will be freezing. Once you're in, however, it is too late to get a jacket or a book. There's no going back.

After you disappear, the world you left behind will go on without you. People usually notice you are no longer there, though not always. When you stop coming to breakfast or fail to show up once a week for your allowance your parents, at least, will wonder if something has happened. They may knock on the door of your room or call your name or the police. But again, by this time you are beyond help.

Once you are gone you will miss everything. You will miss the text messages people write you and the birthday cards they send, and if you were about to receive a prize or go on a fabulous vacation you will miss those. You will miss your mother. You will miss your father. If you were lucky enough to have a brother or puppy you won't see them again. Portals are a one way business.

And if, on your desk in your room, your old computer suddenly springs to life with a line of bold, excited print, with exclamation marks flashing on and off, you won't see it. But the words will be there. In Preston's case the words on the screen read:

"Preston Oliver Nowak *I knew it was you*! NOW THE *REAL* PROGRAMMING COURSE BEGINS!!"

This is the end of Book One of The Spynncaster Sequence.
Book Two, <u>Schrödinger's Prince</u>, will be available in 2024.

About the Author

From Kevin: *The game in this book, Spynncaster, is a real game. I'm an application developer, and I created the game to extend and add richness to the Spynncaster world. My plan is to release the game when I publish Book Two in the Spynncaster Sequence. If you'd like an advance look at the application, game play, and amazing art, join the Spynncaster mailing list at kevinhincker.com and check the Einstein Extras box!*

The second book in the Spynncaster Sequence will be published in either 2024 or 2025, depending on reader enthusiasm for said second book :) I do promise to produce it, so leave an Amazon review if you'd like it sooner rather than later. Happy Reading!

Kevin Hincker lives and writes in Los Angeles. You can connect with him on Goodreads or Facebook. You can also email him, after joining the list on his website. He appreciates hearing from readers.

Remember, the best way to get more books in a series *faster* is to leave a review. They inspire any author.

f

Also by Kevin Hincker

The Little Queen